# J.L. CAMPBELL

# FLAMES OF WRATH

BLACK
ODYSSEY
MEDIA

WWW.BLACKODYSSEY.NET

Published by
BLACK ODYSSEY MEDIA

www.blackodyssey.net
Email: info@blackodyssey.net

FLAMES OF WRATH. Copyright © 2023 by J.L. Campbell

Library of Congress Control Number: 2023900482

First Trade Paperback Printing: December 2023
ISBN: 979-8-9855941-5-7
ISBN: 979-8-9855941-6-4 (e-book)

Cover Design by Navi' Robins

10 9 8 7 6 5 4 3 2 1

Manufactured in the United States of America

Distributed by Kensington Publishing Corp.

Dear Reader,

I want to thank you immensely for supporting Black Odyssey Media authors, and our ongoing efforts to spotlight more minority storytellers. The scariest and most challenging task for many writers is getting the story, or characters, out of our heads and onto the page. Having admitted that, with every manuscript that Kreceda and I acquire, we believe that it took talent, discipline, and remarkable courage to construct that story, flesh out those characters, and prepare it for the world. Debut or seasoned, our authors are the real heroes and heroines in *OUR* story. And for them, we are eternally grateful.

Whether you are new to J.L. Campbell or Black Odyssey Media, we hope that you are here to stay. We also welcome your feedback and kindly ask that you leave a review. For upcoming releases, announcements, submission guidelines, etc., please be sure to visit our website at www.blackodyssey.net or scan the QR code below. We can also be found on social media using @iamblackodyssey. Until next time, take care and enjoy the journey!

Joyfully,

Shawanda Williams

Shawanda "N'Tyse" Williams
Founder/Publisher

# AUTHOR'S NOTE

Flames of Wrath is a journey I likely wouldn't have taken on my own, so I'm grateful to Shawanda Williams and Kreceda Tyler for their vision in creating a publishing house that's focused on shining a light on stories involving minorities. Here's to Black Odyssey Media's longevity and success.

Suspense with romance has always been one of my favorite combinations to read and write, but this book is something new and different. I give God thanks for my son, who I call "the parent police" for reminding me how this adventure would broaden my scope as a writer. He was actively involved in the plotting stage, letting me bounce ideas off him, coming up with his own, and vetoing concepts that wouldn't work. Since then, I've warned him not to take up a life of crime.

If you've read my work before, thank you for picking up this book I didn't know I had in me. I appreciate each and every reader. If this is your first taste of my writing, welcome to my world. There's plenty to experience and I appreciate you, too.

# PROLOGUE

**G**RANDMA IS GOING *to kill me…maybe it won't matter, since I'm already dead.*

A brilliant cluster of stars littered the sky, as though someone had scattered handfuls of them with no care for where they fell. She'd been discarded in the same way, like trash scattered by a pack of hungry dogs.

But Alexia wasn't garbage, and her friends had done this.

Pain pulsed over every inch of her body.

The pounding of dancehall music saturated the night air as a chill settled in her bones. Somewhere in Montego Bay, another party was happening.

She turned her head and, through the slit of one eye, realized she was spread on the grass surrounding the deck. The reflection of moonlight from the water in the nearby pool splintered into shards that magnified her headache. They'd turned off the lights on the back patio, as if to forget what they had done.

How much time had passed? An hour? Two?

She inhaled, and it was as if an arrow struck her chest, piercing her lungs. The air hitched in her throat and she mewled, then took shallow breaths. Anything more hurt. Her torso and back were aflame. Thick liquid from her forehead blinded her, but she couldn't make either hand obey her commands. *They're probably broken.* The thought amplified the torment racking her entire frame, and fresh tears oozed onto her cheeks.

Time crept by and with it came awareness of her surroundings. Heavy footfalls alerted her to an approaching figure. Alexia angled her head to catch sight of the person but in the soft light, her vision was blurry.

"Help me," she whispered. "Please."

A mature woman hovered next to her, eyes pulled wide. "Dear God. Hold on, chile, mi soon come back."

As tears seeped into Alexia's hair, the agonizing waves of torture won. She released her grip on reality and floated to where the soothing silence waited.

# CHAPTER ONE

## ALEXIA

*Hours earlier ...*

**A**LEXIA EASED AWAY from Derek, whose muscular arm tightened around her waist as they grooved to Yung Bleu's lyrics under the moonlight.

"Come on babe, relax," the linebacker whispered against her neck as his moves went from casual to sensuous.

"We don't know each other like that." She put a few inches between them and pointed at the villa over her shoulder. "And isn't your girl inside?"

"Chloe isn't my girl. She's ..."

As a sheepish expression crossed his face, Alexia smirked. "Just a friend, right?"

He shrugged, his stringy brown hair falling into his eyes. "It's not that serious."

Howls erupted from the people dancing on the other side of the pool as Mateo fell in, still fully dressed in his Sunday finest. He floundered while they ignored him, dipping and rising with the studio-engineered rhythms. One girl held up a phone as Sancia flirted with the camera and swung her hips in a circle, oblivious to the drama being played out. Her brother, Jonathan—the more sensible of the two Jackman siblings—was nowhere in sight.

"Can someone get him out of there, please?" Alexia cried, breaking away from Derek and taking rapid steps toward where Mateo was now treading water. He'd been drinking, like most of the others, and now threw his head back and howled at the moon.

A muscular blond in a T-shirt stretched a hand along one side of the rectangular pool and Mateo grasped it. Instead of lifting himself out of the water, he let out a burst of laughter and pulled the other guy in with him.

Phil didn't find being drenched amusing and punched Mateo in the face.

He fell backward and sank like a boulder.

The metal chair legs scraped across the deck, and Deja, a quiet sophomore who Alexia was friends with, rushed to her side. "What on earth?"

"Are you an idiot? Don't leave him in there like that," Alexia yelled, trying to be heard over the music.

"Who are you?" Phil asked, scowling. "Holy Mary?"

"No," she shot back. "But you have me confused with someone who wants to be stuck in a room with a cop because you couldn't be bothered."

He stared at her, his pale face expressionless, then turned back to the pool.

Alexia exchanged a glance with Deja, who shook her head as she glared at Phil.

Mateo now floated with his arms spread wide, jabbering to himself. Phil poked him with his sneaker and hauled him up by his garish shirt, dotted with planets in a range of colors. He sputtered and dragged himself to the steps, then crawled out to lie on the lip of the pool where he swore at the sky and laughed at something only he saw.

At the other end of the deck, which stretched around the corner at a right angle, her other friends sat at a table with a glass top. A cluster of fan palms, arranged for privacy, hid them from sight. For a while now, they'd been hunched over their phones, the screens reflecting on their faces. Now and then, they sipped from the fruit punch that someone had laced with what Alexia described as thousand-proof rum. One sip and it would blow a hole through her brain, not to mention her stomach. Earlier, she ditched her cup inside the kitchen.

Backing away, Deja tugged the loose curls at the back of her afro, the way she did when off-center or irritated. "Talk about a total a-hole. I'm out. See you at the airport tomorrow, Lexi."

"Sure. I won't be here much longer anyway." The party had thinned out, and only a handful of people who weren't staying at the villa were still on property.

Deja marched toward the gate that opened onto the beach, slipped off her sandals, and disappeared onto the sand.

Two girls Alexia had never seen before joined them on the patio. They shouted hellos, then looked around for a place to sit.

Jason, a second-year student at the University of Miami, slid over to them. He'd been on the prowl since they arrived in Jamaica, and though they were scheduled to fly back to Miami in the morning, he hadn't given up on scoring with any available female. He was good-looking with a bad-boy vibe—tall with jet-black, tousled hair and intense eyes—but desperation made him unattractive.

The slim brunette tipped her head back and glared at him, as though offended by what he'd said.

Over his shoulder, Jason scowled as he said, "Just so you know, I've got some *good* stuff."

"What you got?" Phil asked, pulling off his wet shirt and throwing it on a lounge chair.

Lowering his voice, Jason shared details Alexia didn't hear while removing an item from his pocket. The two leaned closer as they chuckled.

Derek had settled next to two young women who were giggling in the spacious living room. One was Chloe, a cheerleader with jet-black hair that extended to her waist. The other, Mia, had an olive complexion and sipped from a plastic cup between laughing and staring at her phone. When Chloe climbed into Derek's lap and his hand slid under her tank top, Alexia figured it was time to leave.

She'd been there for several hours and didn't see a reason to stay. Her boyfriend, Chad, hadn't been able to make the trip because of work, so she was on her own. She wasn't staying at the villa, but had borrowed her grandmother's car to attend the party.

If Jason and Phil knocked heads, the party could go in a direction she didn't like. Heading toward her friends, she moved past them.

Jason grabbed her arm. "Where you going?"

"To the other deck where my friends are sitting, then home," she said, prying her arm from his grip.

"You're too pretty to be such a nerd." Jason held on tighter. "Why not stay and have some of this *good* stuff?"

"Thanks, but I'll get along without it," she said, twisting her arm. She'd never put anything harmful inside her body, except liquor. Truthfully, she'd had more than enough in the time they'd been on vacation. Plus, she was driving. On top of that, her mother would kill her if she wrecked her grandmother's car.

He didn't release her. Instead, his thick fingers cut off her circulation. "Hey, what's your hurry?"

"My man's waiting," she lied.

"Awww, come on now." Phil wriggled his eyebrows. "Be nice."

"I won't be for much longer, if your friend doesn't let go of me."

Jason sniffed, then leered at her. "I bet you'd loosen up a little if you stayed a while longer."

An image of them forcing whatever poison they wanted to share down her throat made Alexia's desire to leave more urgent. Stranger things had happened on these spring break jaunts, and she didn't want to be a story or a statistic.

The new visitors wandered over to investigate, shaky on their feet and wearing brilliant smiles.

"We heard you talking." The petite female with an hourglass shape and curly hair looked at Jason as if daring him to deny it. "What d'you have going on?"

"A little peyote over here." Jason held up two transparent bags and grinned. "And some ecstasy on this side."

"That does *not* sound like a good idea," Alexia said, rubbing her chafed wrist when Jason finally released her.

"You were just leaving, remember, narc? This has nothing to do with you," he spat.

"You're right about that." She stood straight and was about to tell him what she thought of him for manhandling her when Nisha walked into her line of sight.

"What are you guys arguing about?" Her words carried a slight slur, and her brown eyes were out of focus.

Alexia grabbed her arm. "How much of that rum punch have you had?"

"Nunya." Nisha laughed at her joke and jerked her arm, which knocked Alexia off balance.

She grabbed Jason's shirt to steady herself and the packet of white power landed in the pool. The bag containing the pink, blue, and green pills fell at her feet and she stepped on them, the heel of her shoe crunching the bag into the concrete.

"You little bitch." Jason advanced on her and shoved her in the chest. "You did that on purpose."

Struggling to stay upright, Alexia slapped him on the arm and shouted, "It was an accident."

His face twisted and spittle flew from his mouth. "Accident, my ass."

Jason prodded her a second time, and she stumbled. "If you touch me again—"

"Hey! Watch what you're doing." A shrill voice hit her ear, and someone pushed her toward Jason, who punched her in the belly. She bent over, retching. The contents of her stomach spewed over the feet of the female who stood closest to her, and she screamed obscenities at Alexia, who was still heaving.

"That's it," Jason hollered. "Time to take out the trash."

A sharp jab to the spine sent Alexia crashing to the cement. As the skin of her knees scraped across the hard surface, a blow to the ribs put her flat on her back. The air rushed out of her lungs, and she couldn't seem to catch another. A shower of blows rained on her, and she instinctively curled into a fetal position.

When a rough hand sank into her thick hair, Alexia screamed and clawed at the person's skin. Clumps of strands separated from the follicles as she was pulled toward the yard. She bumped down the two steps that led to the mowed grass, kicking and screaming. Her hip and thighs struck the edges of the treads, numbing them instantly. Someone stomped on her knee and she was sure it was either dislocated or shattered. The battering continued from every direction as she jerked and twitched. Then bitter liquid spewed from her lips. Seconds later, she lost consciousness.

"What the heck?"

A warm hand touched her cheek, and a man hovered next to her.

"Why don't you do what you really want to do?" A mocking female voice came from behind him. "What you've been dying to do?"

"What are you talking about?"

The voices faded, and the couple argued while Alexia tried to make sense of what was happening. She knew these people. *Christian. Sancia. Need your help.*

A light breeze wafted over her thighs, and she moaned as someone moved her from side to side, shifting her clothing and amplifying her pain. A weight settled on top of her. She shifted but couldn't make it go away. Alexia pulled in a breath to protest, but no sound came from her throat. The crushing sensation brought her pain sensors back to life. Agony, like nothing she'd experienced before, shafted through her lower body and between her thighs. The darkness claimed her once more.

After a while, a cool draft of air replaced the unwelcome pressure.

A sharp object poked Alexia's side, then the female said, "You're not all that anymore, huh? Let's see how you like this."

A white-hot line marked Alexia's forehead, leaving fire in its path, and she fainted.

# CHAPTER TWO

## GENEVA

**T**HE SNAKELIKE TUBES ran everywhere. Unlike real serpents, these plastic hoses sustained life. They kept Alexia in the land of the living. The IV lines delivered medication and sedatives her baby couldn't do without.

Geneva Leighton struggled to inhale without sobbing. The tightness in her chest put her close to hyperventilating. The drainage tube protruding from a dime-sized hole at the front of Alexia's head triggered her gag reflex. Then, there were the casts on her arms. She counted slowly to five, then forced her feet forward to the angled hospital bed.

Her flight from Miami to the island was smooth but passed in a blur. Her mind had been consumed with nightmarish images. What would she find when she stepped inside the hospital where Alexia had been admitted? Could she handle everything else that needed to be done while they made arrangements to bring her home?

Geneva brought a hand to her mouth and blinked tears away to focus on her daughter. Everything else was secondary.

The doctor and nurse on the far side of the bed watched silently, their gazes filled with sympathy.

Alexia's eyes were half open, but she wasn't conscious. The doctor had explained a moment ago that Alexia was in an induced coma to stabilize her system. Aside from head trauma, she suffered broken bones, a dislocated knee, and a long list of internal injuries. Only God knew what brain function she'd have when they woke her up, and whether she'd be able to breathe without the ventilator. The neck brace was another source of worry. The doctor didn't think she'd have permanent spinal damage, but they couldn't be sure.

A slash, closed by neat stitches, marred her forehead. Vivid red trails leaked across the white of one sunken eye, and the area around Alexia's cheek was bruised and swollen. Her smooth, reddish-brown skin was otherwise unmarked. Alexia's nails were broken, which brought Geneva a tinge of satisfaction. *My baby fought back.*

"What happened to her face?" Geneva's voice was loud in the small room.

"Her cheekbone and the lower part of her eye socket were fractured. We did a closed reduction to reset …"

His voice faded against the nightmarish reality Geneva faced. What kind of animals would do this to a friend? What could Alexia have done to deserve this beatdown? The little Geneva's mother knew about what was supposed to be a farewell party in no way equated to the ravages visited on Alexia.

With a gentle touch, she stroked Alexia's cheek. "Will she be able to see?"

The light glinted across Dr. Harewood's glasses as he nodded. "Her vision may be blurred for a while but should return to normal."

She sank in the chair next to the bed, her mind a hive of jumbled thoughts. The questions tumbled over each other, demanding to be asked. For now, only one was critical.

"How soon can we fly her back to Miami?"

The hunched doctor with pale skin glanced at the nurse, then said, "As things stand, that's not a good idea. To be on the safe side, I'd give it a week or more before moving her, especially since she's had several seizures. That will allow us to stabilize her."

"So, the breathing tube …?"

"Part of that process."

Geneva's gaze drifted back to the bed. "This is a lot to absorb."

"I understand." He bobbed his balding head.

Frowning, Geneva asked. "Was anyone else brought in with similar injuries or from the same location?"

Eyes narrowed, the doctor shook his head. "Not to my knowledge."

"Thank you. My mother is waiting to see her, so I'll allow her to come in."

"I'm sorry, but—"

Geneva held up one hand. "I know, only one person at a time. Can I come back in after she sees her?"

"Of course."

She discarded the gown, gloves, and mask, then left the room behind the doctor, who faced her outside the door. "We're doing everything we can for her, Mrs. Leighton."

Looking him dead in the eyes, she asked, "What would you say are her chances of survival, in terms of percentages?"

He lowered his head, then cleared his throat. "At this point, somewhere between five and ten. Her injuries …"

Geneva stopped listening.

Dr. Harewood was duty-bound to convey what he saw as the facts laid out on the bed inside that room. She didn't have to accept them.

This was her child he was talking about. Alexia had always been a fighter. She'd arrived at twenty-four weeks, after everything the doctors did to keep her in the womb. Barely a pound, she'd hung on and improved steadily, having been given only a 40 percent chance to live.

Despite this heartbreaking situation, they'd work through it. Somehow.

At the sight of the familiar slender figure of her mother, Geneva said, "Thanks again" to the doctor.

He used a finger to slide his glasses back into place, gave her a sympathetic smile, and then walked away.

"Can I go inside?" Lorna Wright's shaking voice and trembling lips reminded Geneva that their lives had raced off the tracks in a way that made no sense. Nothing about this situation did.

"Yes, sanitize, suit up, and you're good to go. The nurse is still with her." Pointing down the hall, she added, "I have to call Spence."

Geneva sat and pulled out her phone, which she'd silenced earlier. When she swiped the screen, she found that her husband, Spencer, had called several times. She dialed his number, and he picked up immediately. "Why haven't you been answering my calls?"

"Why d'you think?" she ground out through her teeth. "I've been with our daughter."

"I'm sorry." He sighed, then continued, "I've just been worried and trying to check in."

"She's the same as when you left." She stared at her manicured toes as she said, "I take it your meeting is over."

"I'm on the way back to MoBay now."

Geneva rubbed her grainy eyes as an awkward silence filled the airwaves. "Um, I had planned to visit the police station this afternoon to—"

"Let's do it together. I haven't gone because of…well, everything."

Her shoulders sagged and she leaned against the seat. She'd been worried about another argument. She didn't have the energy to spare. These days, everything in their marriage was a battle. He'd told her the police had been called to the hospital after Alexia's arrival because of her condition. Spence hadn't caught them before they left, and his efforts to contact them had been fruitless. The one good thing he'd done was to have Alexia moved to this private facility. He'd already been on the island because of business, which was what consumed the majority of his life. His role as the CEO of a Caribbean-focused shipping company meant frequent trips across the region.

*Your daughter is near death, yet you went to a business meeting fifty miles away.*

"Okay. See you when you get here."

She was about to hang up when he said, "Jen, are you okay?"

After biting her lip to steady her voice, she changed the lie she'd been about to tell and gave him the truth instead. "No, I'm not."

"Stupid question. I'll get there as soon as I can."

On her way back to the intensive care unit, the charge nurse met her at the door. "I'll let your mother know you're back."

"I appreciate that. Thanks."

By the time Geneva sanitized her hands, her mother emerged from the room. She hugged the slight woman, who stood a head shorter, and stepped back. "Go home and get some rest. When Spence gets here, we have to leave for a bit. I'll call you before he comes."

"If you're sure." Her slumped shoulders and lined face reflected exhaustion, but Lorna wouldn't admit it, no matter what. She was that stubborn.

"What did Marlena say Alexia told her about the group at the villa?" Geneva asked, in reference to her mother-in-law. Alexia had spent the last few days with her paternal grandmother, who lived in Ironshore, where the party had been held.

"She told her the group was flying out today."

Her stomach clenched and Geneva wanted to be anywhere but in the hospital watching her child die. She corrected that thought—despite Alexia's condition, she would not give in. Without another word, Geneva pulled on the necessary gear and stepped into the room. This time, her reaction was different. She was devastated, but she'd be darned if she accepted Alexia's lot based on the current situation.

For several minutes, she stroked the back of Alexia's hand, preoccupied with various scenes from her childhood. The latest triumph had been her joy at making it into the university early. This trip to Jamaica was supposed to be a celebration. Now, it had turned to ashes.

Leaning close, Geneva spoke next to Alexia's ear. "Lexi, I don't know if you can hear me, but Mommy and Daddy love you. And whatever it takes, we're going to make these people pay for hurting you."

# CHAPTER THREE

## DEJA

**S**HE CAME FACE to face with Christian Skyers outside the tiny bathroom at the back of the airplane's cabin.

"Hey." His juicy lips curled in a fake smile, but he didn't know who she was. Not really. He probably didn't have a clue about her name. A superstar like him, who was at the top of the food chain, had no time for someone who didn't deserve his attention. That would definitely include her, but it didn't stop her from responding, "Hey, yourself."

She'd known him for years, since they lived in the same city. They had also attended the same schools, but she'd never been considered good enough to be in the popular crowd. She hovered on the fringes. A part of the scenery, but never calling attention to herself, or doing anything to stand out. Being in the limelight had caused her more grief than anything else.

Christian was the opposite—so entitled, he was a cliché. Talented, good-looking, self-centered; the typical football jock. The qualities that set him apart were his intelligence and the lack of a working conscience. His major at the University of Miami was accounting and finance. While he'd been playing football since high school, Christian had no real ambition to compete professionally.

His heart was set on taking over his father's investment company, located at Alhambra Circle, the financial hub of Coral Gables. He was all about the high life and taking what he felt was his due. That had always been his attitude.

After making use of the cramped bathroom, she moved up the aisle, passing Christian and his friends on the way to her seat. When she sat, one of the guys with him said, "Wasn't she at the party last night? What's her name? She'd be hot if—"

"Yo, man, who cares?" Christian snickered. "I wonder how she got an invite."

"Did you see her, though?" another guy asked. "She looked pretty damn good to me."

"Yeah, but the thing with you is that anything on two feet is fair game." Christian paused, then added. "Even her."

They laughed as if he'd said the funniest thing they'd heard all year.

At that point, she inserted the earbuds and scrolled through the playlist on her phone. Their words didn't hurt because she was used to being a nonentity. She liked it that way. Or so she told herself.

Most of them from last night's party were booked on this flight. A couple of the guys turned up at the Donald Sangster International Airport looking like the angel of death was calling their names. Others slept while waiting in the departure lounge. The rest of them scrolled on their phones and engaged in pointless teasing. If the plane went down, the world would definitely be better off without them.

The sour thought chilled Deja.

Early this morning, she'd called Alexia to offer her a ride to the airport, but her grandmother answered the phone. When she asked to speak with Alexia, Mrs. Leighton stifled a sob. "She won't be going home today."

"What happened?"

Mrs. Leighton's explanation left Deja weak. Someone had attacked Alexia and left her in the backyard at the villa. She'd been found at dawn.

She shouldn't have left the party without Alexia, but those knuckleheads were the limit. If only she'd waited. After all, Alexia had said she'd be leaving shortly, too. But her aunt's house was a short walk down the beach, and Alexia had a ten-minute drive. Dragging both hands over her face, Deja asked herself what she'd say to Alexia's mother.

Aunt Jenny—Geneva Leighton to other people—had always treated Deja as if they were related. She'd lived and worked in Coral Gables for some time, same as Deja's Aunt Camille. Despite the three years between them, the girls had clicked, and Alexia was the one who told Deja the group had decided on Jamaica for spring break. The two of them had tagged along because the trip would serve a dual purpose. They'd both get to see their relatives.

Everything worked as planned. Until yesterday. The crux of the whole situation was that she shouldn't have left Alexia behind.

After scouring the internet for any hint of *the* incident, and finding nothing, Deja reclined her seat the few inches it would go and stared at the ceiling. It was too early for any news to have come out, and only images from the start of the party had been shared with the hashtags #ironshore #islandescape #islandvibes #jamaicavibes #montegobay #springbreak #villasettings #villaparty.

A couple other people from the group also had relatives in Jamaica, so they hadn't needed accommodation. The rest of them, a loose group of friends, and friends of friends, had crammed into their parents' timeshare.

Only God knew whose idea it was to have that party, but wasn't that what spring break was about? Mindless amusement from dawn till dusk in an exotic location. Half of them remained at least slightly high and drunk from the time they arrived until the time they left.

Friday night had simply been a culmination of their stay. A time when everything was fair game and nothing was off limits. They would all go back to their lives and prepare for classes on Monday, but nothing would ever be the same for Alexia. That knowledge settled in her soul. She wondered if any of the others around her heard what had happened, but at least a few of them *had* to know since Alexia was found on the property.

OCD tendencies had her picturing faces and listing names. By the time she'd done it twice, she remembered everyone who'd been rooming inside the five-bedroom villa and who'd been invited to what had started as a barbeque and turned sinister when darkness fell.

After speaking with Mrs. Leighton, Deja had returned to the villa before going to the airport. In front of the house, she'd picked up the Wi-Fi and did what she was compelled to do, using her laptop. As she scanned through the footage to find what she was after, she hung her head outside the car, puking. When she was back in Miami, she'd have the time to make sense of the pictures now stuck inside her head.

Something alien, and yet familiar, had come over her as she watched Christian and Sancia take advantage of Alexia. She'd managed to forget the past, shut away the painful parts, but it had slammed her in the face. Made her remember being used in the same way. Woke up the demons that lurked but weren't allowed to control her life. Now, they threatened to run loose.

Willing herself to take deep breaths, she grabbed the armrests of the seat and closed her eyes. If she focused hard enough, her mind would remain in the present. The horrors of yesterday would destroy her if she wasn't vigilant.

A loud guffaw startled Deja, and she jerked. One of the earbuds was dislodged.

"Wow. Good thing the housekeeping staff came in after we left," Christian said.

"Why? Did someone trash the place?"

"Alexia was still there, and someone called the police." Christian lowered his voice but sounded as if he was choking when he said, "They're searching for everyone who was at the villa."

# CHAPTER FOUR

## ALEXIA

*IF I MAKE it out alive, I'll need some serious time with whoever put me here. They should have let me die.*

She had no clue how long she'd been held down by whatever was keeping her motionless. Everything was hazy, aside from the unbearable pain washing through her body in non-stop waves. The medication was a blessing and a curse. The endorphins she'd read about were missing in action, and her throat was a dry wasteland where nothing went up or down. Even if she wanted to, she couldn't beg for relief from the continued torment.

In a moment of clarity, she remembered trying to yank the tube out of her mouth. That had not gone well. The next thing she recalled was having a needle that felt like the size of a drill bit inserted in her arm. Since then, she'd been in a kind of no-man's-land that shifted when it was time for more medication to enter her system.

"Alexia." A gentle hand stroked her wrist. "Lexi?"

She struggled to open her eyes but nothing happened.

"Can you hear me? Alexia, baby?"

The voice was familiar. If she could force her eyes open, she'd be able to connect with whoever was calling the name that clearly belonged to her. Her lids twitched, but nothing else moved. She tried again, but the only thing that shifted was her level of discomfort. Even her eyelashes hurt, and frustration made it worse. When she could not force her eyelids to do as she commanded, a tear leaked and rolled down the side of her face.

With a gentle swipe, the woman at her side brushed away the warm liquid. Another followed and the soothing touch was repeated, then confusion set in. Was it a nurse or someone else? Who was her family, anyway? She couldn't remember.

The woman sniffed, then whispered, "You are *not* a quitter. Despite all of this, you *will* get better."

After a soft rustle, a warm hand enfolded hers. "Alexia, if you can hear me, squeeze my hand."

She tried. Oh, how she tried, but all she managed to do was wake up every pain cell that hadn't been alert before this moment.

The door opened and closed, then a man greeted the person at her side.

"Good to see you." As the woman spoke, she touched Alexia's skin in a gentle sweep. "Have you decided when we can fly her out?"

"It will be a few more days yet. She's still having seizures. Once we have those under control, she'll be fit to travel."

Alexia sensed the disappointment in the woman's sigh and wished she could reassure her. Since she'd been in this bed, she discovered that every person who came to visit had a different aura. The two older females were different, but the same. They didn't speak except to whisper prayers. Even then, they radiated gloom rather than hope. One said the rosary. The other begged God to either restore Alexia's health or take her home.

The person with her now carried a much stronger vibe—positive, yet tender. Someone who believed in action. Now and then, Alexia caught a familiar scent. A perfume she knew. This woman had to be her mother.

If only she could remember.

The air around Alexia shifted, and the lady kissed her forehead. "I love you, baby. I'll be back in an hour."

She stepped away but didn't close the door, so her conversation floated to Alexia.

"Thanks for calling me, but you're only telling me what I already know."

After another few seconds, she added, "I'm beginning to think the police couldn't find water in a well, even with a bucket. I know the people who did this are now out of your jurisdiction, but surely you collaborate with police departments in places as close as Miami?"

In a more forceful tone, she said, "If you won't do what's necessary, then it means that I will. Don't you understand? *My child has been violated in the worst way.* Whatever information I need to ensure she gets justice, you can be sure I'll find it, no matter what I have to do. I have to go. There's an important call coming in."

When the woman spoke again, her voice sounded as if she was about to cry. "Yes, I'm still in Jamaica. We won't be back until the seizures stop."

Alexia thought she'd left, but footsteps approaching the bed pulled her back from the edge of sleep. "Thanks, Syl. I appreciate it. Tell Tavia and Janet to keep praying, too."

The door clicked shut minutes later, and Alexia was left alone.

Scenes from some violent incident spooled through her mind, but the wicked combination of pain and sedative would not allow her to concentrate. Weird how she couldn't remember her name but kept snatches of what had happened to put her in this place. She could help the woman she was convinced was her

mother with the important details. The question was how, since
Alexia couldn't stay awake, and nobody knew when she was close
to alert.

A looming figure silhouetted by the moon invaded her mind.
What he took from her was more precious than anything else she
lost that night. But she was here, with a warrior fighting on her
behalf.

*"He who fights and runs away may live to fight another day;*
*But he who is battle slain can never rise to fight again."*

If there was ever a time when she needed to hear those words,
now was that time. *Daddy.*

She couldn't picture his face, but knew with certainty that he'd
quoted those words when she'd been beaten up in kindergarten
and hadn't defended herself. She'd been too young to understand
what the phrase meant, but grew past that experience, using
brainpower and snark to defend herself as she grew smarter. Those
things hadn't helped her at that party. Not when her friends and
other people she knew had gone past the point of good sense.

Recovery would put her on the level with those who had
taken away her life. Since she hadn't died that night, she sure as
hell wanted to live to face them down.

# CHAPTER FIVE

## GENEVA

THE URGENT BEEPING from the machines woke Geneva from a light doze.

Alexia arched and flopped back on the bed. Her head beat against the pillow, and the whites of her eyes made Geneva shudder. She leaped to her feet, bolted for the door, yanked it open, and shrieked, "We need a doctor in room four."

An unfamiliar doctor and a nurse rushed past. Then another hurried in, rolling a crash cart. One of the nurses gently guided Geneva back to the door. "I'm sorry, Mrs. Leighton. Please wait outside. We'll update you as soon as she's stable."

Tears brought on by anxiety and frustration stung Geneva's eyes.

One solid week and the police still had not given her anything she could use. They were dead silent on the people responsible for Alexia's condition. Geneva had memorized a list of names from a conversation with Alexia, when she mentioned several friends who were part of the trip. They had likely settled back into life as they had known it before they left Miami. Her daughter didn't have that luxury. That made her furious.

Worse than everything, Alexia's best friend had not come to Jamaica. She'd opted to fly to Aruba with her family. Her mother was recovering from a bout with cervical cancer, and Danielle wanted to be near her. Geneva certainly understood that. Her only regret was knowing that if Danny had been in Jamaica, Alexia might have fared better. The two had been looking out for each other since they connected on their first day in high school. Her boyfriend also hadn't made the trip. So far, Geneva had spoken with him once and updated him several times by text.

Spence hurried down the corridor, his long legs making short work of the ceramic tiles. "What happened? I heard them asking for Dr. Harewood for room four on the intercom."

A vise gripped her throat, and several seconds went by before she spoke in a strangled voice. "Alexia. She had another seizure."

"Oh, God." Spence put a hand to his forehead and stepped out of the way as Dr. Harewood raced toward where they stood. He gave them a grim nod, then stepped into the room and closed the door firmly behind him.

Spence leaned against the wall with his eyes closed. Deep lines bracketed his mouth and marked his forehead. The skin beneath his eyes was dark and puffy from lack of sleep. His sun-kissed skin, several shades lighter than Alexia's, was pale, and his mouth drooped at the corners. At forty-eight, he was quite an attractive man. That, and his inclination to stray, had brought trouble to their marriage.

Geneva switched her mental channel and said a prayer. Two days had gone by without a seizure and here they were again. This private hospital was the best in Montego Bay, but she knew the first-world facilities in Miami were what they needed for Alexia. If she required more specialized treatment, that would also be available. They had already made the reservation to air lift her off the island, if only she'd remain stabilized long enough to travel.

The door swung open, and a nurse hurried down the corridor. Through the crack, Geneva couldn't see anything other than the pale-blue gowns and scrubs worn by the treatment team. She was startled when Spence touched her arm and moved her out of another nurse's way.

Her phone vibrated in the back pocket of her jeans, and Geneva eased it out to look at the screen.

Jaden was calling. "Hey, Mom. What's happening?"

"We're at the hospital." She glanced at Spence, who now sat staring at his hands. "Lexi just had a turn again."

"Ugh. I just landed. I'll get Grandma to bring me there."

"Fine, but you may not get to see her right away."

"I understand." Jaden raised his voice above the sound of heavy-duty equipment. "See you soon."

She was about to end the call when he said, "I have something to show you."

"Good news, I hope."

"Depends on how you look at it."

Gaze fixed on her sandals, Geneva frowned. "That doesn't sound positive."

"Don't worry about it. You can decide when you have a look."

"Sure, baby." Spence shifted and their eyes met. His were red and watery. He needed sleep. "Tell Grandma to be careful on the road."

Jaden chuckled. "In that case, maybe I should drive."

"Don't even play about that, boy." Her tone was light, but they both knew she meant every word.

Taxi drivers were notoriously reckless. That was part of the Jamaican landscape. Nearly three-hundred-and-fifty persons were killed in road accidents every year, with 80 percent of the victims being male. Not good for such a small island.

The last time he visited, Jaden had been in an altercation that almost cost his life. The cab driver who caused the crash had threatened to stab Jaden if he reported the incident to the police.

Jaden did exactly that, with the result that the police detained the man overnight, then charged him for the threats made.

Sometimes, Geneva regretted that both her children were as hard-headed as she. Spence's calm demeanor was a good foil for her fiery disposition, but a little more of him in their kids would have been a blessing.

The door swung open, and Dr. Harewood stepped into the corridor.

"How is she?" Geneva searched his face for the truth he might be holding back.

"She's resting now. We gave her some medication. This one lasted more than five minutes."

Geneva knew that wasn't good news, but she was thankful. The way she looked at it, with the level and number of injuries Alexia had, any of them could be fatal.

Spence slipped a hand around her waist. The gesture would have been the norm for a longtime couple, but not for them. Instead of inching away as she wanted, Geneva focused on the doctor. "I'd like to get her out as fast as we can. If she doesn't have another seizure in the next two days, I think we should try."

Slowly, he nodded. "If it happens in the air, the medivac team will know what to do."

As the other medical staff filed past, Geneva touched his upper arm. "Thank you. We appreciate all you're doing."

His dark-brown eyes shone with sympathy as he included Spence in his response. "You're welcome. I have a daughter her age. No parent should go through what you're facing."

Spence shook his hand, but Geneva only nodded, unable to speak because the unshed tears held her throat in a chokehold.

As if he understood what was happening, Spence pulled Geneva closer. She stepped back, and he whispered, "I know I don't deserve to, but let me hold you."

His haggard features stirred her heart, and she allowed Spence to do what he wanted. Her eyes smarted, but she didn't have the luxury of crying. The doctors and nurses never knew for sure, but Geneva had convinced herself that Alexia could feel her presence. She talked to her every day and was determined to be positive, despite the situation.

"I love you." Spence tightened his embrace, then kissed her forehead.

His whispered words interrupted her thoughts, but she didn't respond. The disappointment in his eyes reminded her that they had issues to resolve, but now wasn't the time. She pulled away from him, put on the equipment from the dispenser, sanitized her hands, and opened the door wide enough for him to see Alexia. "I'll be out in a bit to give you and Jaden a chance to go in."

Spence nodded, assessing her with a resigned air.

She rushed to the side of the bed, caressed Alexia's shoulder, and ignored the network of tubes and cables as she kissed her forehead. "Keep fighting. We love you so much. Jaden's coming to see you. He just got off a flight. Daddy's also here and will see you next. Love you, sweet girl."

Geneva was sure a faint groan came from Alexia, but she didn't want to think about the aches she might be feeling after thrashing around and convulsing. The fact that she'd been sedated brought some comfort. Seconds later, she trashed the protective gear and squared her shoulders before stepping outside. "Your turn," she said to Spence, who leaned on the wall, staring through the panes of glass that lined the other side of the corridor.

The squeak of someone approaching in sneakers and the familiar cadence of the footfalls had her craning her neck down the corridor. She expected Jaden to be there in ten to fifteen minutes, but it had taken twenty. Road usage was another thing that was different from when they had lived on the island. Every hour of the day seemed to have peak traffic.

After slapping his father on the back, Jaden threw both arms around her. "Hey, Momzel," he murmured. "How are you holding up?"

"Like I told you, I'm fine." Throwing a glance at Spence, she said, "Why don't you go in, then Jaden can spend some time with her."

"Okay, babe."

A flicker of a frown creased her forehead, which she hoped Jaden hadn't caught. If Spence was making some attempt at normalcy, the least she could do was meet him halfway. Their son was no fool, but he didn't need the added pressure of navigating a minefield between his parents.

When Spence entered the ICU, she looked up at Jaden, a younger reflection of his father clothed in her cinnamon complexion. "Where's your grandmother?"

"She went back downtown. Said she had some errands to run."

Geneva believed Marlena Leighton was avoiding her, but didn't comment. Spence's mother probably thought Geneva held her responsible.

"What were you going to tell me?" she asked.

Jaden's thick eyebrows drew toward each other as he swiped his phone screen. "It's something I came across on social media, a new site called Social-Invyte. Looks like the same party Alexia was at."

When he found what he needed, Jaden cued the video and handed it to Geneva. She tapped and watched as a blonde, holding a plastic cup, toasted the camera while gyrating.

"Look behind her," Jaden instructed.

In the background, Alexia was talking with two young people. Seconds later, she moved out of the camera's range.

Geneva played the video once more, then said, "Send it to me."

She'd been mystified that very few pictures of the party had surfaced. Today's kids lived out in public, so the silence around Alexia's incident was unnatural. Finally, she had something useful. Danny had spoken to her earlier in the week when she couldn't reach Alexia. Although Geneva wanted to ask for the names of the people who had taken the trip to Jamaica, she knew it wouldn't be a good look. She'd circle back to it later. Or the police could, if they moved fast enough.

She squinted as some detail teased the edges of her memory. When the revelation came, she sucked in a deep breath and released it in a slow tide. Deja Johnson, the other girl who completed their trio, had also been part of the group. She must have been the person who called her mother-in-law to ask about Alexia.

Geneva would find her when she was back in Miami. A message wouldn't do. She needed to look that child in the eyes to find out what made her abandon Alexia. And if she had anything to do with harming her baby, there wouldn't be any place on earth where she could hide. "She can stake her miserable life on that," she whispered.

"Huh?"

Jaden's voice pulled Geneva from her thoughts. After studying her for a couple of seconds, he said, "We all want to know what happened at that party, and who's responsible. But, please don't do any of that high-tech stuff that will be considered cyber stalking and invading people's privacy."

Jaden was on his way to following in her footsteps and was already proficient in his chosen field, but preferred working with hardware. His next stop would be a master's degree in computer engineering; he was dedicated and focused—like her. He'd learned much from her over the years during which she operated as a cybersecurity expert in the corporate world. She now ran her own consulting company and was always in demand.

Her master's in the same field gave her an up-close-and-personal knowledge of computer science and electrical engineering, which would give her options as she navigated through these next few months and brought her daughter's attackers to heel.

Smiling to soften her next words, Geneva cupped Jaden's cheek. "You may be grown and everything, but you don't tell me what to do."

# CHAPTER SIX

## DEJA

IN THE THIRTY-SECOND video clip, Sancia swirled her hips in time to the dancehall recording. Like the typical party girl, she couldn't help herself. Had to be a showoff and post it for the world to see. Social-Invyte wasn't the typical social media site. They'd only started up three months ago, but now people were flocking to join because of the untraceable disappearing posts.

She kept the sound off because of where she sat in the food court. It took her a while to decide how she could help Alexia. She hadn't been around to help her friend that night, but her mind had been going in circles.

Since coming back home, she was sick with remorse. Those who hadn't turned on Alexia had been caught up in doing their own thing. A few were probably too drunk to even know their own names. And that disgusting pair had arrived like hyenas at the scent of a fresh kill.

Every action was set in motion due to a couple of packs of poison meant to chase a temporary high. After forcing herself to watch the video again and again, Deja threw up and couldn't stop crying. Nor could she sleep. She'd had to lie to her roomie, pretending to be ill from something she'd eaten.

The rumor mill at the university churned out several stories as to why Alexia hadn't returned to school. She'd been attacked by unknown persons. Been in a bad accident. Remained in hospital in Jamaica. None of them mentioned that her luck had taken a dive at *Island Escape*.

"I left before whatever jumped off, so I don't know what happened," was all Deja could manage when Aunt Camille shared Alexia's condition. Sick at heart, she made the appropriate sympathetic sounds while being fed the details of her friend's injuries. Since then, she stayed away from her aunt to avoid the risk of breaking down.

That update had set Deja off again, and her mind had tumbled back to her teenage years before Mom had finally brought her to Miami. She was the last of her three children to leave Jamaica.

The things she could have told her mother, if she had a mind to do so. If she weren't protecting other people. Even now, she knew Hyacinth Redgrove wouldn't believe her. So, she kept both her business and pain to herself—as she had for many years.

Aside from the names of the spring breakers she carried in her head, Deja now had a plan. The only decision left was where and who to start with. But if she were honest, the decision wasn't hard.

Sancia had a reputation for running her mouth, and her need for attention was legendary. Another entitled girl who thought the world owed her everything, she said whatever came to her mind and didn't care who was listening. Like now, for instance. She sat with two other girls several tables away, speaking at the top of her voice.

"Jamaica was so tame." Sancia flicked several stands of blonde hair over her shoulder. "Next time, I'm going to Cancun. Daddy said if my grades are the same or better, it won't be an issue."

Her friend's response didn't carry far, but Sancia's reply did.

"There's *nothing* my father won't give me. He got me here, didn't he?"

"I thought applying like everyone else and having good grades was how people got into the university," the brunette said, with an irritating nasal twang.

Sancia's laughter was supposed to be a delicate tinkle, but it fell on the ear like nails on a chalkboard. "That's how it works for most people, but not folks like Jonathan and me. And definitely not when your parents are movers and shakers, who put money into all the right organizations and charities."

This wasn't the first time Sancia had made reference to not having to go through the same process as other applicants, or "jumping through hoops like trained animals," as she put it.

A rocket scientist wasn't needed to figure out what she meant, but Sancia had planted a fresh idea.

Sliding lower in the seat, Deja weighed her thoughts. The pounding of her heart said this was one way of leveling things up, but it would only be the beginning. After one slow drag of her green smoothie and stashing the phone inside her backpack, she rose and walked in the opposite direction without looking toward Sancia and her group.

With her classes over for the day, now was a good time to head to Tyler's place. The small space was his lab, where he worked as a ghostwriter for comic strips to supplement his day job and cover his student loan. When he wasn't doing that, he scoured the internet for inspiration and got into things he shouldn't. But only she knew that. Tyler had a knack for research that had come in handy in her studies. The human mind fascinated her, and, more so, her reaction to much of what had happened in her life. Psychology had been a natural choice when she entered the university.

Her older brother, Curtis, had introduced her to Tyler years ago, and when he mentioned that both of them were computer whizzes, their connection was instant and hadn't slacked off since then. A fifteen-minute ride in her ocean gray Nissan Altima took her through Coconut Grove to his one-bedroom house on South West Street. She stepped on the concrete walkway and turned her face up to the sun. Miami reminded her of Jamaica, and that was half of what she appreciated most about it. The other had to do with the greenery and the nearness of the ocean, which had a calming effect on her senses.

She climbed the shallow steps and rapped on the door, which he pulled open after a few seconds. A bright smile split his dark-chocolate skin. "Hey. Shoulda known it was you. What brings you here today?"

"I need you to help me look for some info, but I don't want anyone to know I was looking."

The intensity in his dark gaze heated her skin. "Mind telling me what it is?"

"It's nothing illegal."

He turned away, then looked at her over his shoulder. "Which is why you want me to go incognito, right?"

"You got it."

They both laughed as she scanned his compact living space furnished with a sofa, coffee table, television, and shelving that contained books on technology and cartooning. His computer equipment was spread across his dining table, which was rarely used for eating. That happened in front of the television.

Tyler approached the laptop connected to a large monitor, and she drew up a chair next to him. Although he dwarfed her in size, his presence was comforting. With one elbow propped on the sheet of glass placed over the wooden surface of the table, she looked at him sideways.

"So, what am I looking for?" he asked.

"I need information on the Jackmans of Coral Gables."

His eyebrows flew upward. "*The Jackmans?*"

"Yes, those." Angling herself to stare directly at him, she continued, "How do you even know about them?"

"I live here, that's how. He's in politics and they are everywhere." He tapped the keys in a clatter that highlighted his efficiency, then peered at the screen. "Okay, so what specifically do you want to know about Charles and Rachel Jackman?"

She edged closer to the edge of the chair and tapped the screen. "Can you tell me how much cash they've poured into the university?"

"You know how to do this stuff as well as I do. You've watched me often enough."

"But I don't know how to get certain kinds of data."

"Like what?" he asked, glancing away from the screen.

"Like bank accounts and bank statements."

His head swung toward her, and he huffed. "That's jail time, sweets."

"Maybe for me, but not for you." She tweaked one of his locs. "Your skills make me afraid of you."

"Mmm-hmm, this is the part where you talk to me nice to get what you want."

Laughing, she said, "Your mama didn't give birth to no fool."

"No, she didn't."

When they stopped laughing, Tyler sat back and rested both hands on his thighs. "Seriously though, why do you need this stuff?"

"To right a wrong, so you can't leave any trace."

He sucked his teeth. "Am I good or am I good?"

Placing a hand over his, she said, "We both know you're *great* at this stuff."

Tyler squinted at the screen then asked, "How far back are we talking?"

"From April of last year, and give me twenty-four months before that, as well."

"Girl, are you for real?" he asked, rubbing both hands together.

She hid a smile. The challenge already had him excited.

"I wouldn't ask if I didn't think you could do it."

He shook his head, then said, "Give me some space while I do what I do."

"No problem." She rose to pace the room, peering through the grilled front window until he cleared his throat.

"You got a thumb drive?" he asked.

She plucked it off her keyring and eased into the seat beside him. "Here."

The moment he handed it to her, she asked, "Can I use one of your laptops?"

"Sure." He flashed a brilliant smile, which was infectious. "It's like nothing is off limits with you."

"You know you love me." She grinned and kissed his cheek.

Something shifted in his eyes before he said, "Yeah, you know I do."

She grabbed a closed laptop and set it on the low table, then sat on the end of the leather sofa. After scrolling through all the material Tyler gathered, she highlighted one name that appeared with several bank transfers while beating back excitement.

A quick search confirmed the man's identity and his connection to the university. She cut, pasted, and compiled the transactions to fit on one page. Then she added the bank's header that contained the Jackman's names and account number.

When she sent the information to Sancia, it might take her a minute to figure out what she was looking at, but she'd understand the implications eventually.

Deja smiled as she stared across the room. Hitting that family where it would hurt most made her giddy with delight.

# CHAPTER SEVEN

## ALEXIA

THE CONSTANT PAIN was like a frenemy—always present and taking digs at her. Alexia had no idea how much time had passed since she'd last been awake but her mother's comforting touch made up for the frustration of dealing with the lapses in time and memory.

"This isn't a good time, Spence." The silence continued until Geneva spoke and her words took on a cutting edge. "Because I was online with a client."

Aside from her even breathing and the occasional beep from the machine, the lull was complete. Alexia wanted to protest, because as long as her attention was focused on her mother's words, she could forget being locked inside the hell her body had become. She fell into a doze then jerked awake, wishing they would dial back the stuff that kept her drugged up. Although the medication held the pain at a manageable level, she was frustrated.

Her brain was blank, as if she'd been born yesterday and her only memory was the darkness of the womb. Flashes of some horrific incident came and went, but she couldn't hold on to it long enough for it to make sense. For some reason, her brain had been failing her. She focused back on her mother when the conversation continued.

"What are the police saying?" She paused, and Alexia prayed her mind wouldn't go fuzzy again.

"Are you serious? Well, at least they had the good sense to collect a statement from the housekeeper. That can be used in court." The irritation in Mom's tone was clear when she asked, "What else do they have?"

She let out a sigh filled with impatience, and the chair creaked as she shifted.

"Thank God Mom had the presence of mind to collect Lexi's clothing and her phone." She gripped Alexia's hand tighter, then whispered, "She insisted they do a rape kit."

Alexia's willed herself not to fall asleep but was disappointed when her mother didn't say anything else on the subject.

"If the situation was different, I'd be back down there in a flash to give them hell." Her voice cracked, and she added, "Distance or not, they'll be hearing from me until they get off their asses and do something about this situation. For heaven's sake, it's been …"

If she could, Alexia would have pumped her fist or applauded. She didn't remember what date Mom had said, but hoped too much time hadn't passed. Even she knew that the longer the police took with the details, the more likely it was that her case would fall to the bottom of the pile of whatever they were working on. Both her grandmothers said crime was out of control on the island. *There, she remembered something! Two grandmothers.*

Her fingers twitched, and her mother pulled in a sharp breath. "Alexia? Baby, can you squeeze my hand again?"

Alexia kept trying, but her luck didn't hold.

The door opened and the air shifted.

"Hi, Chad. All is well?"

"I'm fine, Mrs. Leighton." Chad cleared his throat and lowered his voice. "How is Alexia?"

"She hasn't woken up, if that's what you're asking."

When he spoke again, he'd come closer. "I guess. Did the doctors say anything different?"

"They reversed the induced coma, but ..." Her mom breathed in deep, then added, "When it's time, it's time. She's doing better."

A smile Alexia couldn't feel tried to make it beyond the static space of her useless body. The first time she knew he was there, Alexia understood the sadness that cloaked the room. Chad wasn't dealing with her situation well. She wasn't a vegetable. She was still alive and conscious of the world around her. If only she could tell him. Weird that she remembered him and not her family.

He dropped a warm hand on top of hers and squeezed gently, as though she'd break if he applied more pressure. With her throat blocked by whatever was wedged inside, she couldn't make a sound. A warm liquid splashed on her hand, and he wiped it away.

"Chad?"

The chair creaked, and Chad withdrew his hand, leaving hers cold. His shoes squeaked on the floor as he rushed from the bed and opened the door.

Although Alexia tried hard to prevent it, a tear trickled from the corner of one eye.

"Mean and senseless." The choked-out words pierced the no-man's-land where Alexia now lived.

The person standing somewhere close breathed hard, as if she'd been running. But in a hospital, that was never a good sign. This individual wasn't staff, though. If she was, she'd be fiddling with the equipment. She pulled in a sharp breath and touched Alexia's arm. "I'm so sorry I didn't—"

The door swung open, and she sniffed and withdrew her hand.

*Darn it!* The rhythm of her words was familiar, like someone whose family also came from the island.

Mom's comforting voice intervened. "Thanks again for coming, Deja."

"It's no problem. D-did anyone else visit?" she asked, her words hesitant.

"Not from your group." Her mother's tone was harsh, then she sighed. "Can I ask you something?"

Several seconds passed before Deja answered, "Sure."

"Do you have any idea who did this to Alexia?"

The silence stretched and the machines hummed while Alexia struggled not to fall asleep.

"Um…I left her at the villa."

"So, you didn't know about what happened until …?"

"Wh-when I spoke with Mrs. Leighton the next morning." Now, Deja sounded as if someone was twanging her vocal cords, making them vibrate. "I'm so sorry."

"Didn't anyone else think it strange she didn't fly back with the group?" Mom asked softly, in that voice Alexia recognized. Her mother was poised to pounce and ferret out the truth, something she'd done all her life. If Alexia could, she'd have smiled. Another detail had surfaced from her memory bank.

Deja, though, she believed was a friend. Otherwise, she wouldn't have come. Unless she'd helped put her here and came to check if Alexia was conscious and able to tell what had happened. That would come soon enough. She strained to hear Deja's answer.

"No one said anything, so I didn't, you know?"

"No, I *don't* know. Friends check on each other." The air shifted and Mom added, "Isn't that how it normally works?"

"Yes, ma'am, but …" Deja's words faded, then she sighed. "I'm sorry, Aunt Jenny. If I could change anything…Alexia doesn't deserve this."

"No, she doesn't." Her mother's voice was like the crack of a whip, then the room descended into cold silence. If Alexia had a way to communicate, she'd have told Mom not to be too hard on Deja. After all, she wasn't responsible for what those at the party had done.

She waited, but neither of them said anything. A flurry of footsteps followed, then the door opened and closed.

Mom's heavy sigh disturbed Alexia. What she wouldn't do to emerge from this place now to share what she knew. Which was what, exactly? Shifting images that came and went each time she woke. Angry voices and blows directed at her. Pain like she'd never imagined was possible. Despair that she'd ever again be "Alexia the Great." Her father's teasing voice echoed in her ear, making her want to scream in frustration.

"We may be down, but we're not out, you hear me?" Mom squeezed Alexia's hand, which pulled her back inside the room. "That girl knows something she isn't saying. Whatever it is, I'll get it out of her."

And she would, too. Geneva Leighton wasn't someone to play with when she wanted results. Alexia's thoughts drifted until Mom said, "The worst thing she could have done was to leave you at that villa."

# CHAPTER EIGHT

## GENEVA

GENEVA CLOSED HER eyes, praying for patience. "Even if your father was the Commissioner of Police, I'd have done the same thing."

"You could have given me a heads-up and—"

"How much more warning did you need, Spence? We've been back for a month and what progress have we made? Tell me that."

Everything annoyed Geneva. Her daughter lay broken, and they had gotten next to nowhere with law enforcement. Stateside, the police were reluctant to do anything, since the crime was committed outside their jurisdiction.

In her opinion, the Montego Bay lawmen were sleeping on the job, and Spencer wasn't making much of a difference in spite of his father being part of the police hierarchy in that region. Aside from a statement released by their public relations department about following clues, the silence had been telling. The police had done less than nothing.

Both major papers on the island had been only too happy to listen to her story. Maybe the articles released today would light a fire under them. That, and the event she had lined up for this afternoon. But all in good time.

"You know it takes time to build a case. Dad called me this morning." A horn blast drowned his words for a few seconds. "Couldn't you have found another way, outside of going to the newspapers?"

"It's not like you or your father—"

"You know damn well you're being unfair," Spence snapped.

"If you had tried harder—" She glanced at Alexia, then rose and went to stand in the corridor. "Like I was saying, you've been back in Jamaica twice since this happened. *Twice.* And you still can't tell me anything about Alexia's case. Did you even take the time to visit the divisional headquarters?"

He didn't answer and she sighed, exhausted in body and mind. "I guess that's a no. Because the fact is, you were likely paying more attention to your job, and other things, than finding answers."

*Especially since you're the same kind of man as your father. Work comes before family. Every. Single. Time.*

"That's not true. After we spoke yesterday, I found out the police accessed the tape from the villa."

She didn't bother to tell him that was one of the first things she'd been trying to do while she was on the island, but the agent for the villa had refused. "And? How has their case advanced?"

"They'll be working with the police in Miami. I'm guessing some kind of facial recognition software will help them tie down all the youngsters."

"All of that could have come on the back end. Surely, the reservation agent would have the names of the people staying in the villa," she snapped. "And I suppose at this rate, it will be a few more months before we know anything else."

"That's unreasonable. The police are working with limited resources and are short staffed."

"You sound like your father."

That shut him down, as she knew it would. Spencer had a love-hate-despise relationship with his father. He loved the man. Hated him for the things he'd put his mother through. And despised him for not rising above the rank of superintendent.

Sometimes, talking with Spence was pointless. Now was one of those times. Forcing herself not to snarl at him, Geneva said, "I have to go."

After a tiny pause, he said, "Sure. I have a meeting in a few minutes. Talk later."

Geneva rehashed the conversation as she massaged her forehead on the way downstairs to grab a cup of coffee at the cafeteria. As she sat staring outside, she realized how much life had changed. She now ran her business at Alexia's bedside and had all but given up on physical activity, which had her feeling sluggish. But she wouldn't have done anything differently, if given a choice.

The awful-tasting black coffee would give her enough energy to keep moving for the next few hours. A moment later, she threw the cup in the trash and walked briskly toward Alexia's room with her thoughts still churning.

Since Jaden had shown her the picture of that young woman at the villa, she'd been following her movements on social media. Knowing what she did about young people, the sudden blackout was a big clue that something was wrong. Sancia Jackman's wall had been full of sun, sea, and sand photos, which was how many people viewed Jamaica.

Then nothing. That one video and not even one photo or live clip for the rest of that evening or the following morning when they left the island. Her profile was now mostly selfies and shots with her friends.

The sight of them crowding together and grinning at the camera brought tears to Geneva's eyes and a lump to her throat.

Life was unfair, but she knew that. She entered the hospital room and her gaze went to Alexia, who was a shadow of the vibrant young woman she'd been a month and a half ago.

If—*when*—Alexia recovered, her baby girl would …

Glancing at the other empty bed several feet away, she reminded herself of what could have been. A tic developed under Geneva's eye as she opened her laptop. She'd sat in this same chair and gathered every scrap of information she needed about *Island Escape*.

One email and a response from the villa rental agency had given her a way inside. Plus, the timeshare arrangement had come as a sweet bonus. Charles Jackman and Desmond Skyers were among the businessmen with shares in the villa where Alexia's life had been nearly beaten out of her.

"Don't worry, baby girl," she whispered, smoothing her hair with one hand. "We're about to do something about that."

In all her years of work and study, Geneva had never limited herself in terms of theory versus know-how. She had equal knowledge of how to do things the right way and what to do if she didn't want to leave digital footprints. Sitting at Alexia's side had given her ample time to work out exactly how to implement the first step of her "get even" project, which she'd roll out today. She'd dubbed it Flames of Wrath. Everyone who had a hand in hurting Alexia would get a taste of revenge—Geneva style.

She had not been able to access the recording from the day of Alexia's attack, but she'd discovered that the agent's computer was wired into the surveillance system of several vacation properties. Since the incident, she had studied the building and its amenities, and knew when the last guests checked out three days ago. The log at the agency revealed that *Island Escape* would be empty for the next week.

The skeleton maintenance staff left promptly at four o'clock each afternoon. All she needed was the twenty-minute gap that existed when the security guards made their rounds to each property handled by the Dynamic Vacations agency.

Inside the villa, a small office was tucked away, complete with every modern office accessory to suit businesspeople who needed contact with the real world while on vacation. *Island Escape* was not only furnished with appliances connected to the Wi-Fi—the personal computer, fax machine, and printer were also on the same network. Talk about internet addiction overload.

Her first step was to erase and then rewrite the software of both the fax machine and printer, then infect both with a malicious code. Experts might say that the built-in thermal breakers would prevent the fusers inside both pieces of equipment from overheating and starting a fire, but Geneva understood that any piece of machinery could be breached, if one knew how.

The fax came as a surprise. Nobody used those anymore, but it would work in her favor. If one piece of equipment didn't get the task done, the other would. Both machines were connected to electricity and neither had ever been powered down in the time she'd been watching. The crucial element was paper, which had also been left in the trays. A few keystrokes meant the point of no return, but she was ready. The loss of a building and the income derived from it could not compare to the devastation of a life and family, but it was a place to start.

She glanced at Alexia before typing in a series of commands. Then she sat back and watched until a few curls of smoke emitted from the paper stacked in the printer tray. Her tiny smile widened when several sparks shot from the laser printer and fell on the wooden desk.

In a house with a partial wooden structure and furniture to match, it wouldn't be long before the fire spread. By her watch, eighteen minutes would elapse before the guards did another drive by. Even so, the office was located toward the back of the building so by the time anyone noticed the flames, it would be too late.

Her gaze went back to Alexia, but her mind settled on Jaden. She had another task to complete, so she rang his number.

"Hey, Mom, any changes?"

"No, love." The top of the desk at *Island Escape* was covered in flames when she said, "Did you do what I asked?"

"Yeah. The laptop is set up inside your office."

"Thanks, love. Be safe."

She'd shut it off in a moment of absentmindedness. The program she needed would allow her to access the laptop owned by her father-in-law, Superintendent Desmond Leighton.

# CHAPTER NINE

## GENEVA

DEJA WAS A pretty girl but didn't seem to care about her appearance. The baggy T-shirt and jeans screamed that she was trying to avoid attention. She may have had reasons for that, but Geneva wasn't there to focus on her problems. Only one thing occupied her mind: avenging Alexia.

The loss of the villa would touch the pockets of those affected, but she wanted them to experience the heartbreak she was living. But as her mother always said, "time is the master." Planning and strategizing occupied the hours when she wasn't working for her clients.

She let two days go by before asking Deja to come to the hospital. After her visit with Alexia, Geneva took her downstairs to the cafeteria. Around them, people came and went, focused on their business. Deja sat with her fingers wrapped tight around the cup of coffee Geneva had bought and stared at the fiberglass table.

Geneva cleared her throat to wake Deja from whatever rabbit hole she'd fallen into. "I know you feel bad about Alexia, but I need to ask you something."

"Okay." As she sipped from the cup, her wide eyes struck Geneva as comical, but she'd never felt less like laughing.

"Do you remember the people who were at the party when you left? And who else might have been on the property?"

Her gaze darted over Geneva's shoulders, and she lifted the cup to her lips a second time. A sip turned into a swallow that scalded her mouth. She uncapped the bottle of water close to her hand and downed a few mouthfuls. Not once did she look at Geneva.

"Um…I'm not a hundred percent sure—"

Geneva pulled out her phone. "Start with what you remember."

While she already knew the names of the youngsters who'd been staying at the villa, Geneva wanted to be certain of which individuals were inhouse at that particular time.

Deja lowered her head and chewed her lip, deep in thought. When she finally spoke, Geneva's fingers sped over the phone's keypad and made a list in her notetaking app. At the end, Deja sighed. "That's it."

The girl had an excellent memory, but Geneva pushed a tad harder. "And you're sure you haven't forgotten anyone?"

Deja pulled the hair at the base of her scalp and squinted, as if jogging her memory. "Just the ones who had disappeared, but were around somewhere."

"And who are those?"

Her gaze turned suspicious, and Geneva let out her breath. "I'm sure you want the people who hurt Alexia to face what they did, right?"

"Yes," she whispered.

"Then you're doing the right thing."

"Yes, Auntie." She sat straight and mentioned four additional persons.

Last names didn't matter. It would be easy enough for Geneva to gather that information. She smiled at Deja, a reward for her cooperation, but she wasn't feeling it. Helping was the least she could do after leaving Alexia behind. She wasn't done with her. Not by a long shot.

She forced another smile to her lips. "If you think of anything else, or you have anything that will help, please reach out to me."

"Okay." Deja nodded like a bobble-headed toy, eager to please. But her eyes said something else. She knew much more, but Geneva didn't want to be intimidating. Not at this minute.

After putting away the phone and picking up her handbag, Geneva left the table with bitter thoughts circling in her head. None of them deserved to be walking around whole and healthy while her child had been cast aside like a bit of garbage. They were the refuse, not her baby.

As she did when this ordeal threatened to overwhelm her, Geneva took several deep breaths. By the time she stood inside the room where Alexia lay, she was back in control. She sat next to her, stroking her hand.

"Lexi, darling," she whispered. "You *will* recover from this, but until then I'll make sure they don't forget what they did."

Tears threatened, but she had no time to indulge herself. She kissed Alexia's cheek, then sat at the small table in one corner. She booted her laptop, masked its IP address, and opened her browser. She'd already taken note of two people on Deja's list, whose names she knew. Sancia and Jonathan Jackman—the children of a popular businessman and politician. She had also created a dossier on both and had formulated a plan. Their father would find out the fire was merely a mole hill compared to the heap of troubles to come. Another half-hour of research netted her more valuable material. Digging deeper unearthed exactly what she wanted.

Charles Jackman was like most privileged and influential men, conscious of his place in society and not afraid to flaunt it. He threw money around in an obvious attempt to align his name with highbrow charities. The pattern of his donations to the

University of Miami had aroused her suspicions, and she now had everything needed to make the first strike against the Jackmans.

Aside from donating to several foundations, some of Jackman's payments had gone directly to the vice president in charge of finance. A deep dive into their banking records cemented that connection. Four installments that totaled five hundred thousand dollars, paid more than a year ago.

She had looked up the VP on the university's website. George Falloon was a distinguished middle-aged man with a full head of steel-gray hair. The right kind of individual needed to facilitate the deal the Jackmans had made. The fact that their money had also gone into several of the school's foundations had smoothed the path through admissions for his children.

Geneva assumed all parties had walked away from the exchange satisfied.

The information she had wasn't conclusive proof. Who was to say the payments weren't made for another reason? Even if they were, just the hint of scandal would be enough to make the right people take a second look. Also, anyone with two eyes didn't have to look far to see that the two Jackmans enrolled in the university didn't belong there. Her foray into the university's vast system revealed that both barely had passing grades.

She pulled up a mind-mapping software she had created and opened a document. For a moment, she stared at the bubbles. Each one carried a name and details about the person, and a network of lines ran in several directions. To the casual observer, her mind map may not have made sense, but each stroke connected people with each other by interest and other commonalities.

Geneva rose from the seat to pace the width of the room. From time to time, her attention went to Alexia, and her throat closed tight. With both hands nestled inside the pocket of her linen pants, she studied the ceramic tiles, finetuning her next move. The pieces were already in place; all she had to do was fit them together and execute. She released a breath and rubbed her chest, which ached every time she focused on her daughter.

Pulling the laptop closer, she settled into the seat and her next task. Within minutes, she created a glitch in the university's messenger app, which allowed her to blast a status update and accusation against the Jackmans. *Rumor has it that Jonathan and Sancia Jackman are at the top of a list of students whose parents may have provided donations and special favors in exchange for admission. #admissionscandal #donorsociety #jackmanandjackman #sanciaandjonathan*

Let them explain that to the people who mattered, including the police.

# CHAPTER TEN

## CHRISTIAN

HE'D PLANNED TO ignore the text, but something told him to read it.

*Some kinds of dirt rise to the surface, even if you sweep them under the carpet.*

His gaze darted around the nearby benches where his friends were clowning between classes. The jokes about football practice went forgotten. The breeze rushing in his ears replaced the sound of Blake, Kadeem, and Mick's voices. The text could have been misdirected—a message meant for someone else—but after that blast about Sancia and her brother, he had to wonder.

Christian's radar for trouble was always on high alert, although he'd avoided getting into any serious mess. There was that one time with that girl, Donna-Marie. A chill raced up the back of his neck, but he rubbed it away with one hand. The last time he'd been careless was during spring break in Jamaica, but he'd breathed easier as the normal rhythm of school took over and the days ran into each other. For all he knew, someone had the wrong number. No need to worry about something that might be a mistake.

"Hey, what are you staring at?" Mick leaned sideways to get a look at the phone screen.

"Nothing that concerns you," Christian snapped when his phone pinged again. He slid it into his pocket. The new message was also from an unknown number. He'd check what it said on the way to his last session for the day. After that he had practice.

He slid sideways off the back of the bench where he had perched.

"Hey, where are you headed?" Blake, another football player, asked as Christian walked away with his mind wrapped around a petite girl with a headful of curly hair that he was checking out.

"Finance. Class starts in a few."

"I'm going in that direction, too," Kadeem chimed in, hefting his backpack to his shoulder.

The phone vibrated in Christian's jeans and brought him back to the message he'd received a few minutes ago, but his thoughts shifted to Sancia. Technically, they were in a relationship that neither of them had given a name. They were more friends with certain benefits that flowed on both sides. She did favors for him and those same favors kept her satisfied. He got the action, and she liked watching. They'd been friendly now for close to eight months and, in a sense, were kindred spirits. Both of them liked living on the edge.

When they arrived at the lecture hall, Christian sat at the back of the room and eased out his cell. Three unread messages. Two from an unknown number. One from Sancia. He opened the one from her first.

*Let's meet later.*

That wouldn't fly. Not with the mood he was in. *No. Meet me in an hour at that café you like.*

He cut the sound on the phone and opened a video clip that came with one of the messages with an unknown number. People were trickling into the hall, so he hunched over the Samsung. At first, all he could make out was the fact that the area on-screen was dark. Then, he recognized himself and Sancia crouching in the grass outside the villa. The reel ended where he unzipped his pants.

His lunch threatened to make a sudden return, while his heart thundered in his ears. This couldn't be right. Who had filmed them, and was there more of it somewhere? At the thought of the last unopened message, he broke into a sweat. Conscious that he was breathing through his mouth, Christian read the text.

*This forbidden fruit will be your downfall.*

Christian swore his heart thumped directly against his chest wall.

*Who was toying with him, and what the hell was he going to do?*

The minute the lecture ended, he headed to that expensive café where Sancia and her friends seemed to spend half the day. When she stood before him, makeup perfect as always, he put the phone in her face, then pulled it back so she could watch the clip.

Her eyes widened and she grabbed his arm. "Where did that come from?"

So, she was going to try and act innocent? "I was about to ask you."

She glared at him, eyes glittering. "Why would I do anything like that, and who would have done it for me?"

"How should I know?" He ran one hand over the back of his head. "And I'm wondering if there's more of it anywhere."

Sancia licked her lips with the tip of her tongue. "I don't know what to think and why you're still looking at me like that."

"Like what?" he snapped, his irritation getting the better of him.

Her gaze flicked to the phone in his hand. "Like you think I had something do with it." She pulled her shoulders back, then added, "There's something else that's freaking me out."

Sancia was such a drama queen, he simply waited for whatever bit of fluff she'd come up with next.

"You know when somebody's spying on you?" She raised both brows and glanced around before continuing, "I've been feeling like that lately."

Christian flipped his wrist and shook his head. "Come on, you *always* have eyes on you. That's some BS."

"Right." She rolled her eyes and scoffed. "After what you just showed me, how can you be so certain nobody's watching us?"

She switched her book bag from one shoulder to the other. "Something about this doesn't feel right. First someone spreads those lies about me and my family, and now there's this."

Christian's head was about to explode, so he took a calming breath before he said, "We both know what a first class bish you can be without even trying, so that might be a matter of someone getting back at you."

Cutting her eyes at him, she said, "I haven't had time for anything. Classes have been busting my butt."

Now, it was his turn to scoff. "Seriously?"

"For your information, I've been staying in and minding my own business." She ran both hands through her hair then pulled the long strands into a loose bun. "You'd think people would learn to mind theirs."

While searching his eyes, she pouted. "Are you going to tell me you're the only one on campus who didn't receive that disgusting lie about me and my family?"

"I don't like your tone," he said, stepping in closer. "Are you accusing me of something?"

She eased back and forced a smile. "N-no, I'm not, but when stuff like this happens, I can't help thinking that someone close to me might be jealous enough to pull something like this."

"Do you ever think about anything but yourself?" he asked, losing his patience.

Sancia pointed at his phone while her cheeks turned a blotchy red. "Are you saying you wouldn't be concerned if someone was spreading news like that about you? Everybody was looking at me funny today."

"And you're being extra, as usual."

"You don't understand, and I can't tell you what else might be out there." She raised one hand, her palm facing him. "This could ruin me."

"Newsflash." Christian held up the phone. "This shit is way more serious than your *precious* reputation. You better get your head on right and keep your mouth shut. If this gets out, we'll have way bigger problems than what people are *saying* about you."

# CHAPTER ELEVEN

## GENEVA

GENEVA'S GRIEF SETTLED into something darker.

If Deja knew what was good for her, she wouldn't have given in and revealed that she had a copy of that video. Watching her baby losing a female's rite of passage to a predator was heartbreaking. The live feed with Alexia being mauled by those savages almost did her in. Again.

Days before, Geneva had taken what she needed from her father-in-law's laptop. For a policeman, Desmond had to be the most careless officer when it came to confidential information. She understood that had to do with his age and the fact that he only looked at the computer as a tool and not an instrument that could be dangerous. This, despite the growing problem with internet banking fraud and scamming on the island. Still, she wouldn't be too hard on him because his lax attitude had been to her advantage.

She cried a thousand tears and railed against God and the brutes who did the worst to Alexia.

"How could they?" she'd muttered, wanting to look away, but knowing that if Alexia had suffered all she had and was still alive, the least she could do was bear witness to her daughter's agony.

Inside her office, she paced for what felt like hours with the blinds drawn. Each time she walked by the credenza, she touched the framed photos with Alexia's image.

Geneva would have said she wasn't sentimental but the evidence suggested otherwise. The odds and ends from Jaden and Alexia's early years were in storage and wouldn't be discarded, no matter how they teased her about keeping junk. She hadn't thrown out the "artwork" Alexia had crafted in school and presented her with over the years. They were a touchstone to the past that acted as a bridge to the future. One that was now in ruins.

When Spence came to let her know he was home, she'd waved him away with the excuse that she was working on a system for a client.

"I'm fine, honey," she insisted when he stared at her, his head tipped to one side.

"If you need anything, I'll be around for a bit," he said, studying her as if he could tell what was going on in her mind. That endearment she dropped also had him confused.

The last year had been rough. She'd told herself she was done with Spence, because she could no longer trust him and keeping tabs on him wasn't something she planned to do. If he didn't value what they had at home, then to hell with him. But he'd been more attentive and hadn't given her reason to suspect he was being unfaithful. Forgiveness wasn't her strong suit, and it played havoc with their marriage. Yet, Spence refused to give up on her.

She patted his chest to reassure him. "I'm good. Really."

He half believed her because that was her modus operandi when she was thinking. Pacing until she tired herself out, if her ideas didn't coalesce into workable solutions. A slow nod signaled his acceptance of her explanation before he withdrew and closed the door.

Hugging herself, she considered every action she'd watched on that tape until plans to expose Alexia's attackers morphed into something dangerous. Gathering and collating information was part of her skill set. That would only be a small fraction of what she needed to do in the next few days to put her plans into play. Those bastards that called themselves friends would suffer just like her daughter. If they didn't, whatever she chose to inflict on them would be exactly what they deserved. Patience would be key. Too close of an interval between each incident would attract attention she didn't need.

⸻

Deja was another matter that needed special consideration. The girl sat inches away and wore guilt like a shroud. Geneva sensed that she wanted—no *needed*—to purge herself of the weight she carried. After buying her a green juice this time and gently encouraging her to share what was bothering her, Deja handed Geneva a thumb drive.

With her stomach shriveling into a tight knot, Geneva angled the computer screen so they both could see it. Although she guessed the reason, Geneva didn't ask why she'd spliced the video into several chunks and she didn't care—not in the moment.

She sat like a statue, separating herself from what was happening on the laptop by focusing on the camera, which Deja had covered with a tiny bit of tape. The marker she'd used to color it made the tape nearly unnoticeable.

Meanwhile, Deja came close to blubbering as they watched.

Without looking at the girl, Geneva passed her tissue from her handbag.

Deja went silent, but continued to dry her eyes. Since they were seated in a corner of the hospital cafeteria, she had to maintain some semblance of composure. While she sniffled,

Geneva watched exhausted workers and dry-eyed visitors topping up on bad coffee and empty calories.

"What's done is done," Geneva eventually said. "There's no use crying over it now."

When Deja's eyes welled with fresh tears, Geneva wanted to smack her. Something other than what happened to Alexia was bugging her. Whatever it was didn't matter to Geneva. She had one aim in view and would not be deterred. At the end of the tape, she touched Deja's hand. "You know, there *is* something you can do for me."

"What's that?" she asked, eager to please.

Geneva scanned her shapeless hoodie, baggy jeans, and sneakers. This child had some serious issues. She'd never dressed like other teenagers. No tank tops, tight jeans, or flashy footwear. On the three visits to the hospital, she'd looked the same. Like someone deliberately trying to avoid attention. That was to Geneva's advantage.

She patted Deja's hand and chose her words. "Those two boys, Jason and Phil. Your friends."

The girl winced but didn't interrupt.

"You're a whiz." She smiled, and Deja responded with one of her own. "I'm talking about the computer and the internet ..."

Nodding, Deja sniffed and wiped her nose. "Yes, Auntie."

"And you want to help Alexia, right?"

She dipped her head once more.

Pointing at the laptop, Geneva continued, "Based on how this madness started ..."

The undeserved agony Alexia went through stole her breath for a few seconds, and she paused to relieve the tightness in her chest. "I realize these boys are into some things that aren't good for them."

Another extended sniff from the girl at her side made Geneva close both fists to prevent herself from losing her cool and slapping her. Why people thought tears would resolve anything was beyond her. Not to say she didn't experience the same weakness, but she never wallowed. Action and mind control had been the thing that got her through every difficult situation in life. If she used the brain God gave her and combined that with everything she'd learned along the way, success would be hers at some point. Always.

She brought her mind back to the present and put on a winning expression.

"I'd like you to keep an eye on them. See what they're dabbling in."

When Deja opened her mouth, Geneva applied pressure to her hand. "The police need time to make their case. There's nothing wrong with us helping them, is there?"

Deja pulled at the silky curls at her nape and squinted, as if thinking. Then her eyes cleared.

Geneva knew she had her, but added a touch of sweetener. "You'd be doing something to help Alexia, and I'll be extremely grateful."

She clasped both hands on the table and stared at her fingers. "I'd do anything to help Alexia."

After a sharp inhale, Geneva removed the flash drive, closed the laptop, and slid it toward Deja. The time when her assistance was critical had passed, but the future was important. A few more carefully planted seeds in the form of complimentary words brought a sparkle to Deja's eyes.

As she stood, Geneva touched the girl's shoulder. "Stay and finish your drink. There's something I have to do now. I'll reach out to you."

She stepped away, already putting the next steps of her plan in place. Geneva couldn't do everything at once, but knew how to create a domino effect.

"Aunt Jenny?"

That word "aunt" twisted her stomach and made her mouth bitter. Friends took care of each other. Relatives were supposed to be even more vigilant. Deja had failed on both counts.

"Yes?" she said, over her shoulder.

"If I had the chance to do anything differently, I would."

"Not to worry." Geneva laced her words with empathy. "I'm sure the opportunity will come for you to do better."

# CHAPTER TWELVE

## PHIL

**J**ASON'S WIDE EYES reflected his terror as he gripped the steering wheel. "What the hell, man?"

Without a word, Phil ran a hand down his face, then hit replay on Jason's phone screen and watched the short video again.

The girl, Amelia McGhee, stumbled down the front steps of his home and into the yard toward whoever was holding the camera. Her long, red hair and clothes were rumpled and her eyes out of focus. She held up one hand as if to ward off the camera, then mumbled to herself and staggered down the sidewalk into the darkness.

"Oh, man," was all he could manage.

The time stamp told him exactly which day that had happened. Two weeks ago, when his parents were out of town celebrating their anniversary weekend. He'd brought Amelia home after a movie and they had the same intention and followed through in his bedroom. By the time he let Jason into the house, she was more than prepared. He'd slipped her some molly in a diet soda at the theater.

Jason had given her a fright when he appeared by the side of the bed and slid in.

Her eyes popped wide, and she made halfhearted attempts to fight him off, but had been too far gone to defend herself.

The minute Jason stepped out of Phil's room, he went inside and helped her back into her dress. Amelia cried the entire time as if she would never stop, but he sent her on her way.

"At least we didn't leave any marks on her," Jason said, as if that mattered. And as if they hadn't done worse.

Phil's thoughts flashed to Alexia and what happened in Montego Bay. She still wasn't back in school, and he didn't ask questions when he heard she was back in Miami, but in the hospital. Word was, the police were on the hunt for those who were with her on spring break. No one had contacted him, and he hoped that episode would die since they were back in the States.

He scratched his skin, which crawled when he remembered moving Amelia through the door and leaving her to fend for herself. She only lived a few blocks away in a one-bedroom unit that she shared with another student, but he should have taken her home. He couldn't lie to himself that he'd been relieved when he saw her on campus days later. Anything could have happened to her in the state she'd been in the previous evening.

At the sight of him, her face flamed. She clutched a stack of books to her chest and took off down a pathway as if being chased by a pack of wild dogs.

"What are we going to do?" Jason shoved one hand through his hair and stared through the windshield of his black Mazda. They were on the way to Phil's house when the message notification interrupted their talk about a girl they had their eyes on.

"Don't lose your cool," Phil said, trying to keep his voice even. The thought of anyone knowing about any part of what they'd done made him weak. He was at the university on a partial scholarship, which he couldn't afford to lose. Although they lived in a nice neighborhood, they weren't rich, and his father worked hard to maintain their lifestyle.

"Dude, this didn't come to *your* phone." Jason cut his eyes at him. "It's not about not having it all together. If this got out—"

The driver whose bumper Jason almost touched blasted his horn.

"Watch the traffic, man. Anyway, we could play it off and say she was sloshed." Phil shrugged and pulled in a calming breath. "Nobody can prove otherwise. And it's not like she was caught stumbling down *your* parents' driveway. Just chill."

"Easy for you to say."

"Look, we were both careless." Phil sat sideways in the seat to make his point. "We should at least have taken her home."

"Then we would have been farther up a dark, smelly place." Jason dragged one hand back and forth on his forehead. "You're right. The best thing for us to do is stay calm and say nothing. Nobody knows what happened except you, me, and Amelia."

"Right."

Amelia hadn't accused him of anything, and he understood how she felt. Just like all the other girls they had given ecstasy, who hadn't been able to look them in the eyes afterward.

He shook his head and pushed those thoughts aside. If anyone came out of this looking bad, it was Amelia, not them.

Jason was still messing with his hair that now looked as if he'd stuck a fork in a light socket.

Patting his arm, Phil said, "Relax, man. This is probably a prank. If it's Am—her idea of a joke—I'll take care of it."

His words sounded hollow, but Jason would buy it. He didn't question much. Amelia had nothing to gain, and her reputation to lose, if she were exposed. But just in case, he'd make sure she didn't get any other bright ideas.

He sank in the seat, satisfied that he'd found a solution. Then, his message tone sounded. His mouth went as dry as the Sahara and the back of his neck crawled.

"Stop being an idiot," he muttered, as he tapped the recording that had come in.

Phil squinted at the scene for a couple of seconds, until it made sense.

His heart stopped. Someone had recorded Jason attacking and then stomping on Alexia.

# CHAPTER THIRTEEN

## ALEXIA

TODAY WAS THE day. She sensed it.

Sometimes, when her eyes were half open, her mother would get excited. Until the doctor killed her enthusiasm with news that Alexia's reaction was a natural part of being in a coma. Her gaze wandered around the white-painted walls and ceiling but she couldn't focus on any one thing. That made her panic, and Alexia's heart boomed in her ears as if someone had given her a shot of adrenaline. What if she wouldn't be able to see properly when she was better?

The machine next to her beeped, and someone moved to her right. She turned her head as far as she could and met the gaze of a woman who looked familiar. *My mother?*

Somehow, Alexia knew she'd be the first person she'd see when she woke up. But was she really awake? Or was she in the middle of another episode where she hovered between sleep and waking? She seemed to be stuck in this place with no option to check out.

Her mother's eyes were round as she stared, then her attention went to the monitor on the other side of the bed. The equipment continued its racket.

"Alexia, baby?" the woman whispered and her smile widened in her dark-caramel face. She wasn't wearing makeup, but she was good-looking. Her hair was pulled into a low bun and she wore a suit, as if she'd been to a business meeting. "You're really awake?"

She attempted to smile but couldn't make her face do what she wanted. The hose hanging from the front of her head was in the way, making her eyes cross.

Her mother leaned in, her tone urgent as her words spilled out in a quick sentence. "Can you blink twice if you hear my voice?"

When she was able to do that, Alexia wanted to celebrate, but the door burst open and a pair of nurses crowded around the bed.

"Mrs. Leighton, you should have alerted us." A tall nurse with a piercing gaze spoke from behind a face shield.

"Her eyes have barely been open for a minute." Her grip on Alexia's hand tightened, as she continued, "and you're here now, aren't you?"

The second nurse, petite with dark hair, pursed her lips in disapproval before slipping the chart off the foot of the bed to study it. While she did, someone else hurried into the room with their shoes squeaking.

"Dr. Waite …"

The doctor didn't respond but lifted the chart from the nurse's hands, then turned his attention to Alexia, whose vision still hadn't settled. His face was a blur, but she kept blinking, hoping her sight would improve.

The tall man with olive skin and a thick mustache smiled. "Miss Leighton, welcome back. You've been giving us cause for concern these last six weeks."

She tried to respond but could tell from the slight shift around his forehead that she wasn't making much sense.

"Don't worry about your speech," he said, glancing at the clipboard. "That's common for someone just emerging from a coma. We'll be running some tests to see where you're at."

To her mother, he said, "Mrs. Leighton, I'm going to ask you to wait outside while we do the checks. I'll speak with you afterward."

She stood and kissed Alexia's cheek. "I'll be back soon."

Instead of trying to mash words together that might not make sense, Alexia nodded then watched her leave.

One of the nurses left the room and returned with another clipboard, which she handed to Dr. Waite. He came closer and explained what he was about to do, then asked her several questions and made notes. Dr. Waite handed the clipboard to the tall woman next to him and said, "I'm going to check your motor responses, as well as other functions."

He looked into Alexia's eyes, spoke to her as if she were deaf, and asked personal questions in between instructing the nurse what numbers to write. By the time he watched her move her fingers, toes, and feet, she was exhausted and ready to drift into sleep. But he wouldn't let her.

"I need you to speak with your mother before you rest."

Alexia let her eyes do the talking when the woman who'd been her champion returned and sat at her side. She might not be able to say thank you in a coherent way, but she was grateful for the time and encouraging words while she was in between worlds.

Her warm hand settled over Alexia's as she faced the doctor.

Dr. Waite cleared his throat, then asked, "Alexia, can you tell me your mother's first name?"

Staring into her eyes didn't reveal the answer. An album of faces, nicknames, and titles swept through Alexia's head, but none of them felt right. Nothing she reached for filled the gap.

"Do you remember your father's name?"

The question brought on panic, which also sent the machine into signal mode.

Her eyes stung, and she struggled to focus while Dr. Waite spoke. "…worry too much about it…fairly common in cases like this…will pass."

A wind tunnel developed inside her head, and when she emerged, the doctor and her mother were on their way outside. The fog cleared when he said, "…case of post traumatic amnesia."

# CHAPTER FOURTEEN

## GENEVA

"**I**'D LIKE TO report a crime."

The young officer, Rodrigo Cruz, sat with his pen poised to take Geneva's statement. "What's the nature of the crime?"

"Assault." The ringing of several phones distracted her before she added, "One which caused grievous bodily harm."

He scanned her from head to feet, as if to determine where she'd been hurt.

"My daughter is the person who was attacked."

The light glinted off Officer Cruz's glasses as his focus shifted to an officer going past the desk. "Where is she, and where did the attack take place?"

Geneva didn't bat an eyelid when she said, "She's currently at the Coral Gables Hospital but she was hurt in Jamaica."

The policeman ran one hand over his close-cropped hair and frowned. "Jamaica, New York City, or Jamaica, the island?"

Geneva ignored the buzzing of her phone to answer, "The country."

Cruz laid his pen down and looked her in the eyes. "Why would you report the incident here, and if I may ask, when did it happen?"

Leaning forward and resting one elbow on the desk, she said, "Because the people who did it live in this city. My daughter was hurt during spring break in Montego Bay."

The confusion on his face cleared, which gave Geneva a spark of hope. When she'd walked into the building that functioned as the headquarters for the police and fire department, as well as the emergency operations center, she was prepared.

An internet search revealed that only a minute percentage of the officers looked anything like her. Cruz had come closest to any of the qualities she wished to see in law enforcement. He was polite and had a face that hadn't been hardened by the things he'd seen on the job. Experience had taught her that the eyes were indeed direct windows into the soul of a person. Rodrigo Cruz's were kind and open.

In terms of expectations, if she had to bet, she'd say she had a 2 percent chance of receiving any help, which was fine by her. Knowing what she was up against gave her the advantage. Her visit today was meant to plant a seed. When it germinated into something bigger, the department would be aware of her name and the fact that she'd asked for help.

Cruz rubbed his jaw, as he said, "I don't believe we can do anything about it since the incident took place outside this jurisdiction …" He glanced at the form in front of him. "Why haven't you reported it before today?"

"Based on how badly my daughter was beaten by this group of students, I believed the Jamaican police would have made contact by now …" She shrugged. "But clearly …"

He held up one finger. "If you'd give me a moment, please."

"Sure."

She waited while he squinted at a computer screen and tapped the keyboard.

While he did, her cellular pinged, and she removed it from her bag and looked at the screen.

Spence had texted her. *Any update? Call me when you can.*

She sucked her teeth quietly, then sighed. His timing was off, which always seemed to be the case these days. But there was a point in their relationship when she wouldn't have hesitated to answer. Despite his flaws, Spence was trying and had been faithful with staying in touch each day when he was traveling. She needed to show him some grace.

Yesterday, after Alexia woke again later in the evening, Geneva had video called him in Suriname. She had explained that their daughter had temporary memory loss, but he was still disappointed when she didn't recognize him. The pain in his eyes had aroused her own anguish, and she'd had to pretend they weren't dealing with what was in front of them to get through that phone call.

Geneva looked up to find Officer Cruz watching her. She typed a message. *Talk in half-hour. At a meeting.*

She saw that he'd received the message and looked up the moment the policeman folded his hands on the desk pad. He waited until a group of uniformed officers were several feet away before he spoke. "I'm sorry, Mrs. Leighton."

Cruz's regretful tone told Geneva everything. The police department had received nothing from Jamaican law enforcement. If he'd given her good news, she would have had difficulty believing him. That's where she was with those bungling island policemen who had no sense of urgency.

"Thank you for your time." She dropped the phone in her bag, then handed Cruz a business card. "If anything changes, here's my contact information."

He slipped it under the side of the desk pad and nodded. "I'll keep it in mind."

"I appreciate that." As she rose, the message app sounded.

Thinking it was Spence, she waited until she was sitting in her car in the parking garage before looking at the cellular.

Jaden had sent her a screenshot of an article. *Businessman Charles Jackman Questioned as Investigation into Admissions Scandal at University of Miami Deepens.*

She scrolled up and read the short article.

*After recent allegations that the Jackman family was involved in securing places for their children at the University of Miami by bribery, the board of directors has launched an investigation into the claim, even as they deny any knowledge of wrongdoing. In the meantime, the police have detained Jackman for questioning.*

Before she could read further, Jaden sent another text. *Remember, the daughter was at the villa.*

She sent him an emoji with clasped hands to convey her thanks. This time she had it right, which made her smile. According to Jaden, she was clueless when it came to using a fitting emoji most of the time. Her cluelessness tickled him because he claimed it was ironic that someone with so much knowledge of all facets of the internet and the technology surrounding it had no idea about the social media side of things.

Geneva put aside the phone and started the engine of her Honda-CRV. Jackman's detention, no matter how fleeting, would keep him safe in the meantime. His daughter, not so much.

# CHAPTER FIFTEEN

## SANCIA

SANCIA SLID INTO the chair across from Christian, whose blank expression told her nothing. She set the orange juice and a sandwich on the table, then let her gaze land on his stiff face. He'd texted her half-hour ago, and she told him where she planned to have lunch. The café was a popular spot close to the university that served a long list of soups and sandwiches. She wasn't a big eater, so their menu items were ideal.

Christian leaned forward, and she couldn't mistake the fury in his eyes. "You trying to set me up or something?"

She pulled back and frowned, but didn't get a word in before he snarled, "Reels are *still* coming to my phone."

"What are you talking about?" she asked, then lowered her voice. "The same as what you showed me?"

Christian barely moved his lips when he answered, "Yes. Montego Bay."

A gasp clogged her throat, and Sancia sucked at the straw to settle her nerves. She leaned over the tiny table. "You have to show me."

He sucked his teeth and slouched in the seat. "I don't have to show you anything. You know what happened."

Angling her head sideways she said, "What if you're just fooling with me?"

The dark eyes she found so mesmerizing shot fire at her. "Do I look like I have time for that kind of stupidity?"

Now that she thought about it, Christian looked as if he hadn't slept a lot recently. This was serious. She sipped from the cup while gathering her thoughts. Five days had gone by since the police had asked her father to visit the station. That had been a rough stretch, and only self-confidence helped Sancia act as if the whispers didn't matter. But they were true. She knew because someone had sent her a bank statement from one of Daddy's accounts. How that was possible, she didn't know. Of course, she couldn't say anything to Daddy, because he'd snarl at her and expect her to know where the information came from.

This business with her and Christian looked bad, and it had to go away. She couldn't afford any hint of scandal now. Her father would kill her.

When Christian closed his fist, she met his eyes. "Honest, I don't know where those came from. Like I asked you before, what would I gain by sharing that? And you haven't told me how I would have filmed it."

"How should I know?" The finger he pointed at her shook as if he was freaked out. "And if I find out you had anything to do with that wild goose chase you sent me on two times in the past couple of weeks, you're going to be sorry."

His tone reminded Sancia of the one Daddy used to keep the family in line. But while she had to put up with his shit, she didn't have to take it from Christian. "Don't threaten me."

"Don't get it twisted." His scowl made her shrink, then fiddle with the gold hoop in her ear to hide her response.

"That wasn't a threat," he continued, gripping the phone tight. "It was a promise."

Her phone rang, and she fumbled to pull it out of her jeans. One look at the screen pulled a sigh from her. Jonathan was calling.

"Hey, you need to get down to Dad's office at three o' clock."

Now, her stomach was queasy but Sancia kept her voice even. "What happened?"

"He's having a press conference."

As her stomach sank, she asked, "What does he need us for?"

"Window dressing, lame brain. His PR people probably told him it would look good to have us there. The whole all-American family look."

A glance at her designer watch had Sancia rolling her eyes. "It's gonna be tight. It's already after one, and with traffic, plus going home to change—"

"Do whatever you have to," he said, sounding like their father. "And be sure not to turn up looking like a slut."

"Go to hell."

Christian's head snapped up, and he searched her eyes before looking away.

Her brother only snickered. "Just be grateful I don't tell Dad half the things you get up that you think I don't know about."

She was on her feet by the time she ended the call. "I have to go. Family matters."

Christian stood and shoved his chair back, then slipped his backpack over one shoulder and walked with her toward the exit.

With slow and confident movements that disguised the panic she could barely hold in, Sancia unlocked the Benz SUV that was parked curbside. As she got in with Christian watching, she remembered how much she hated the vehicle because it was pre-owned. But after she crashed the Porsche Macan after a night of drinking and partying, Daddy had been livid. At first, he swore she'd have to get around on foot like most other people, but she'd begged and pleaded until he gave in and bought her another ride.

She supposed she should be grateful, but she was used to having only the best, and the come-down still griped her. Still, the Benz was better than what 98 percent of the students drove.

She switched on the engine, then wriggled her fingers at Christian who had his phone out. He barely dipped his head in response, which made her face flame. She wasn't accustomed to being ignored, but she'd forgive him because he was worried about the video.

After cuing up Ava Max's latest song, she pulled away from the sidewalk. Going to the mall would be a chore she didn't need, but she couldn't turn up looking less than her best. She spent the ten-minute drive hoping she'd find something ideal. Her mind snapped back to the road when the power locks clicked three times in a row. Weird. The SUV probably needed servicing.

She eased up on the pedal upon approaching the shopping center and signaled to turn. The vehicle continued past the entrance. Frowning, she sat up in the seat, gripped the wheel hard, and turned down the music. Despite laying her foot hard on the brake, the SUV kept going.

"What the hell?"

The edge of panic to her voice forced Sancia to settle her nerves and take deep breaths. "In. Out. In. Out," she muttered while pulling the fitted shirt away from her skin.

A glance at the dashboard monitor showed nothing out of the ordinary, but no matter how hard she tried, the brakes wouldn't work. As if the Benz had a mind of its own, they were now headed down Coral Way toward Miami. The heating system had kicked on and the cab was turning into a furnace. The seat was hot, and she wanted to rip off her jeans plus her shirt. Not only was the center console at a searing temperature, so was the passenger seat when she touched it.

"This can't be happening." She clawed at her shirt collar, hoping this was a nightmare she'd awake from at any minute.

The music increased to a deafening level, switching to a different station every few seconds. Jabbing the button to make it stop was a wasted effort. Perspiration trickled from her hairline, racing toward her cheeks. As she swiped at her forehead, the temperature in the cab lowered to normal. In the next moment, the sweat dried on her skin as the air grew chilly.

No matter what she did, the Benz careened down State Road 972, which had four lanes divided by a median with huge trees. Sobs tore at her throat as she jammed both feet on the brake to bend the four-wheeled monster to her will. Then, a cold voice interrupted the mayhem coming from the radio. "What you did in Montego Bay followed you home. Goodbye, Sancia."

Gasping and shivering as tears blinded her, Sancia yelled, "No! This isn't possible."

The radio cut off and the Benz accelerated, then veered onto the grassy median. As the SUV raced toward a row of ficus with thick, gnarled trunks, warm liquid gushed from her bladder and flowed onto the seat.

At the moment of impact, she screamed.

# CHAPTER SIXTEEN

## DEJA

**T**YLER'S DIRECT GAZE made her uncomfortable, but when had that ever been different?

"Am I looking at a crime being committed?" he asked.

She focused on one of the large monitors a few feet away. "In a manner of speaking."

"Wild." He watched for several more seconds, then shook his head.

She dreaded what he'd ask next and debated how she'd answer.

"Where did you get this footage, Deja?"

"It's on my phone, isn't it?"

Frowning, he said, "The angle tells me that you got this from surveillance equipment. What I can't figure out is what the hell they were thinking."

Staring over his shoulder, she said, "I don't understand it either."

They sat silent at the work table for a few more minutes before he sighed. "What do you want me to do with this?"

When she made a funny face, Tyler held up both hands. "You came here to ask me something. What is it?"

She grabbed his upper arm and rubbed her forehead against his cheek. "So, I've broken this recording into several segments and—"

"Why not give it to the police? You could do it anonymously."

"In case you didn't notice, two of the people in that video are Black. The other person is not. Do you really believe they would rush to do anything about this situation?"

He tugged one of his locs while staring at the huge poster of Bob Marley with a guitar and his head thrown back.

"See, you can't even answer. You know what I know." She stared him dead in the eyes. "And in any case, it didn't happen here."

He laughed, but in disbelief. Deja knew what that particular sound meant because this wasn't the first time she'd heard it. Tyler was wondering what angle she was coming from and still trying to work out what she wanted. With one elbow propped against the table, he said, "Surely, you're not gonna hold out on me now."

"This was in Jamaica."

"And you happen to have this recording because …"

She sighed and closed her eyes. "I got it from the villa."

Moving his head side to side, Tyler asked. "Why would you do that?"

She explained about the phone call to Mrs. Leighton, then added, "I thought I'd need it."

"Again, I ask why?"

"After talking to Alexia's grandmother, I had a hunch."

Tyler rubbed one palm over her forearm. "Sounds like you just needed to do something. Anything you figured would help,"

While nodding, Deja blinked away tears. Instead of regaining control, suddenly she was crying harder. The sobs racked her body, and Tyler left her side and returned with a wad of hand towel.

"You act like such a rebel, yet …" Tyler didn't continue, but she understood what he was saying.

While drying her eyes, Deja gave him a weak grin. "So much for your rebel theory."

She didn't want Tyler to know why this incident affected her so deeply. As hard as it was to face what Alexia had been through, it was worse to let it go without doing anything. Aunt Jenny hadn't asked her to make contact with Christian, but Deja wouldn't allow him to forget the disgusting thing he'd done. When they met again, she'd give an update on Jason and Phil, who she'd also been watching.

Tyler's hand shook as the recording continued. When it stopped, he cleared his throat. "Tell me what you want."

After she explained what she intended to do, he shook his head. "Baby girl, I can't say it strongly enough. You should give what you have to the police. If they do nothing, at least you tried. It's either that or—"

"Forget it happened, huh?"

They both stayed quiet until Deja pulled in a deep breath and shuddered. "I can't forget."

"How did I know you were going to say that?" Tyler spun toward her. "It's never the easy way out with you."

"The path to anything meaningful has never been *easy*."

Smiling, he said, "Now you've gone philosophical on me."

"So, are you going to help me?" she asked, barely able to hear over the pounding of her heart.

"I'll tell you what you need to know, but I'm not going to help you do it."

She pulled in her breath too fast, which ended in a coughing fit. "You can't leave me hanging on my own."

"Like I've said a million times before, you know almost everything I know."

"Almost doesn't count."

"You just need confidence." Tyler gripped Deja's chin and made her look into his eyes. "You should let this go."

"But you know I won't." She lowered her gaze, then added, "So, I guess you're going to answer *all* my questions."

He tapped the phone. "There's the matter of the legality of what you plan do with this."

She gave him a side-eye. "You don't know what I'm going to do."

"That's exactly what worries me."

Frowning, she asked, "Can you see me rolling up on these two and demanding hush money?"

"No, but I can picture you spreading it all over the internet."

She shook her head in a regretful way. "You seriously underestimate me. The information on the Jackmans belonged in the public forum. They deserve exactly what's coming to them for that kind of dishonesty."

Tyler sounded irritated when he said, "But it's not your duty to make them pay."

"That wasn't me." She stood and pushed the chair away to stalk his compact living space. "Someone did it before I could."

"D'you have any idea who it could be and why?" Tyler released his locs and massaged his scalp, as if the elastic band holding them together had given him a headache.

"Who knows." Deja shrugged. "People like the Jackmans step on other people's toes every day."

"I don't like the sound of this. Be careful you don't get in over your head." Rubbing his forehead, Tyler asked, "What exactly is your aim?"

She stopped, with both arms folded under her breasts, and couldn't help noticing how fast Tyler looked away from the front of her T-shirt. Keeping something in reserve, she told him she intended to contact Christian, whom she deliberately didn't name.

For several seconds, Tyler didn't blink or move. "At least you're sensible enough not to confront him on your own. Right?"

She didn't answer, but didn't know what to expect when he rose from the chair. He gently moved her out of his path and disappeared into the bedroom. When he returned, Tyler placed a canister in her hand. She'd never handled mace before but was grateful for his concern. Smiling she asked, "Care to tell me why you have this?"

"Something told me you'd need it, so I didn't second guess myself when I decided to buy it."

Moving in close, she stood on tiptoes and kissed his stubbly cheek. She stepped back and discovered his eyes were closed. "Thank you," she whispered.

His Adam's apple bobbed, and the shadows in his eyes shifted. "If you can't be good, then at least be careful."

# CHAPTER SEVENTEEN

## CHRISTIAN

**S**ANCIA WAS DEAD.

"This shit is unreal."

At any moment, Christian expected her to call or message him. But two days ago, she'd run her Benz into a tree. He'd seen the notice and condolence message on the school app. First, he was shocked and had been stupid enough to ring her phone, as if she would answer. Now, he was just shaken and couldn't seem to think about anything else.

He threw himself into the office chair and spun toward his computer screen, scrubbing his face with one hand. Outside of that, he had bigger problems. Whoever had been sending the clips of Alexia, Sancia, and him had gone overboard. He now had a half dozen thirty-second reels that left no doubt about what he'd done. The scenes were out of sequence, but it didn't matter. Sancia and he were identifiable, even in the shadows just outside the range of the light bulbs at the corner of the villa.

Some of the things she liked in the bedroom were downright strange, but they didn't bother him. Hell, she was helping him score more hits with women than half the guys at the university. His intention had been to blame her if things escalated. Since she was no longer around to defend herself, he had the perfect cop out if any accusations came from Alexia or her people.

He tipped the chair back and folded both hands behind his head. It was too late for regret. Whoever was sending these pictures had an aim. Sooner or later, he'd find out what they wanted but he had no intention of giving up his life for what was nothing more than a bad decision.

He nearly launched out of the seat when someone laid a hand on his shoulder. Then his nerves settled. Anoushka, his father's latest toy and wife of three years, stood next to him. Radcliffe Skyers moved her into the house two years before that. She was fifteen years younger than Dad and looked like someone who had everything money could buy. Of course, she went through his father's money, shopping and visiting the beauty salon the way other people bought groceries. She was one dangerous brown Barbie.

"What are you looking at?" she asked in that annoying, breathy way that grated on his nerves.

His father probably found it attractive, but to Christian she sounded as if she were in the middle of an asthma attack. Every damn day.

He wheeled the chair backward to get out of her reach. Christian didn't always steer clear of trouble, but this woman was off limits. He liked the many luxuries his father's money provided and didn't plan to mess up the future that was waiting for him within the walls of the business.

Since the fire that gutted the villa, his father had been in a foul mood, so Christian kept out of his way. The good thing was Sancia had been the one to make the booking. Otherwise, Dad might have found a way to blame him for something that didn't even happen when they were in Jamaica. When he was raging over his losses, he could be irrational.

"What can I do for you?" he asked Anoushka, knowing it was the wrong thing to say the minute the words slipped out.

She glanced at the bed before her red-painted lips formed a smile. "Your door was open, so I stopped in to chat."

Christian's gaze went to the entrance, then back to her. She obviously thought he was stupid. His room was out of her way, so she'd deliberately come looking for him.

"Where's Dad?" he asked, tipping his head sideways as if expecting to see his father. The fact that she was here meant Dad was probably where he couldn't see Anoushka coming on to him.

Her smile widened. "Upstairs."

*Wrong answer.*

She shifted and cocked one hip toward him while glancing at his phone, which he grabbed off the desk and slid into his pocket. He stood and cleared his throat. "I need a drink."

The phone vibrated against his leg, and he flinched.

"Is something wrong?" Anoushka leaned against the desk as if she had nothing better to do.

"No." His tone was sharp when he said, "Shouldn't you be preparing Dad's dinner or something?"

"That's what I was doing in the kitchen." She licked her lips before she said, "I have something tasty for us that I'd like to share with you."

Christian shook his head because her meaning couldn't be clearer. "Thank you, but I have to be somewhere else."

She tipped one brow, poked out her lips, then put an extra swish into her hips on the way to the doorway. "It's your loss."

Christian closed the door behind her and leaned against the wooden panel as he swiped the phone screen.

*Meet me at Miracle Mile. We can talk about the entire reel.*

His heart thumped hard enough to make him uncomfortable, and he put a hand to his chest. This had to be a trick.

A follow-up text told him the exact location for the meeting.

What was he expected to give in exchange for getting the film? He'd be a fool to think that would be the end of this bit of drama. But at the same time, he couldn't ignore whoever was sending these annoying and frightening messages. What if they released them to anyone else? He had to get his hands on the whole video, but how?

The number had been blocked so he couldn't respond, and he suspected whoever was behind this hadn't been using the same SIM card each time. He dropped on the mattress and looked back at the message. Before he could type a response, another text came in.

*Make it 6:30. Don't be late.*

<hr />

Merrick Park's design, with its many nooks and crannies, made him nervous. The palms and shrubs scattered around the large property didn't make him feel any better. He was too easy a target. Since this foolishness became a thing, his mind seemed like it no longer belonged to him. He kept seeing shadows where none existed and danger behind every bush. He scoffed. *Get your head together and focus on what you came to do.*

He walked into the small courtyard from between two columns with both hands tucked into his jeans. While he peered at the phone screen, he perched on the edge of the nearest bench, bouncing the balls of his feet on the concrete. Without raising his head, he scanned the open space around him.

The phone beeped with another message. *Don't get impatient. Patience is a virtue.*

The fear in his gut shriveled and anger replaced it. He'd had enough of being toyed with. He shot off the bench to circle the area, scouring the surroundings with his gaze. His fists opened and closed as he swore.

Christian squinted as a Black man in dark glasses, a hoodie, and jeans approached from his right. His gaze swung in a wide arc, then went back to the guy, who had slowed his steps as if looking for someone. This had to be the person who was dogging him. Christian didn't recognize him, but would find out how they were connected in a minute.

"Hey, you!" Christian barked as he rushed toward the tall man and shoved him the chest.

The dude stumbled, but when he righted himself, both hands slammed into Christian's chest. They tussled with each other, while people at a nearby table gawked before hurrying away. In no time, a security guard would be on them. Two Black men causing a disturbance in this upscale mall wouldn't go down well.

Christian threw a punch that connected with the other guy's cheek. He staggered, and Christian gripped him in a headlock, trying to search his pockets for any kind of storage device.

The man pummeled his stomach, sucking away the air and numbing his mid-section. Christian released him and doubled over, gasping. As he straightened, the man drove his foot into the side of his knee. The fire that spread through his joint made Christian think it had been shattered. He screamed and crashed to the ground, cursing.

# CHAPTER EIGHTEEN

## GENEVA

GENEVA ENDED THE call and turned to where Spence leaned in the doorway.

His eyes lit up as he walked into the room, as if he was happy to see her, but there was something beneath the surface. Geneva suspected she knew what it was.

"How have you been since I left?"

This time, he'd been gone for a week.

"I have good and not-so-good days," she said, "but seeing Alexia getting better each day is a major plus."

"Yes, that's true." He sat on the edge of the desk, facing her. "I stopped at the hospital, and she does look better. When did they say we can move her to a rehab facility?"

The weight of the responsibility was heavy on Geneva, but she put it aside temporarily. The physical demands had proven exhausting, but she'd do everything again if they were faced with the same situation tomorrow. Thank goodness they could afford to provide what Alexia needed. They both made good money, which they had invested well over the years. Plus, they had insurance coverage.

"I have to confirm that with Dr. Waite and his team." She glanced at the laptop screen, then at Spence. "She might not be at that point yet, but I've been checking out a few options."

"So, it's impossible for someone to provide home care for her when she leaves the hospital?"

Geneva massaged her forehead, wishing the tension would lessen. "Actually, I put that aside when I thought about the equipment she may need that we don't have. A facility might be easier. At least for the first few months of rehab."

He stifled a yawn as he said, "Do what you have to and let's discuss it."

That *you* stung, as if he was detached from everything to do with Alexia's care, but the reality was that Spence was never around.

He made himself more comfortable on the edge of the desk and folded both arms across his chest.

"By the way," he said, "did you hear the villa the kids were staying at was destroyed?"

"How?" she asked, keeping her breathing even.

"Apparently, there was an electrical fire. At first, the Fire Brigade thought it was arson, but couldn't find anything conclusive."

"Really?" She flipped a pen between her fingers, avoiding his gaze. "Thank God the police got the evidence they needed before that happened."

"I'm surprised you didn't know about it considering the close watch you've kept on everything since Alexia's ..."

He couldn't find a way to describe the horror their daughter had been through, and yet, he kept trying to put a leash on her. Geneva pulled her mind off that track and looked at him, the way she would if she had nothing to hide. "I've been busy. I can't keep tabs on everything."

His close study of her face made Geneva tip her head sideways. "Is there something you want to ask me?"

"It's not so much a question as an observation." He scanned the office, his attention focused on the whiteboard in front of her, then on the desk where she had several files open to one side of the computer.

She tipped one brow, although she suspected where he was heading.

"I don't know how you did it, but you've accessed details that the police have not released to the public."

"Which police?" She frowned, waiting for his response. "And do you have proof to stand behind the accusation you're making?"

A moment slipped by before he said, "You're the smartest woman I know. Scratch that. You're one of the smartest people I know. Don't do this."

She said nothing, and eventually he sighed. "Only the police knew why the information on the villa rental wasn't released, and only they, and our family, knew certain other things about the case. You're impatient, but splashing this all over the newspaper isn't helping us or their case."

Geneva sat up, glaring at him. "Their case? They have only one job to do. Make the people responsible for this crime pay. Instead, they're pussyfooting around while my daughter …"

She shuddered and stopped herself from saying something she'd regret, by putting a hand over her mouth. When she had control over her anger, she exhaled and stood to confront him. "I'm not admitting anything, nor am I going to rest until I have justice for my daughter…even if it means fighting alone."

Spence's brows drew together, and his eyes turned stormy. "That's unfair and unnecessary."

She curled her lips. "But it's how I feel."

"You're acting as if I have influence over the police and can make them do as I wish."

"That's not what I'm saying, but I'd think that since it affects his granddaughter, your father would help move this forward."

"You're being unreasonable again." Spence rubbed the back of his neck. "How do you know he isn't doing all he can?"

"If he was, they would have put the evidence they had together and submitted it to the Miami police." She flicked her wrist in a dismissive gesture. "But it's all right."

"I don't like your tone. We should be working as a team." He shook his head, as if exasperated. "If you let me know what you need, I'll do it. You know I'd do anything for you and our family."

"That's sweet, Spence, and I know you love me, but there are questions I'm sure you can't answer. Things I need to know."

His curiosity was clear as he asked, "Like what?"

"Why are they hiding the fact that the police got paid not to release the names of the people staying at that villa?"

Spence pulled his head back as she continued, "And why did they quietly transfer the policeman involved? Where is the fairness in that, Spence? Where's the justice?"

# CHAPTER NINETEEN

## ALEXIA

How WAS IT possible to remember Chad but not her parents? She still didn't get that. An image of them laughing in the Ramsays' kitchen flashed across her mind. Behind closed eyelids, she pictured the muscular twenty-year-old charmer with golden-brown skin, who she'd been in a relationship with for the past year. Before that, he'd simply been Danny's older brother...until the day Alexia was at their house studying, then sat down to dinner with their family.

Chad had been warm and funny, and something sparked between them that evening. He'd waited several weeks before asking her on a date, and after that they were as close as chewing gum and the wrapper. Her relationship with him was like being snug in a warm sweater on a cool evening. He was affectionate and treated Alexia as if she meant everything to him. Not a day went by that she didn't hear from him by phone or text. He also hadn't been big mad when she wasn't ready to have sex.

He hadn't returned to see her, which made her wonder. But, she didn't blame him. Looking at her would have been hard to stomach. She cleared the sawdust from her throat to whisper, "Where is Danny?"

Her mother stroked her skin as her face twisted into something than wasn't quite a smile. "She hasn't handled your—*this*—well, so she stays away."

She retreated to the small table near the door. Did looking at her also upset her mother? The thought made Alexia sink deeper into her doubts and fears.

The hose had disappeared from the front of her head in the last couple of days, and some of the smaller tubes had been removed. Now that she was fully conscious, the nurses had tilted the bed at a more upright angle.

She'd counted off her injures—at least the ones she could see—over the past week. A newly-closed hole in her head, one hand broken, the other fractured, one leg immobile and the scar on her forehead. Then, there was the wreckage on the inside that the hospital dialed back with medication. No wonder Chad and Danny couldn't deal with being around her.

Mom had refused to let her look into a mirror, but she'd convinced one of the nurses to bring her a compact last night. She hadn't recognized the person looking into her eyes. If she'd been pretty, that certainly wasn't the case now. That fact grieved her.

Alexia assumed she'd been in a car crash, but hesitated to ask her mother. The shadowy images that attacked her mind told her differently. She didn't shy away from them, but nothing was clear enough for her to be certain of what had put her in this bed.

No matter what, she wanted her memory back. Sooner, rather than later. This reality meant a long road to the life she'd had before she was broken. But for now, she needed to do something productive while lying in the hospital like a vegetable with only light exercise to break the monotony. "I need a journal."

Mom looked up from the laptop and her gaze went to Alexia's hand.

"I can teach myself to use my other hand."

After lowering the screen of the laptop, her mother said, "I'll get it for you."

Her words surprised Alexia, who was sure she'd been about to say no. "Aside from physio and reading, I'm not doing much of anything. I'll go crazy if I don't fill in the gaps in my memory."

"The doctor did say you weren't to pressure yourself—"

"This isn't his life and he's not the one trapped in this bed," she snapped, then was sorry she'd lost her temper.

"Love, I know you want to get better." Mom pushed both hands into her hair and ran her finger to the ends, ruffling it. "But let's take it one step at a time. Please."

Alexia sighed and turned her head away to hide the tear that ran across her cheek. Her inability to do anything without help made her want to scream and throw a tantrum, but that wouldn't be a good look. She sensed it wasn't Mom's intention, but she was smothering Alexia's efforts to do more. Although the light physiotherapy she was on was agonizing, she'd do the exercises a dozen times a day if it meant being out of the hospital faster.

"How do you feel about a blog?" Mom asked, breaking the strained silence.

That was kinda simplistic for a woman with her mother's skills, but at least she was trying to make things better.

Alexia smiled, then grinned, and her mother said, "What's that about?"

"You're a cybersecurity expert!" Her tone was that of a young child who had discovered an exciting fact. She wanted to pump her fist, but didn't. Her weakness was disgusting. Half the time she felt like a wet noodle.

Mom's face reflected Alexia's glee, and that was good enough for her.

"So, you remembered something else. That's wonderful."

Pleased with herself, but doubtful about her mother's idea, Alexia stared into her eyes. "What will we be writing about?"

"Your experience. How we're managing the journey. What we'll do to get your life back on track."

"Mom, please level with me. What has been my *experience*? I mean, what put me in this hospital?"

Instead of giving her an answer, Mom pulled in a sharp breath. Her jaw trembled, then she sat up straight. "The medical team prefers if you remember on your own."

"But what if that never happens?"

"You will, baby." Mom cleared her throat and tried smoothing her hair. "Just give it some time."

Somehow, Alexia knew Mom wouldn't give in to her curiosity about what happened, so she asked, "Won't that mean having people up in our family business?"

Hiking one shoulder, Geneva said, "Yes, but if we can help anyone else, I'd say it's worth it. We'll start from where we are and work backward. You never know, that might jog your memory."

"I get that." The thought of something to look forward to exited her. "When do we start?"

Wearing a mysterious smile, her mother said, "As soon as today. I have a few ideas."

She wasn't certain of the reason, but Alexia felt as if an army of ants was running over her scalp. "Promise me you won't share anything about what happened to me unless I agree with it, *when I remember.*"

Mom's shoulders rose and fell in slow motion, then she dipped her head once. "I'll do my best, baby."

"You have to do more than that." Alexia's voice was stronger when she said, "Don't tell the world anything I'll regret."

After setting the laptop aside, her mother rose and walked from one wall to the other. The empty bed a few feet away reminded her that the woman who'd occupied it in the last few days hadn't survived. She'd been a victim of domestic violence and died without regaining consciousness. Alexia's attention returned to her mother when she stopped and slid both hands into the pockets of her floral sundress. "You've got it."

Alexia held her gaze, trying to gauge her mother's intention. This woman would keep fighting for her, no matter what. Yet, she was uncomfortable and searched her mind for what was wrong. A moment later, it came to her. The thing that disturbed Alexia's spirit was the determined light in her mother's eyes. She'd seen that same look many times in the documentaries she'd watched on the Discovery Channel. Her mother reminded her of a hungry leopard or lioness. The kind that had cubs and wouldn't stop hunting until she had tracked and killed her prey.

# CHAPTER TWENTY

## PHIL

**"I** KNEW YOU WEREN'T** going to introduce me to Cassidy," Jason said, grinning over his shoulder as he let Phil inside his parents' house. The plan was to do some business and then study together.

Phil smiled but had no intention of discussing the one girl he wasn't going to share. Physically fit and bubbly, Cassidy was a member of the women's golf team and dope.

"She's hot." Jason wriggled his eyebrows and stuck out his tongue in a suggestive way that made Phil want to clock him.

"And you're out of your league."

Jason switched his backpack from one shoulder to the other and pulled his head back, as if offended. "Excuse you? If she's good enough for you, then it's the same for me."

"Just met her," he lied. "She's not up for that kind of thing, man."

Smirking, Jason asked, "Were any of the others?"

"This is not a joke," Phil snarled, glanced around the huge living room, then glared at Jason.

"So, it's like that, huh?"

"I don't know what you're talking about." He sat on the beige leather sectional, while Jason threw his bag on a chair and pointed the remote at the massive television screen.

"Sure." He snickered. "Then I guess you won't mind if I look her up."

Phil didn't respond but his face flushed with the effort to ignore the deliberate provocation. Why had he agreed to study with this clown? He'd just pick up the steroids and go home before he lost it and hit him.

After a bad attempt at whistling a tune, Jason said, "Maybe we can still smash her together."

Stifling a curse word, Phil clamped his jaw shut and relaxed his fists.

Jason was always hungry, and perhaps that's why he stuck to Phil, who had learned to work what he had. His long, sandy-blond hair and handsome face, combined with regular workouts and a tendency not to talk too much, made him irresistible to the ladies.

The molly Jason was peddling didn't do Phil any favors. It simply gave Jason access to his dates. If it wasn't for Jason's direct link to the plug who sold the steroids that kept Phil in the money, he'd ice him out. Matter of fact, he'd find a way in and get rid of him altogether. That meant more money from each deal. Jason wasn't the sharpest tool in the kit and could become a liability.

A day ago, Phil caught up with Amelia and knew for sure she hadn't sent the video. The poor girl almost jetted out of her skin when he tracked her down. That whole episode still bothered him, but he'd met a roadblock. A notification from the phone snapped him out of his head, and he yanked the phone out of his jeans.

He scanned the screen in disbelief, then met Jason's gaze. The same fright that seeped through him covered Jason's features. This was getting old, but he asked a question for which he already had the answer. "Are you seeing what I'm seeing?"

Jason swallowed hard, then nodded while focused on the iPhone.

Looking away from it hadn't stopped the madness. Rows of text—the details of their conversations—filled the screen.

"This is unreal," Jason whispered and jammed one hand through his hair.

Phil dragged a hand down his jaw and covered his mouth. "Oh, shit,"

How was this possible? The one thing they agreed on was that they'd delete their shared messages once the conversation was over. It ensured they left no evidence if anyone ever caught up with them. Sure, there was the thing about "digital footprints" but since Phil didn't have long-term plans for dealing steroids, he was reasonably safe. Until now.

He frowned, "Have you been deleting the stuff like we agreed?"

Jason dipped his head, but his gaze wavered.

"Don't lie to me." Phil rubbed the back of his head as his temper flared. "If you had done what we said, this wouldn't be happening."

"Honest man, I've done it most of the time."

Phil leaped from the seat to shove him in the chest. "Well, you better make sure you get *all* of it."

With his mouth twisted at one corner, Jason said, "It's not like it matters because it's here in front of our eyes."

This had to be some kind of phone malfunction. Nobody they knew had the skills to do anything like this, and in any case, they didn't have enemies.

*Except for all those girls.*

He shook his head to kill that thought. None of them was brave enough to accuse them of anything. The way things were set up, people would blame them for leading him on. His shoulders relaxed. This was only a hiccup. Something like the one about

Sancia's family the other day. Except, something serious had come of that. But she hadn't lived to feel the effects of that scandal.

His attention snapped back to the phone when it pinged again. The relief he felt slid away, and his heart sped up like a runaway train as a final line of text appeared.

*When all is peace and safety...then comes sudden destruction.*

Jason swiped his forehead and pushed his hair back. "I don't think we should worry about it, man. Let me grab a quick shower and we can get to work. You want a drink?"

Still distracted, Phil said, "Um...sure." A moment later he cracked open the can of Pepsi Jason handed him.

Phil's attention soon strayed from the action movie, and he focused on the expensive furniture and artwork on the walls. His parents were at a different level, but he didn't envy Jason. The steroids kept him in the money, plus the side hustle of trading funds. One day, he'd get to where he wanted to be.

A scream parted the clouds in his brain and made him frown and sit up. The sound had come from upstairs. Another loud wail had him jetting off the sofa and running up the stairs. The panicked cries continued, leading him to Jason's bedroom. He burst through the door and into the bathroom.

"Help me!" Jason shrieked while beating against the glass enclosure.

The atmosphere was thick with steam, and Phil could barely see in front of him.

Jason slammed against the glass with the side of his body before tumbling to the floor. The rainfall shower system poured jets of water in every direction.

"Get out!" Phil shouted, while reaching for the metal rail to slide the door open. "Don't touch the handle!" With both fists, Jason pounded the bottom of the glass while cowering. "Turn off the ..."

Phil yanked his hand back and looked around him. Nothing in the bathroom could break the thick glass, so he ran into the bedroom, scanned the space, and grabbed a computer chair. He drove it into the glass with all his strength. Three more attempts shattered it, and showered Jason with shards.

He had stopped moving, except for his limbs that kept jerking like someone who'd been electrocuted.

Phil reached into the cloud of smoke and scalding hot water. It took a few tries before he yanked Jason onto the floor. Blood and water swirled together on the tiles. Trying not to look at the angry, red patches that covered Jason's skin, he threw a towel on top him. With shaking hands, he reached for the phone. He was in the middle of calling for an ambulance when Jason started twitching and frothing at the mouth.

# CHAPTER TWENTY-ONE

## GENEVA

"**O**H. MY. LORD." Geneva squeezed her eyes shut and clung to Spence as the waves of pleasure washed through her body. She arched her back as he reminded her of one reason they made a good couple. Their chemistry had been in the stratosphere from the start of their relationship. His betrayal threatened to contaminate the cloud of ecstasy she rode, but she wrapped her legs around him and let the sensory overload sweep his flaws away. Momentarily.

"I love you, Jen."

By the time the pure cotton sheet at her back signaled a return to reality, Spence had wrapped his arms around her and was sprinkling kisses on her forehead.

Her lack of reciprocity said everything about the state of their marriage.

If it wasn't for the fact that they hadn't made love in more than a month, and that it was so good, she'd have rolled to her side of the king-sized bed. But Spence wasn't one to give up once he had the advantage, and the truth was, she hadn't realized how she missed his lovemaking. But that was his fault.

A year was a long time to hold a grudge, but that was part of what made her uniquely Geneva. As she'd told Janet, Octavia, and

Sylvia—lifelong friends she'd made in college—most men didn't understand their partners. When a woman set her heart on a mate and joined her life to his, she made that choice for life. The way mute swans and gray wolves settled into permanent pairs. Men didn't understand how gutted and insecure they left their partner for what sometimes turned out to be a momentary diversion. Even now, she still didn't trust him. Spence had shattered her heart and her belief in him. Twice—that she knew about. God help him if he cheated again and she found out about it.

He kissed her cheek, rolled off the bed, and picked up his shorts on the way out of the room. The light went on in the hall, and she released the breath that had been trapped in her lungs. Her thoughts never left Alexia for long, and she wondered if she was asleep in the facility where she would be for an undetermined amount of time. They would move her when she could manage at home.

As for that boy, Jason, she wondered if he would last the week. The havoc that must have played out earlier in the Blalock's home made her smirk. She didn't take pleasure in other people's pain, but all bets were off when it came to her daughter. Jason got only what he deserved for making that evil move on Alexia. Right now, he'd be in agony—except for the medication. He wouldn't be able to rest on any part of his body without his skin being on fire. Hell on earth. Just like the punishment he'd rained on her daughter, for no good reason. If that other boy hadn't been there to help him, Jason wouldn't have made it out of the shower, and she'd have been done with him in one go.

Phil's presence was a tad inconvenient after she put her plans in motion and set that timer, but he'd remember this painful lesson when she got around to him. While on this mission, she'd always have the advantage. People didn't realize how vulnerable they were with everything in their home automated, computerized, or connected to the internet. She'd played around with the

Blalocks' appliances, air conditioning, and lighting until the idea of breaching their heating and electrical system combined, turned into a viable option.

Their bathrooms were the dream of the hedonistic—underfloor and shower floor heating, plus heated towel rails. The metal handle that controlled the sliding doors housed an electronic panel which controlled the water temperature and was the perfect conduit for electricity. She'd been surprised to find that the water jets adjusted to 60 degrees in any direction. A pleasant experience on an ordinary day, but not so much at scalding temperature or combined with electricity. Jason's shower stall had turned into the perfect death trap.

Her thoughts went on hold the moment Spence appeared in the doorway, balancing their large cheese board in both hands. She chided herself. Spence might be intuitive, but he couldn't see inside her head.

As he approached, she rose and went to the bathroom to freshen up. A few minutes later, she returned wearing his bathrobe.

He'd switched on a lamp and straightened the sheets. His smile widened when she climbed into bed, but he didn't comment on the oversized robe. She sat against the headboard and accepted the glass of port he offered. "What are we celebrating?"

"You have to ask?" His slow smile was suggestive as his eyes traveled the length of her body. With one hand he circled her foot, stroking the inside of her ankle. "To us. Thank you, babe."

She didn't ask why Spence was thanking her. They both knew. She'd made him work hard to get back in her good graces, but the truth was that the family crisis had put their hostilities on hold. The way he'd made love to her tonight made their ceasefire so worth it. Inhaling deeply, she tapped the glass against his. "To us," she echoed.

Geneva's gaze panned the selections he'd made—apple slices, grapes, cashews, specialty salami, crackers, aged cheddar, brie, and her personal favorite, pepper jack. The port was included simply because she liked it. Thoughtful gestures like that had won her heart early in their relationship. Her stomach gurgled quietly, reminding her that she hadn't eaten lunch. "This is quite a feast."

Spence chuckled. "I did say I was hungry before we fell into bed."

"That's true." She patted the space next to her. "Come closer."

Avoiding the questions in his eyes, she held on to the board while Spence settled on the other side.

She popped a grape into her mouth and delicately chewed it. "Tell me about your trip."

"Normal stuff. Meetings and more meetings." He bit into a cracker and a sliver of cheddar, and it was a moment before he said, "But we got some good news from the police."

Her eyes were glued to him, and she went still. "And?"

"That policeman you asked me about? The one you said was quietly transferred?"

She nodded and swallowed the grape. "I remember."

"He's facing corruption charges."

With her gaze lowered, Geneva sipped from the wine glass. "Really?"

"That's what Dad told me." Spence looked directly at her. "Apparently, his bank records somehow found their way into the public domain, and he had no explanation for how he'd come by the lump sum in his account."

Frowning, Geneva asked, "So, how did it come to light? Especially since the police clearly don't get in a hurry there?"

Spence licked his lip, swallowed more wine, then announced, "An anonymous tip made to Crime Stop."

He looked at her again. "The informant was kind enough to provide a trail that led directly to Corporal Marsden's bank account."

Geneva cocked one brow. "So you know his name?"

"It was in the paper." He stared across the room and didn't speak for a while. Then, he pulled in a deep breath. "Geneva, *if* this had something to do with you…would you admit anything, *if* I asked you?"

"Why would you want to?" She patted his chest. "You credit me with far too much. I may be handy with a computer, but I'm not Superwoman."

Spence's response was a smile that told her nothing. He was good at keeping secrets, which she knew all too well. It was clear he didn't believe her, but she had nothing to hide. At least, not anywhere he'd choose to look. If she was careful under normal circumstances, she was meticulous when faced with extraordinary situations—like invading people's privacy and accessing records she shouldn't. But nothing was off limits in her crusade.

They discussed Alexia's next steps on her healing journey, then Spence removed the leftovers from their meal. While he was in the kitchen, she reached for her phone and went to the Social-Invyte platform. Her first stop was on Christian Skyers' page. As she scrolled through the latest pictures of him posted from a hospital bed, she gritted her teeth so hard her jaw hurt.

He'd posted about being attacked by a group of hoodlums, but Geneva didn't believe that's how he came to be injured. Something told her Deja had run ahead of her, which annoyed her all over again. No harm could come to Christian. Not yet, anyway. The plan was to deal with him last. For what he'd done, he deserved special attention.

She navigated to Jason's page, which was flooded with get-well wishes, but didn't waste time there. Earlier, she learned he'd had several seizures and his chances of survival were dicey. Phil couldn't have chosen a worse day to show up at Jason's house.

Unlucky for Geneva. Lucky for Jason.

On Phil's page, someone had shared Jason's shower mishap and Phil's rescue. Their friends and well-wishers had left hundreds of comments.

Geneva wrinkled her nose. Someone had posted a photo of Jason, who was swathed in bandages. These youngsters didn't understand the meaning of the word, or the sanctity of privacy. If she hadn't limited Alexia's visitors, pictures of her would probably have ended up on the internet as well. When—if—they released pictures of Alexia, it would be on her terms.

"What are you looking at?" Spence asked, sitting on the side of the bed.

Geneva pressed a button to blank the screen, then stroked Spence's chest. "Nothing interesting. What d'you say we hit the shower and then go to bed?"

On cue, he yawned. Then he stood and held out one hand. "That sounds good."

When she rose, Geneva ran a finger down to his belly button. "Will you go start the water? I'll be there in a minute."

She waited for the sound of the shower before she sat at the cherrywood writing desk in one corner of the room. All she needed was a moment to tidy up the incriminating digital trails she'd been laying earlier when Spence lured her away from the computer.

# CHAPTER TWENTY-TWO

## DEJA

"**S**O, ABOUT THIS guy …"Tyler propped one elbow on the table and stared her in the eyes. His movement released the aquatic fragrance of the deodorant he wore, distracting her when she needed her mind to be settled.

"Which one?"

"Don't do this."Tyler lowered the screen of his laptop. "Let's start again. It's been a couple of weeks, and you've been scarce, and we both know why."

She shrugged. "In case you developed brain freeze, remember I have school and work."

"That never stopped you coming around here every week like clockwork."

"Look, I'm sorry about getting you into that situation." Her breath hitched as she folded her arms. "I've been following Alexia's new blog and her social media page. Even visited her in hospital."

Deja's gaze shot to his. "She was in a bad way, T, and I didn't realize that until I went to see her. She had all of these tubes and what-not…I definitely had to do something."

A slight frown crossed Tyler's face and he licked his lip, pulling Deja from her story. He was right about her avoiding him, but she'd stayed in touch via messaging. Today she made the time to come and see him, hoping he'd be less salty about what went down with Christian. How was she to know he'd follow her to the plaza and get into a fight with him?

He was staring at her again in *that* way. As if she was the best thing that had crossed his path that day. She couldn't deal with that now, or maybe never, so she pretended not to notice.

"It's all right to be sympathetic, DJ, but when things go sideways like they did that evening, what happens then?"

Her gaze shot to his. "I didn't ask you to do anything."

"No, you didn't." He pushed back the chair and paced the room. "But think about what might have happened if the police had come along and caught the two of us? I'd be facing an assault charge, and for what? Something you should have told the police a long time ago."

While he continued to rant, her thoughts strayed. Tyler was right. He might have been in a world of trouble if the altercation had gone any other way. Still, she couldn't help the satisfied smile that escaped. Although she'd been horrified to watch Tyler and Christian fighting, she didn't approach for fear he'd recognize her. The plan to leave a copy of the video vanished, and she didn't know whether to stay or go. She'd stumbled away after Tyler ran off and she was certain he got away.

For several days after that, no new posts appeared on Christian's page, so she didn't know how badly he was injured. But the grapevine had given up several nuggets. He'd suffered tears to all the ligaments in his knee. If that was true, Christian wouldn't be able to play football again.

"Are you even listening to me?" Tyler asked, standing akimbo.

She couldn't afford to aggravate him any further, so she focused on him and nodded. "What makes you think I'm not listening?"

"The fact that you're cheesing because something terrible happened to someone—"

"And why would you be sympathetic to a guy like that?"

He sighed and ran one hand through his locs. "You know my views on violence."

"For a guy who hates it, you did pretty well for yourself."

The flashing of his eyes stopped her from making any further comment. Then, Tyler shook his head. "I can't believe you're happy to know I ruined someone's life."

"That's not exactly what happened." His fierce glare cut her off, and she held up one hand. "Trust me, Tyler, he'll be fine. His father has plenty of money. He can be anything he wants to be."

"He sure as hell won't be playing any more football, from what I heard."

Throwing back her head, Deja sighed. "For what he did to Alexia, that's a small price to pay."

"I don't agree with you."

She cut her eyes at him and scoffed. "You're such a bleeding heart."

"Better that than what you've become over this whole thing."

"That's pure drama and your emotions speaking." She raised both hands as she pleaded for his understanding. "All I'm doing is making things right."

Tyler's head snapped back and he closed his eyes. "And who appointed you to be the avenger? Why are you so hell-bent on taking revenge on people who've done nothing to you?"

"You wouldn't understand."

"Damn straight, I don't."

"All I'm asking is for you to trust me." She grabbed his arm and stood. "I've got this."

Tyler sucked his teeth and stepped out of her reach. "Trust you? In case you haven't noticed, you're in over your head." Pulling his shoulders back, he added, "I'm done helping you. Any funny business you want done, do it yourself."

"T, you can't be—"

"I'm serious all right." He gripped her shoulders, his frown fierce. "You have to stop this madness before it gets out of hand."

She stepped away, forcing him to release her. "I have to pick up a few items. Catch you later."

Tyler took in her sneakers, sweatsuit, and hoodie in one sweep. She'd worn the same outfit when her plan to meet Christian went sideways. He cocked one brow, but didn't remark.

"What?"

He opened the laptop and stared at the screen. "Nothing at all. Like you said, we'll touch base."

When he let out a heavy breath as if she'd trampled on his nerves, Deja picked up her knapsack. "So, this is what we're doing?"

Without looking her way, he said, "Just go."

"If that's the way you want it."

Tyler sat as still as a Buddha statue until she walked away. She needed him, but refused to allow him to hold her to ransom. She'd done nothing to help herself when her uncle repeatedly raped her. Not this time. It felt good to get even with Christian. Pity Sancia had gotten the easy way out. What happened to Jason was accidental as far as she knew, but just desserts all the same. Phil's day was coming. She'd make sure of that.

# CHAPTER TWENTY-THREE

## GENEVA

*G*OD FORGIVE ME.

For the first time since Alexia's trip to Jamaica, Geneva was glad to end their visit with her. Alexia had months, if not years, of rehabilitation ahead. Her baby girl struggled to do something as simple as take a few steps, and Geneva's eyes burned at the unfairness of it. Always graceful, Alexia now moved like a newborn giraffe who didn't yet understand how to make its legs work in a coordinated way.

When Geneva opened her eyes, Spence met her gaze. He covered her hand and squeezed.

"This is heartbreaking," she mumbled and leaned closer as he hugged her.

"I know, but Lexi is a trooper."

As if to prove him right, the subject of their conversation grinned, waved, then clung to the steel railing to support her weight when she took the next step.

Geneva waved back, pasting on a bright smile and hoping Alexia wouldn't see through it. Her throat closed with her next words. "Do you remember how she pulled herself up on the edge of that center table the first time? She wouldn't go back to creeping after that."

Chuckling, Spence nodded. "Yes, she ran everywhere."

Amused despite the heaviness weighing on her, Geneva quipped, "If you can classify her staggering all over the place as running."

They laughed and focused on Alexia, who turned and took hesitant steps in the opposite direction between the rails, encouraged by her therapist.

Geneva wished she had her daughter's forgiving spirit. But she wasn't made up that way. She held on to grudges the way a baby clung to a security blanket. In this case, her character flaw wasn't a bad thing. If she was like Alexia or Spence, she'd suck up their misfortune and hope that natural justice and the law prevailed. Since neither had manifested so far, she'd had to stand in the gap. To date, she hadn't regretted that decision.

Spence spoke softly in her ear. "The important thing is her determination, and that's half the battle won."

Still focused on Alexia, she said, "I'm calling your father when we get home."

He didn't respond right away, and she thought he'd missed her words, until he said, "I may not agree, but I understand."

Geneva glanced sideways because she expected him to ask her not to call. His attention was fixed on Alexia, and the indulgence in his gaze was clear. She drew strength from Spence's strong grip that went from her waist to sealing her hand inside his. Staring at their fingers, she counted off her unfinished tasks. Last week, when Deja called and asked to visit Alexia, Geneva gave an excuse. Seeing a stranger would confuse Alexia, and it was best she regain more of her memory before accepting visitors.

Deja's disappointment was almost tangible, but Geneva didn't want her interacting with Alexia yet. Let her stew over how she'd let down a close friend. Whenever she produced more useful information would be time enough to throw her a crumb.

"Good going, sis." Jaden cheered from behind them and laid a hand on Geneva's shoulder. He'd just arrived and would stay with Alexia a while after they left. They had worked out a roster so that she had company most of the time. Geneva wanted her focused on recovery and occupied with reading and writing for her blog. She'd already made the decision to use online learning to continue her education. They would follow up with the university when she was able to concentrate better.

While Alexia was transferred to her room and situated in bed, Geneva chatted with Jaden. Although they lived in the same house, sometimes she didn't see him except at mealtimes and even that had changed with their new, irregular hours. The irony didn't miss her. Years ago, her decision to work from home had come partly because of the need to watch her children grow and mold them into independent individuals. Jaden was a loner who loved computers and gaming. Give him food and hardware and he'd be satisfied for days. She was proud of the resourceful man he'd eventually become.

"I'll go check on Lexi." She got to her feet and hugged Jaden. "Talk to you later."

"Yeah, see you at home. There's some stuff …"

He didn't continue, and she wondered what he wanted to discuss but didn't press. Jaden would seek her out when he was ready.

◆———◆

"I received a copy of the video from *Island Escape*, which makes me wonder why nothing has happened in your granddaughter's case."

Desmond and Marlena Leighton stared at their computer screen without moving for so long, Geneva thought she had lost them, except that her internet connection was working fine.

Next to her, Spence also sat motionless, but the heat from his gaze almost burned her skin. She'd blindsided him, which was unfair. But she had good reason. If she'd shared what she intended to do, he'd have tried to stop her. Not even he would keep her from getting to the root of the problem facing them.

Desmond blinked hard and stroked a non-existent beard, then sat up straight as if her words just registered.

"What video?" Marlena asked with one hand pressed to her chest.

"The one from the night when your granddaughter was beaten and violated."

Marlena's hand crept to her neck. Her dark-brown eyes that were so much like her son's flashed to her husband. "What does she mean?"

When Spence gripped her hand, Geneva ignored him. She'd had enough of tiptoeing around her in-laws. "One of those boys raped Lexi."

Now, Marlena covered her mouth and deep wrinkles formed on her forehead. "My God." She turned to her husband. "Did you know about this?"

At her side, Desmond shifted and the color drained from his face. Spence had inherited his good looks, including his tawny skin and sculpted lips, but thankfully not all his character traits.

"Well …"

"Desmond, please answer the question."

He sighed and rubbed his forehead. "It came up in the report."

Marlena's eyes glistened as she turned back to Geneva and asked, "They caught all of this on camera?"

"That's right." Easing her hand out of Spence's, Geneva added, "So, it's a mystery to me why nothing happened with the rape kit that was done. Nor does the Miami police have anything on this case."

When Desmond stared directly at the laptop, she continued, "At least, not when I checked."

Taking a breath to settle her nerves, Geneva pointed at the screen. "This is exactly why Jamaican people don't trust the police. Good God, it's been three months, and all I've been given is a runaround."

Her father-in-law rubbed the bridge of his nose. "I understand your frustration, but this is more complicated than you think, Jen. The incident took place at a tourist rental property, so it has to be handled with sensitivity—"

Her tone was strident when she snapped, "Don't you mean it has to be shoved under the carpet and forgotten because the villa belongs to a set of rich assholes?"

Her in-laws gasped, and Desmond folded both arms across his chest. "It's much more than that. Jamaica has a bad enough reputation, and the police are under pressure with the—"

"Pardon my language, but I don't give a rat's ass about Jamaica's reputation or the police having a hard time. I. Care. Only. About. My Daughter. This is *your* granddaughter. What are you doing about that? Does it even matter to you?"

His face reddened. "How can you say that? You know how I feel about Alexia."

"I'd ask the same questions," Marlena snapped. "I thought the case was now being handled by …"

How on earth could she miss the fact that nothing had been done? Marlena was the limit. Too docile and trusting. While she fussed at Desmond, Geneva collected her thoughts. She needed to access Desmond's laptop again. The local authorities had had more than enough time to do their work while she was busy with Alexia's so-called friends. She was done waiting.

Spence sat with his head lowered between his hands, but Geneva was beyond caring. He'd have plenty to say about keeping the video to herself, but she'd climb that mountain when it stared her in the face. For now, she had one aim in view.

"I know you don't want to hear this, but I'm tired of waiting for *nothing* to happen."

"Are you threatening me, Geneva?"

"You're family, so that's not something I'd do." She smiled at Desmond, while rage threatened to cut off her air. "But if the Miami police do not receive that rape kit by Wednesday, I'll write to your police commissioner about this matter. And that's only the beginning."

"That's not necessary," he protested.

"Don't you dare tell me what's necessary and what isn't." Her voice cracked, and she blinked hard at the memory of Alexia's painful effort to walk and how that boy had assaulted her. "I'll do whatever it takes to hold every person who has a hand in this matter accountable."

Spence stood and left the room without a word. A moment later, a door slammed.

It was just as well. She didn't have the bandwidth to deal with his issues. Not right now. Without bidding Desmond and Marlena goodbye, she closed the program but was too tired to rise from the sofa. She allowed herself a moment to breathe and clear her headspace, then used the laptop to access the computer in her office.

To settle her mind, she stared across the living room where she'd insisted that all of them spend part of their Sunday afternoons together as a family. The accent wall in a deep shade of pink complimented the flecks of matching color in the drapes. They'd originally hired a decorator, but late last year she and Alexia had re-decorated and included the adjoining dining nook to better reflect everyone's combined taste.

The common areas they shared were no longer showpieces created by a designer, but places where they connected and spent time with each other. But Alexia's trip had shattered that aspect of their lives. Now, their home was silent, as if occupied only by the ghosts from their previous life.

Casting the memories aside, Geneva let her fingers fly over the keypad as she cemented the next phase of her plan.

# CHAPTER TWENTY-FOUR

## ALEXIA

**H**ER "RECOVERY SPACE" as she called it, occupied the top floor of the hospital. The rehab center was semi-private, with lounges and activities organized in communal rooms. She had internet service, all the comforts of home, extensive menu items, and even the option of having a stylist for hair and makeup. All of this had to be costing her parents a fortune, but Mom wouldn't discuss those matters with her.

"Leave the finances to us. Concentrate on getting better," was all she would say.

The casts had come off her arms and leg, but her kneecap had been broken in several places. The smallest pieces had been removed and the rest stabilized and held together with metal wires. She had pain, muscle weakness, and limited range of motion in one arm and leg, but the physio was encouraging and seemed sure she'd been fine given time.

If only everything got better as the months went by. This minute, she was sorry she had forced a meeting with her best friend and the guy she was sure would have her back in any situation.

"This place is more like a day spa than a recovery center." Danny cleared her throat and went silent as she gazed through the window at the skyline. She had barely met Alexia's gaze since arriving ten minutes ago.

"Too bad a beauty treatment isn't the reason I'm here," Alexia said, keeping an even tone while her spirit sank. The lounge was spacious, with comfortable seats meant to make both residents and visitors forget why they were there. But with the low-grade aches radiating through her muscles after today's physiotherapy session, Alexia was all too aware of her situation. She'd chosen this nook and particular table because she'd grown comfortable sitting here and pecking away on the laptop while writing her blog posts. Also, it was set a bit apart from where most of the patients liked to gather, closer to the middle of the lounge. Only a few other visitors were around at this time of the day, so it was quiet.

Her gaze went to Chad, who stood with his back to them and faced the plate glass, as if avoiding her would make the visit any easier. An awkwardness had settled in the air the moment they walked into the room, and their conversation dried up before it even started.

"So, how are things at school and what's going on in the world of golf?" she asked, tempted to pull her arm off the tabletop. She'd always been skinny, but her wasted muscles mocked her, especially when compared to Danny's smooth chocolate skin, thick curves, and shiny twists.

"Uh...well, we have a tournament coming up so we're training hard." She scratched the lobe of her ear and fixed her eyes on the wall-mounted television behind Alexia. "School is school."

Alexia shifted her leg, then asked what she'd been dying to know. "What are people saying about what happened to me?"

After glancing at Chad, Danny shrugged. "They've moved on, especially since there's been no news in a while."

"Really?" Alexia didn't know what she expected, but felt as if she'd been on a group outing and had been left behind without

a road map to get back home—which was her reality. What she
hadn't expected was for these two to drop her as if she'd been part
of a terrible scandal. But wait—for all she knew, that was the case.
It was one thing to get information online and quite another to
hear the rumors people were spreading.

"Well, you were off the grid for some time." Danny stared at
the table as if the words sat on her conscience. She hadn't returned
after the one time she came to the hospital. Neither had Chad.
Nor had they spoken to her before today.

A sudden rush of tears surprised Alexia. Danny had been one
of her closest friends since forever. They had shared everything—
dreams, fears, secrets. But now her life had gone sideways, and
Danny and Chad were acting as if she had bubonic plague or
something. Mom had told her you never knew the true measure
of the people you called friends until you were sick or needed help.

She was right.

Alexia blinked away her tears and glanced at Chad, who still
hadn't moved.

"That's not exactly true. People know about my situation."
Alexia said, staring Danny in the eyes. "Especially since I started
the blog."

"Oh, that." She shrugged with one shoulder and sat back. The
Fitness Freak logo on the front of her T-shirt mocked Alexia, who
dropped her gaze to the frosted glass where Danny's fingers were
locked tight. "I doubt a lot of folks know about that. Busy with
school, life, and all that."

Her tone carried an edge that Alexia hadn't heard before, and
she didn't know exactly what to make of it. To her ears, Danny's
comment sounded as if she was discounting the blog and the fact
that Alexia was telling her story.

At first, she'd been afraid to share her experience, for fear of
what people would think. As the weeks passed, she grew more

confident as the number of encouraging comments grew. The trolls had also come by, calling her names and claiming her need for attention was sick. Mom had kept her boosted, reminding her that life was filled with the good, bad, ugly, and that haters would always need an outlet for their hate.

Unconsciously, she raised her hand, then lowered it halfway to the closed wound where the doctors had made the burr hole in her head.

Danny followed the movement of her arm, then smiled. "The good thing is, you're getting better."

"Hmm." Another glance at Chad sent a shaft of pain to Alexia's heart. Was he going to ignore her for the entire visit? Her eyes watered again, and despite the discomfort, Alexia sat up and breathed in deeply. No matter what, she wouldn't cry in front of them. She also didn't plan to act desperate and ask when they'd come back to see her. She was better than that. Another thing Mom had said when she was tempted to give up or if she'd done anything to disappoint her.

Alexia didn't regret that she hadn't had private time with Danny. She might have made the mistake of telling her *everything*. Danny and Chad were close, and Alexia would have been devastated to have her business discussed by the two of them. She hadn't even told Mom what she now knew for certain about *that* night.

The door opened, and her mother walked into the room. Within five seconds her smile faded. "Chad. Danny."

Her gaze zig-zagged from one to the other, then settled on Alexia.

"Thank you both for coming." The welcome drained from her voice, as she continued, "I need some time with Alexia."

Danny shot to her feet so fast the action was almost comical. But no one was laughing. Her brother dragged himself across the room and hovered next to Alexia. When he spotted the place where the hose had been located and the hair was shorter, he winced before kissing her cheek. With both hands deep in his pockets, Chad spoke low in his throat. "We'll see you."

Her eyes went blurry, and Alexia turned her head as if looking at the mural on the opposite wall. *If I hadn't asked them to come, they would have stayed away.* She was sure they had no plans to return. And maybe that wouldn't be such a bad thing.

They left the room as if they couldn't escape fast enough.

Mom sat in the opposite seat and laid a hand on hers. "At times like these, you know who—"

One of Alexia's nurses stepped into the lounge. "Mrs. Leighton, Alexia has another visitor."

"Who is it?" Mom asked frowning.

The brunette squinted as if searching her memory, then said, "Deja Johnson."

"Send her in," Alexia said, without interfacing with Mom. She didn't want to hear what she had to say right now. Bad enough she had to deal with that kind of reaction from Chad, but that was expected after his first visit. At least he wasn't crying this time. Ignoring her was so much worse, though. He'd acted as if he couldn't bear to look at her. As if she wasn't worthy because she was broken.

*What happened wasn't my fault.*

She wanted to scream at him, but what good would that do? It would only make her seem unhinged.

The nurse disappeared and came back escorting Deja, who approached as if she wasn't sure Alexia would want to see her. When she sat, Mom gave her the evil eye as though daring her to say the wrong thing.

Deja pulled in a sharp breath, then asked, "How are you feeling?"

Alexia picked up a pen and smiled, although she wasn't feeling it. "I've had better days, but I'm glad to be alive."

Returning her smile, Deja said, "I'm glad you're still here, too."

Angling her head toward Deja, Alexia asked, "How did you know where I was?"

Deja coughed and squirmed in the chair. "I've been following your Social-Invyte account. I saw the link to your blog."

She was getting some weird vibes from Deja, but wasn't sure why. Looking straight at her, Alexia said, "It didn't say where I was."

"I know. I asked your mom." Deja's gaze shifted while she played with one her curls. "I met Danny and Chad at the elevator. Danny only said hello and that she was in a hurry."

*They have a right to be.* "Yes, they came to visit."

Deja leaned toward Alexia as if waiting for her to say more, but she was in no mood to talk about what happened or the funk she'd fallen into in the last half-hour.

Mom rose from her seat and her eyes flashed. She threw a warning glance at Deja as she marched to the door. "I'll be back in a few minutes."

# CHAPTER TWENTY-FIVE

## GENEVA

THE STONY-FACED OFFICER waved her to a seat. "Mrs. Leighton, thanks for coming in."

"Of course," Geneva said as she sat, smoothing the skirt of her powder-blue suit. "I've been waiting for the police department to call."

Detective James Harrison brushed at his thinning brown hair while scanning a document on the desk. His scalp gleamed under the florescent light when he glanced at Officer Rodrigo Cruz, who'd dealt with Geneva the first time she visited the stationhouse. His direct gaze settled on her and would have unnerved a lesser person, but not her. Hamilton studied her as if she were under a microscope—an unknown species that he was longing to dissect.

"So, how can I help?" Geneva asked, taking in the glass and metal setup in one sweep. The small office was tidy, with low stacks of files organized on a nearly credenza. Her attention returned to Harrison when he tapped a sheet of paper on top of the metal desk. "We have a few questions for you."

Geneva's heart stuttered as she angled her head toward the policeman. She was careful to keep her breathing even. "About my daughter's case, I assume? Did the Jamaican police contact you?"

"I'm sorry, Mrs. Leighton." He held up one hand with his fingers spread apart. The long, thick digits reminded her of sausages. When she met his brown eyes, the detective continued, "We'll deal with that in a minute, but my questions have to do with a matter that may be related."

She sat forward and opened her eyes wide. "Go right ahead, please."

"The first one concerns the Jackmans—"

"And who are they?" she asked, with the appropriate level of offhand interest. "The only one I know is the politician."

"That's who I'm talking about."

She encouraged him to continue with a hand motion.

Harrison eased back in his seat and studied her for what felt like a full minute. If he thought that was supposed to unnerve her, he had several more guesses coming.

"It seems that somehow, the university which his daughter attends—attended—experienced a glitch in their messaging system, and certain libelous statements were made about Mr. Jackman and his family."

"I'm not sure what you're getting at, but I read about those allegations in the paper." She frowned, then asked, "What does that have to do with my daughter?"

Harrison rested both elbows on the chair arms and watched her over the steeple he made with his fingers. "You're a cybersecurity expert, aren't you?"

Geneva nodded and let both hands rest on her lap. "And what does my career have to do with the Jackmans?"

His focus shifted to the typewritten sheet in front of him, then to Officer Cruz before he said, "Doing something like that is not beyond your skillset, is it?"

She scowled and waited a beat before saying, "Perhaps you should have instructed me to bring my lawyer. You also should have told me I was under suspicion, *if* that's the case. Plus, there's the fact that you're out of order for suggesting that I'd spread gossip about people I don't know."

He gently beat the air with one hand in what was meant to be a soothing motion. "Calm down, Mrs. Leighton. We're not accusing you of anything. Just covering all the angles in this case."

"As a matter of interest," she said, easing forward, "why would you assume I'd care about that family? I'd say they have more to worry about than who's talking about them."

"So, you're aware of the case."

She tipped one brow. "Is there anyone in this city who isn't?"

"So, maybe you know of his daughter, Sancia Jackman?"

"It's more than possible," she said, shifting in the seat. "My daughter also used to attend the university."

Harrison's eyes narrowed and he looked over her shoulder, then at Cruz. "You know she's recently deceased?"

Geneva shrugged. "How would I know that? I've been busy taking care of Alexia. That's *my* daughter, who's been in hospital for months."

She looked at her watch, then picked up her portfolio off the edge of the desk and laid it on her lap. "Look, I'd love to help in whatever way I can, but I can't do that if we're going in circles. Why exactly am I here? I thought it was about what happened to *my* child. That I was finally getting an update."

His nostrils flared and in a harsh voice he snapped, "Sancia Jackman was someone's daughter, too."

Geneva pulled her head back while staring him down. "I'm perfectly aware of that, so again, what can I do for you?"

The policeman's face flushed, and he gritted his teeth. The muscles in his jaw rippled as if they had taken on a life of their own. Harrison picked up a pen and flipped it between his fingers, still eyeing her as if she were a suspect in some heinous crime.

Her intention wasn't to make him lose his temper, but at the same time, he was trying hers. She sighed and decided to give a little. No sense in making an enemy of him. After all, he would be helpful in getting details about Alexia's case.

"Gentlemen." She put on a winning smile, which included both men. "I have another appointment, so please, let's talk about why I'm really here."

"Miss Jackman crashed her car some weeks ago. We suspect there may have been foul play."

*We suspect. Suspicion, but no proof.*

Geneva's hand went to her chest and she gasped. "Gosh, that's tragic. I can't imagine what her parents must be going through, dealing with the death of a child while also being accused of a crime."

"Hmmm." Harrison's dark eyes searched hers as if he intended to see into her soul. "Her vehicle was found way outside of her normal stomping grounds, so—"

Wearing a wry smile, Geneva asked, "Detective, do you have any teenage children?"

He shook his head, then assumed a questioning expression.

"If you had them, you'd know there's no telling what they will get up to, especially if given too much freedom."

He inclined his head in agreement, then raised one finger as if he'd forgotten something. "The SUV she was driving might have been hacked, and since you're connected to her—"

"Now wait a minute." Geneva moved her finger back and forth. "The only connection I have to her is that she ran in the same circles with my daughter. I'm not sure I even know what she looks like. And besides, why would anyone do something that outlandish? It sounds like something out of a movie. Are you sure she wasn't drinking?"

"No, Mrs. Leighton, she had no alcohol in her blood."

With a hand to her neck, Geneva lowered her gaze and shook her head. "Unreal."

Harrison exchanged a sly look with Cruz. "We heard you were among the best in this part of the state, but I guess we were mistaken."

"I'm good at what I do," Geneva said, narrowing her eyes. Did this officer really think a slight would make her stumble? "But, I'm not into mischief or mayhem. That's for the younger folks, or people with time on their hands. As you know, I'm a busy professional, and my consulting work is for corporations, not teaching people how to hack into car computers. And with my daughter's situation …"

She wrapped her fingers around the chair arms and shook her head. "If there's nothing else …"

"Actually, there is," Harrison said. "We've received a video from the Area One police."

He had the grace to look away when he continued, "We won't be able to let you view it at this time, but …"

She shot forward to the edge of the seat. "I've waited *months* for that surveillance footage to surface, and now you tell me I won't be able to see it?"

"Mrs. Leighton, I don't believe that's the best thing right now. Our team has reviewed it." His face took on a sour expression when he added, "We understand that you and your daughter have started a blog and that you might have information we need."

"So, you've been spying on us?"

"I wouldn't call it that." Cruz's voice faded when she turned a vicious glare on him.

"What would you call it then?"

"We've been looking at what has been published and how it might help this investigation." Cruz's sympathy was obvious when he said, "I know it's hard to stay hopeful when it seems like nothing's happening, but rest assured, we'll do all we can to bring the perpetrators to justice."

"Which brings us back to Sancia Jackman," Harrison said, clasping both hands and sitting forward. "Do you know if she participated in the attack on your daughter?"

"No, I don't." The lie slid off her tongue with an ease that frightened Geneva. At times, she thought she was losing her soul. But she reminded herself of Alexia's condition and how far she still had to go before making a full recovery. Seeing that video was the best thing that happened, despite the heartbreak. Picturing what Alexia had suffered gave her direction she wouldn't have had otherwise.

The police didn't need to know she'd witnessed one of the worst kinds of attack any parent had to watch. She still shook with rage whenever she thought about it. After shoving the visual away, a deep breath restored her composure.

"She was one of the young people on the trip, and now she's out of the picture, and under strange circumstances, I might add. It will be interesting to see if any other unexplainable situations crop up for any of the others who went to Jamaica."

"Well, as long as they don't run into the people who hurt my girl, they'll probably be fine." Geneva's lips twisted and her belly filled with gall. "It's my daughter that needed protecting from them."

Harrison closed the file on the desk. "We'll need to talk to you again, as soon as we've dissected the evidence."

Geneva stood, and instead of feeling she'd had a victory, the mixture of anticipation and triumph sat heavy in her stomach. The relief was enough to bring her to tears, but this wasn't the time or place to give in to her emotions. "That's fine. I'm always available when it comes to my children."

The two men remained silent. One watched her as if he understood what she was going through. The other's scrutiny was dispassionate, and distrust lingered in his eyes.

She hadn't made any mistakes. She was too careful for that. But Harrison was much smarter than he looked and seemed convinced she had something to hide.

Now, she was more thankful than ever for her cautious and meticulous approach to everything she did. If she'd run ahead to exact vengeance the way she'd been inclined to do, she might have blundered and attracted attention with a digital trail that led back to her. It was easy to overlook small bits of coding that could identify the way she worked. But she laid clean tracks to her targets before executing her strategy each time. And within the hour, the Special Investigations Division would be busy with another crime.

When she stood at the door, Geneva tipped her head. "Thanks for the update. I'm sure I'll be hearing from you again soon."

# CHAPTER TWENTY-SIX

## PHIL

**P**HIL STUFFED BOTH hands in his pockets and looked at the floor to avoid Jason's mother. Her red, puffy eyes were droopy and sad. The lines in her face told him she hadn't slept in a while.

"He's the same," she said, arms folded across her stomach. Her chin wobbled as she continued, "Thank you for coming."

He didn't know what to say, so he moved his lips to imitate a smile. "It's no problem." Clearing his throat, he added, "I'm just glad I was there to help him."

"So are we." She sniffed and ran her fingers through her untidy brown hair. "I just wish ..." She covered her lips as tears trickled down her cheeks.

Phil couldn't keep his gaze from going to Jason, who looked like a mummy from a horror movie. He was wrapped in bandages, and the sight of his reddened face made Phil want to puke. Although he felt bad about it, he couldn't wait to leave. He shouldn't have come. Seeing Jason like this brought back the reality he tried to forget for two weeks.

"I'm going to—" He stepped back when Jason moved in the bed, but it wasn't because he was awake. Jason was twitching the same way he had when Phil pulled him out of the shower. He was having a seizure.

Mrs. Blalock gasped and put a hand to her throat. "We need a doctor."

When he didn't move, she brushed past him and hit a button on the bed rail. Before Phil could blink, a small army poured into the room and someone guided him outside, along with Mrs. Blalock. She paced the waiting area with her arms wrapped around her middle.

Phil dropped into a chair like a boulder. *Why the hell did I come?*

His leg bounced against the tile, and he looked up each time someone approached them. He clasped both hands between his knees, thinking about the paper he needed to sit tomorrow. Then he sat up and jammed both hands through his hair. This was a nightmare.

He looked up when a thick guy in green scrubs stopped a few feet away. His gaze swept the space that was thankfully empty, except for an old lady who was nodding off.

Phil didn't hear what the man said to Mrs. Blalock, but her scream raised every hair on his body and sent a chill pouring through his blood. He knew, without being told, what had happened. The burn in his eyes startled him, and he lowered his head and blinked hard.

*How was this even possible? Death by showering?*

Mrs. Blalock collapsed in the doctor's arms, sobbing. Her scream pierced the fog in Phil's brain, yet he was stuck. He couldn't move, pinned down just the same as when he woke from a dream and his mind was alert, but his body hadn't yet caught up.

She hollered and thrashed until her eyes rolled back in her head. The doctor caught her before she sank to the floor. As he shouted for help, Phil got to his feet and headed for the elevator.

He couldn't stick around because things would only get worse, and he didn't want to be there. What help could he offer?

He made it to his car, feeling as if he was sleepwalking. This was madness. Jason was young and healthy. He wasn't supposed to die like this.

The ride home was a blur, and he let out a deep breath and dropped his head on the steering wheel when he sat in the small garage. He'd have to pull himself together if he didn't want Mom all over him. She'd notice immediately if he was out of sorts. He rubbed both hands over his eyes and got out of the beat-up Honda Accord that got him from place to place when he wasn't riding with Jason.

His name brought back the nightmarish scene, and Phil wondered if anyone else had heard yet. Not that it mattered. Jason was beyond caring. With a handle on the door to enter the house, Phil's heart almost stopped as he rumpled his hair.

"Oh, shit."

What if Jason had been stupid enough to keep some of the stuff they did on his phone or laptop? He walked into the house, praying that Jason had had the good sense to delete everything that connected them. That way, all the evidence would die with him. But no, he hadn't. They'd argued about that just before he went into the shower.

Phil would have a hard time explaining anything they'd done, *if* they came to light. Of course, if pressed, he could say Jason had coerced him into it. After all, he was the one dealing directly with the plug for their purchases. It would only seem natural that Jason was the one with all the influence in their relationship.

He walked into the kitchen, greeted his mother, and headed for the refrigerator to grab a bottle of water. When he turned around, she patted his cheek. "Looks like you had a rough day."

Avoiding her eyes, he brushed past. "Practice was intense, and I have to study and prepare a paper, so I may miss dinner."

Her concerned hazel gaze followed him. "I'll come and check on you, but you're not skipping dinner. You know how I feel about family time."

"I know, Mom. We'll see."

He felt her stare as he left the room and wondered how he was going to concentrate on the subject of risk management when his mind was a total blank. Inside his room, he crashed on the bed with his thoughts spinning. He'd wanted to cut Jason out as the middle man in his steroid business, but what a way to get that wish. Shaking his head, he wished he could close off the image of Jason on the floor that day. Scalded, bloody, shaking like a leaf. He doubted he'd forget that as long as he lived. Sighing, he dragged himself into the bathroom, half fearing the same fate would find him. He shook his head at his stupidity. The Reids were nowhere near as well off as Jason's parents, with high-tech everything, so he didn't have to fear taking a shower. Still, every time he stepped into the stall, Jason's accident freaked him all the way out.

He showered quickly and was toweling off when the doorbell sounded. A few minutes later, Mom banged on his door. "Phil, I need to talk to you."

The handle turned, and in another second she stood inside his room. "What the hell have you gotten yourself into?" she whispered.

Phil drew the towel tighter around his waist. "What are you talking about?"

"Your father has worked hard to keep you in school, so what's happening now had better be a mistake." She scanned him from head to feet. "Put your clothes on and come downstairs."

He swiped his forehead and pulled on a pair of jeans and a T-shirt in record time. Facing the mirror, he ran a comb through his hair. This mystery would be sorted out in a minute, but his heart had grown to the size of a basketball. He rubbed his chest, praying it wouldn't give out. His gaze slid to the laptop on the desk, but he was confident on that score. It was too early for his father to be home, and he wouldn't have rung the doorbell, so something else was up.

Phil gulped in a huge puff of air and bounded down the stairs. He stopped short when he walked into the living room. Everything was the way it should have been, except for the policemen who blocked the doorway.

"Are you Philip Reid?" the tall, lanky officer asked.

His throat closed, so he nodded.

"And you're a friend of Jason Blalock?"

Phil bobbed his head a second time.

The two officers exchanged a glance before the shorter man addressed his mother. "Ma'am, we'll be taking him to the station with us."

# CHAPTER TWENTY-SEVEN

## GENEVA

*I*'M GETTING SOFT, *but this is my baby.*

She'd never been one to shy away from anything in life. That had been her strength. But today, she was avoiding an unpleasant but necessary task. Maybe she'd forgotten how strong and determined her child could be. Lowering the screen on the laptop, Geneva looked at Alexia across the table. This afternoon, she was her usual bubbly self. The only blip had come as she dove deeper into whatever she was now writing. Alexia had sucked her bottom lip into her mouth and was now staring through the window. She needed a break.

"Lexi, baby. Can I ask you something?"

Her breath hitched while she inhaled. "It has to be serious if you're not sure you can ask."

Geneva patted her hand. "I don't want to upset you, but some questions do need to be asked."

Her eyes clouded, and her baby's hand went halfway to her forehead before she laid it on the table. She hadn't regained all her strength, but the progress she made each day was encouraging and restored Geneva's faith that she'd make a full recovery.

"Um, how much of what happened—"

"I remember." Alexia peered at the screen, then sighed.

In slow motion, Geneva laid trembling hands in her lap. "Everything?"

"Some of it." Alexia turned her head toward the window, then touched the site where the drainage hose had been located. "Most of it."

Geneva waited, then Alexia said, "All of it, I think. It's been coming back gradually."

"Oh, baby." Geneva averted her gaze as hot tears scorched her eyes. After working hard to provide her children with the advantages in life, her daughter shouldn't have the kind of bad memories that were the stuff of nightmares. Hard things that would stay with her until she died. The violation. The pain. The rejection from her friends. It was enough to make Geneva want to scream about life's unfairness. Instead, she strengthened her resolve to see her new, all-consuming project to the end.

The other challenge she faced was Spence. After that wonderful interlude with him, he wasn't talking to her. His attitude disturbed her, because Geneva would have preferred if he'd say what was on his mind. He chose to brood and avoid her company, as if that would solve their problems.

"I'm so sorry…for all of it. When you're ready, we can talk about therapy."

Several micro-expressions flickered across Alexia's face so quickly, Geneva had trouble analyzing them. If she had to guess, she'd say Alexia was uncertain of what she wanted to do.

"Honestly, I think I'll be fine." She pulled her hand from Geneva's grip as a tear streamed down her cheek. "My first time should have been special. I'd never say I'm glad this happened to me, but it certainly showed me who my friends aren't."

"Yes, those people were never your friends."

"Deja—"

"Let's not talk about any of them." Geneva rubbed her arm and sat back. "They sicken me."

When Alexia smiled—a sad replica of her usual bright grin— it was the last reaction Geneva expected.

"What about forgiving and forgetting? You told me that when Jaden wouldn't let me play with his toys and then wrecked my favorite doll."

"That's your brother." She spread both hands. "Family is precious. When the world turns on us, that's all we have."

"Assuming you have the perfect family."

Geneva laughed for the first time in what felt like months. "This is how I know you're getting better. Your smart mouth is back."

As they laughed again, Alexia looked beyond Geneva and her smile brightened. "Daddy!"

The aroma of sea breezes and citrus announced Spence's presence before Geneva laid eyes on him. He brushed her cheek with his lips, then kissed Alexia on the forehead and tapped her chin. "What's going on with Alexia the Great?"

"Mom and I were just talking." Alexia threw a warning glance at her, which almost offended Geneva. Didn't this child know she wouldn't reveal what they'd been discussing? Especially this kind of sensitive information.

Spence pulled out a chair while Alexia quizzed him. "I thought you were going to be away until the weekend."

"I thought so, too, but I got everything wrapped up early."

She'd known he was coming, but wanted it to be a surprise for Alexia, who'd always been a Daddy's girl. While they talked, Geneva studied Spence. He was still everything she wanted in a partner, and yet they operated on different wavelengths. She wouldn't hold it against him, though. They were both driven in different ways, and that, more than anything else, had created a hiccup in their marriage.

Spence complained that she didn't have time for him, and she figured if he was at home more, they wouldn't have hit the glacier that nearly made a shipwreck of their marriage. Instead of communicating with her, he'd found diversions. Even now, they didn't talk the way they used to, and there were so many things she needed to know but was too stubborn to ask.

For instance, why did he think anyone could replace her? She was aware of twice in their twenty-four years together that he'd stepped out, but aside from blowing up at him and making life unbearable, she'd suppressed the urge to go after the women. Doing them damage wouldn't fix the hole that had opened up in their relationship or her self-esteem, so she'd buried the hurt and pain.

Her mother had gone through the same scenario with her father, and Geneva wondered if fate played cruel tricks on people by allowing them to travel the same path as their parents. When her father died, she'd almost been thankful. Her mother would enjoy some level of peace and stability in her golden years.

Spence's laughter jarred Geneva from her thoughts, and she released a harsh breath. He looked her way, and when she pushed away from the table, the light in his eyes faded.

She'd taken her vehicle in for servicing, knowing she could hitch a ride home with him, but now regretted that decision.

◆——————◆

"I know what you were trying to do." Spence threw his keys on the half table near the front door and stalked into the living room to face her. "You would have preferred to stay and have Jay take you home, rather than ride with me."

She sank on the sofa and laid her laptop bag on the seat. "With the way you've been treating me, what else do you expect?"

His side-eye reminded her of the times in the past when she'd treated him like he was dead. Spence paced the other side of the center table then sprawled on the opposite sofa. "Look, it really hurts me when you …" His gaze settled on the vase of red and white anthurium blooms. "When you act as if you're alone in this marriage and parenting business."

"*Nothing* we do together is a *business*, Spencer."

"Well, you sure as hell make it feel that way." His glare pierced her while he continued throwing accusatory darts. "How could you have gotten that video and kept it a secret?"

When she remained silent, he added, "Things like that tell me you don't need anyone and that you feel perfectly fine taking matters into your own hands."

She covered her face, working out how not to hurt his feelings. "I wanted to spare you the horror of it. Didn't want you to see our daughter like that. It would have killed you…the way it almost did me."

"Oh, so you could handle it, but I can't?" Spence dragged one hand down his face and expressed himself with something between a grunt and a groan. "The things you say tell me exactly what you think of me."

"Don't twist my words, please. I never implied any such thing." Not wanting him to go any further down that road, she quickly continued, "Spence, I've always thought the world of you. You know that."

*Until …*

She shooed away those thoughts and waited for him to answer.

He clasped both hands and stared at them. "If I ask how you came by that video, I'm sure you're not going to tell me."

"So, don't ask," she quipped, softening her words with a smile.

His gaze was incredulous when he said, "Do you hear yourself? One day you're going to end up knee-deep in this cyber shit you do. I just hope I'll be able to rescue you from yourself."

Her temper sparked again and Geneva spat, "Trust me, I don't need rescuing. Our daughter is all that matters. I'll do whatever I can—"

Spence raised his hands in a gesture of surrender. "I know, I know. *To get her the justice she deserves.*" He stood, scowling. "That's been your mantra ever since this happened. I just wish you'd remember sometimes that she has a father, who also wants what's best for her."

"I know that."

His thick brows rose and he scoffed. "Do you?"

"I'm not going to answer that." Smoothing her hair with one hand, she explained what he already knew. "I'm here most of the time, and you're not, so it's only natural—"

"That I have to put up with the crap you do that's downright disrespectful?"

She wanted to clap back with something hurtful, but didn't. From the moment their lives had gone sideways in March, she realized their marital issues were secondary. They still were, but she didn't want to do irreparable damage to what had been the most wonderful thing she'd experienced in her life. Spence often said she was the best part of his, and she'd believed him. She loved him, but after he shattered her trust, sometimes he got on her last nerve. Like now.

"That's unnecessary," she said through her teeth. "It's never my intention to disrespect you."

"Yet it's what you do." His lips twisted. "Day in and day out."

"I can't believe this." She glared back at him. "Now, you're being melodramatic."

When he started to speak, she raised one hand to silence him, then opened the laptop bag and slid out the computer. She plugged in the thumb drive with the villa surveillance footage and turned the screen toward him.

She hurried to the kitchen, knowing she had to escape. No need to hear or see what had been done to Alexia. Already, it was on repeat, stuck inside her head. She took a bottle of water from the fridge and uncapped it, but couldn't make herself drink. Instead, she leaned against the counter with tears streaming down her face. With her sleeve, she blotted her cheeks and drew a calming breath.

Breaking down solved nothing. Continued, focused action would bring results. She had to cling to that, or go mad with frustration, because her daughter clearly wasn't a priority with the police.

She was so far inside her head that when Spence released an animal-like cry, she dropped the bottle, spilling cold water over her feet. Then, a door slammed and the squeal of tires hit her ear. Geneva's heart thudded to a slow, painful cadence.

Where on earth had Spence gone?

# CHAPTER TWENTY-EIGHT

## CHRISTIAN

His LIFE HAD gone down the tubes, and he couldn't make sense of it. Even now, he didn't understand how he got to this place. He still didn't have the video of him, Alexia, and Sancia that he'd gone to collect, and no one had made any demands. But the video spooling on his laptop had him shook.

Watching what he'd done didn't make him feel guilty. He hadn't wanted to take Alexia like that before Sancia encouraged him. But now, the thought of being outed frightened him. He wasn't meant for prison life, and that might be the deal if the person stalking him kept sending him this stuff. No telling where it might end up and in whose hands.

"This is some bullshit," he growled.

He stretched his leg, which wasn't fully healed. That one kick had put him out of the game forever. From MVP to obscurity. Craziness like this happened to other guys, not him. People kept asking questions about what had happened, and he'd made up a story about being jumped and robbed.

His father had been livid, and it was next to impossible to persuade him not to get the police involved. Radcliffe Skyers had ambitions for him that Christian didn't have for himself. His dream was to finish his degree and take over his father's business. But that might be in danger if these clips didn't stop coming. Whoever was sending them had some aim in view. He just couldn't figure out what they wanted. If it was blackmail money they were after, that would be a wash, because the only money he had was what his father transferred to him each month for expenses. Maybe he could ask for an increase, which would give him a buffer just in case.

The handle of his bedroom door turned and he cleared the laptop screen, raised his leg, and lowered it on the corner of the desk. Anoushka peeked inside the room, and he sighed. She was sniffing around again. Since he'd been home from the hospital, she kept appearing at random times and getting on his nerves. If his father knew what she was up to, she'd be out on her ass so fast it would make her head spin. She showed him a row of bright-white, perfect teeth. "How are we today?"

"The same as yesterday and the day before."

"No need to be grumpy." She slithered over and caressed his upper arm.

He tried shrugging out of her grip. "I'm not grumpy. Just have some pain in my knee."

"I can help you with that," she said, closing the space between them.

He swallowed the sigh he wanted to release. "And how exactly does that work?"

His leg was in a brace, and he'd come home with crutches that he'd be using for at least another three weeks. According to the doctors, he'd be fully healed in another seven to ten months.

Anoushka tipped her head toward him and cocked one of her hips. The tight dress she wore left nothing for him to imagine. Her surgically enhanced breasts stared him in the face. "Remember, I used to be a personal trainer."

"Oh, that." Christian scoffed. That gig was how she'd gotten her hooks into Dad, but that was none of his business. Tapping the edge of the desk, he asked, "So, what you gonna do? What magic do you have that the doctors don't?"

She flipped some hair over her shoulder and leaned in close to whisper, "You really wanna know, Chris?"

The brush of her hair against his skin, her perfume, and the warmth of her breath reminded him that he'd been put on a forced diet from sex for weeks now. He might not be playing football, but that didn't mean he'd risk injuring himself forever just because he needed to get some. Leaning away, he said, "Right about now, I think you should fall back. Some things are off limits, and you're one of them."

"Oh, really?" She pointed to his lap. "Your sweatpants are shouting something else."

"Well, if you're breathing all over me, what do you expect?"

He gingerly maneuvered his leg so both feet were flat on the floor and hoped she'd get the message that he wanted her to disappear. Instead, she lowered the straps on her dress and gave him a view of her bare chest. He raised one hand and rolled across the tiles, away from her. "What the hell? Didn't I ask you to fall back?"

"Do you really want to tell me no?" She tucked in her chin as her eyes gleamed and she took a step toward him. "What would your daddy think if I told him *you* came on to me?"

"What?" Sweat broke out on his forehead. "Hell no. You wouldn't."

But her smug smile said she would.

"Just try me," she said, running a hand down his chest. "Come on. He's golfing with his buddies and won't be back for hours."

He shook his head slowly. "Listen, you're making a mistake. Don't do this. My father isn't someone to play with."

One side of Anoushka's mouth curved in an evil smirk. "Trust me, I know."

His heart pounded the way it did when he was in the middle of a strenuous round of training. This entire situation was whacked. He'd worked hard to avoid this moment, but had known in the back of his mind it might come. He should have told his father, but wasn't sure he'd believe him. In his cockiness, he thought he could keep her at bay. He should have been smarter. Should have kept his door locked. If he touched her, and his father found out, he'd disown him. That wasn't a risk he'd ever take.

He put on a serious expression and hoped good sense would win out over her hots for him. "Nothing good can come from this. I just can't. *You're my father's wife.*"

"Stop telling me what I know," she said, gritting her teeth.

He rose from the seat and tried to back away, but Anoushka followed him.

With all her strength, she shoved him backward and he fell into the chair, trying to break his fall. His legs splayed on both sides of her, and she shimmied out of her dress. "Now, act like a man and stop this foolishness."

She yanked at the waist of his sweats, and the protest died in his throat when she gripped him in one hand.

# CHAPTER TWENTY-NINE

## GENEVA

CHRISTIAN ALMOST HAD her sympathy, until she remembered what he did to Alexia.

Geneva paced her office while recording Christian and his stepmother. The woman had chutzpah. Not to mention a healthy appetite. She'd give her that, but she could also be described as too stupid to live. Surely, she had options outside her home. But it wasn't Geneva's business. *This* was excellent fodder that would make that boy's life a replica of hell before she rained her fury on him.

She'd been spying on him through his webcam, and this afternoon her vigilance had finally paid off. One fake message from the university, and a link click at his end that led nowhere, gave her access to Christian's computer. Time and opportunity would determine what she did with this new information.

When Mrs. Skyers eventually finished with Christian, Geneva closed her laptop and prepared to visit Alexia. But before that, she had a date with Deja.

Her care and concern for Alexia would have been more appreciated when it mattered. Still, Deja had her uses. Her personal history made her eager to please and easy to manipulate. When she met Deja, the girl had just migrated to Florida. She'd been reserved, but observant. Watching her told Geneva that she didn't like to be touched or fawned over. Geneva could guess why. She kept her own counsel and never said a word about her assessment to Camille. Gradually, Deja grew more confident over time and forged a friendship with Alexia. But all of that was negated that one night in Jamaica. Friends were there for the long haul. They protected each other. Deja had failed that test.

Despite that fact that she was mostly a loner, Geneva took friendship seriously. More so than these young people. Danny had also been a real disappointment, and so was Chad, but from the sound of it, Alexia understood exactly what was happening. People liked perfect people. And Alexia no longer wore that label.

A sudden wash of tears surprised Geneva, and she chalked it up to the stress and tension of being around Spence, who was now behaving worse than ever. He was morose and impossible to live with. Viewing that video had the exact effect she expected. He would have seen it eventually, but she'd known she wasn't doing him any favors by showing it to him.

She put her thoughts aside when she pulled into the hospital parking lot. Deja remained grateful for being allowed to see Alexia, especially when Geneva made it clear that no one else was welcome. But she'd warned her not to say anything in relation to what happened in Jamaica. If she did, she would no longer be on Alexia's short visitors' list.

That kept her mouth sealed.

Within five minutes, she was seated across from the young woman she'd been thinking about. Geneva slid a green smoothie across the table. "Thank you for coming today. It's Saturday and all. I'm sure you have other things to do."

Deja waved away her comment. "It's no problem. I wanted to see Alexia. I'm glad she's recovering."

"So are we," Geneva said. "Was Jaden with her when you visited?"

"Yes, seems he'd been there for a while." A forlorn note entered her voice. "I wish I got along that well with my brothers."

Geneva shrugged. "Well, since there are only the two of them, it would make sense that they're close."

"Yes, it would." She looked away, and if Geneva had to guess, Deja was thinking about her own dysfunctional family.

"Speaking of that, I heard on the news that one of your friends was arrested."

Deja wrinkled her brows, then said, "Phil isn't my friend. He's more of an acquaintance."

Laser-focused on her, Geneva asked, "Do you know why he was arrested?"

Deja sat up straight. "Something to do with an investigation about date rape."

"Wow, someone has been busy."

Deja smirked, then glanced around the cafeteria. "Yes, him and that monster Jason. Pity he got off without paying for what he did to those girls."

"What do you mean?" Geneva asked, leaning forward.

Flicking one of the strings on her hoodie, Deja said, "He died in the hospital."

"What? When?" Geneva asked with a hand against her chest, as if it was news to her.

"Apparently a freak accident at home with their heating system."

"Pity."

When Deja turned a puzzled gaze on her, Geneva smiled. "Like you said, he got an easy exit. I'm grateful that Alexia is still here."

Nodding in agreement, Deja sucked from her straw. "And we both know Alexia is the sweetest—"

Geneva ended her gushing with a hard look. "We know."

Her smile faded, and Geneva cracked one in return, realizing she'd been too harsh. "Thank you for recognizing her for who she is, but that didn't stop those...*people* from harming her."

"I know, and I'm sorry." She stared at the fiberglass tabletop for a moment, then raised her head. "Don't worry about Phil. He'll get what's coming to him."

"Sounds like you know a little something about that."

"Let's just say I know about some of the stuff they've been doing. I've been watching them like you asked."

And so did Geneva, but it didn't suit her to say so. It was fine for Deja to have a taste of victory. She needed it.

"I hope you didn't incriminate yourself in any way while keeping your eyes on them."

Her smile was triumphant. "Oh no. I'm better than that."

The boastful note in her voice twisted Geneva's stomach. This child should have also been better than leaving Alexia to fend for herself. Geneva tipped her head back and pulled in a long breath. She'd dawdled long enough. The sad but true fact was that the rehabilitation center was the best place for Alexia now, but every time Geneva visited was like having a knife twisted in her belly.

Alexia should have been out and about with friends, having the time of her life. Instead, she was tied to a facility filled with elderly and brain-damaged patients.

Time would take care of every battle Geneva was now fighting, including what to do about the standoff with Spence.

Deja slurped long and hard, then slid the cup on the table between her hands. "Thanks again for letting me see Alexia."

"It's no problem." Geneva told her goodbye and was ready to head upstairs when her phone rang. She pulled it out of her handbag and frowned before putting it to her ear.

"Mrs. Leighton, this is Detective Harrison."

"Yes, good to hear from you," she lied as she stepped away from the elevator door. "How can I help?"

"We'd like for you to come down to the station as soon as you're able."

Her stomach clenched, but she didn't allow her voice to betray a sudden case of nerves. "Can you say what it's about?"

"I'd rather not say on the phone."

"I'm on the way to visit my daughter." She waited a beat before adding, "You know, the one that was beaten and raped in Jamaica?"

"I didn't need that reminder."

"Consider it a favor." She made her tone pleasant and added, "Thanks for calling. I'll be down as soon as it's convenient."

For a moment, she thought he'd hung up. Then, Harrison cleared his throat. "Mrs. Leighton, in case I didn't make myself clear, this isn't a request. It's an order."

# CHAPTER THIRTY

## PHIL

*W*HAT A NIGHTMARE.

How could things go wrong this fast? After the policemen carted him off to the station, his mother had scrambled in behind them a half-hour later. They hadn't allowed her to see him right away, and when they finally did, he couldn't bear the disappointment painted in the lines on her face. The same distress slumped his father's shoulders, and he didn't even want to think about how his younger sister was dealing with the situation. He'd now been locked up for forty-eight hours and was edging toward full-scale panic.

Officer Harrison sat across from him and opened a file folder. He scanned the papers inside as if they contained the most interesting details he'd ever read. When he cleared his throat, Phil looked up. His head was heavy and his chest tight, as if the walls were crushing him.

"Based on the data we found on your laptop, we have additional questions."

"Really?" Phil rubbed his eyes, which were grainy from lack of sleep. His belly gurgled and sweat broke out on his body, reminding him that he needed another shower. He wasn't cut out for being locked up. "What data?"

"It seems you've been dabbling in places you shouldn't."

Phil's fingers plowed through his hair and he stared at the table. "I don't know what you're talking about."

"Sit up."

The officer's voice came at him like the crack of a whip, and he did what he asked without hesitation.

Stabbing a finger on the table, the policeman said, "In case you don't understand, you're in serious trouble, young man."

Phil wanted to make a smart comeback but didn't have it in him. He'd been before a judge, who had charged him with sexual crimes. Everything had been a blur. All he grasped was that somehow the police had gotten hold of files from Jason's computer and came knocking at his door.

They had confiscated his laptop before they'd taken him away. He was relieved that nothing on his personal computer could link him to anything they accused him of doing. The only question was what else they had found and said he'd done. He'd always known Jason was stupid, and here was the proof. He'd wait out the police and refuse to answer any questions—that's what he'd been told to do.

The lawyer his father hired shifted next to him and propped both elbows on the table. "What do you mean about my client being in places he shouldn't?"

Brushing one hand over his hair, Officer Harrison said, "I'm glad you asked. Somehow, your client logged into the University of Miami's database and helped himself to information pertaining to several students."

"That's a lie," Phil shouted. "I don't know what you're talking about."

Eric Randall gripped his arm tight. "Be quiet. Let me handle this."

Facing the officer, Mr. Randall continued, "Neither my client nor I am aware of this new accusation."

"Which is why we're trying to sort this out and why he's still in custody." His attention shifted to Phil. "It would suit you to make this easy on yourself."

Adjusting his wire-rimmed glasses, Randall said, "Frankly, he doesn't have the know-how to do anything at that level."

"I guess we'll find out." Officer Harrison sat back in his seat. "It's curious that we've found information on Jason Blalock's devices that leads to your client and nothing at his end."

"Which tells you something, doesn't it?" Randall threw Phil a warning look. "The deceased influenced my client. As I'm sure you know by now, Blalock wasn't an angel."

"And neither is your client."

Phil's fists curled and his temper threatened to get out of hand. He wanted to punch the policeman in the face. That was wishful thinking, because he didn't need any more trouble. When the policeman's sharp gaze rested on him, Phil forced himself to act unbothered. By now everyone would know he'd been arrested. He doubted his mother had stopped crying since he'd been in jail, and the gnawing in his stomach wouldn't give him a break.

His family's situation was the driving force behind the steroids. Bad investments. Expensive schools. Needing money put him in this position, but he'd made a choice. Another round of sweat soaked his T-shirt and his feet bounced on the floor. If he was lucky, the police wouldn't have a reason to visit his home again. He'd stay quiet, let Randall do his work, and hope everything blew over. If good fortune was on his side, his story about Jason influencing him would hold up. The other business was puzzling. He'd never tried to access any information other than research material at the university, but what he couldn't change, he wouldn't worry about.

*All of this will pass.* The mantra played in his head as his breathing grew shallow.

The policeman studied Phil as if he had some other accusation he wanted to lay on the table.

Phil stared back, displaying bravado he didn't feel.

Tapping a pen on the papers, the officer smiled at him. "Okay, so you were influenced by Blalock and you know nothing about the hacking incident."

"That's right," Phil said, lifting his chin.

Harrison gave him a half smile, then tipped his head to one side. "Perhaps you can shed some light on a surveillance video. From Jamaica. Your spring break trip, in case you can't remember."

While his stomach twisted into a tight knot, Phil sat still.

"In that video," Harrison continued, "you were part of a group of students assaulting Alexia Leighton."

For a moment, Phil's brain froze, and he stood in a tunnel as the wind created havoc with his hearing. Then the bottom dropped out of his stomach. He heaved and rushed toward the bin in the far corner of the interrogation room.

# CHAPTER THIRTY-ONE

## GENEVA

**D**ETECTIVE HARRISON HAD his attitude all wrong. He also didn't understand the way her mind worked. Or maybe, he did. But *nobody* told Geneva what to do. Not even the man she had married—despite the love, honor, and obey part of the vows she had taken.

Before she shelved thoughts of the policeman, Geneva made a note to stop at home after she left the rehab center. The drop-in wasn't strictly necessary, but one never knew.

She greeted the receptionist and made her way to the alcove beyond the lounge area, where Alexia sat at a table with her journal open. Instead of writing, she was staring out the window.

Geneva kissed Alexia's forehead at the same time a tear slid down her cheek. By reflex, she swept it away with one finger. The breath rushed out of Geneva's lungs, and she could barely choke out her question. "What's wrong, honey?"

After laying her laptop sleeve and handbag on another seat, Geneva sat down, her heart racing. "Lexi, what happened?"

Alexia swiped her face, then glared at Geneva. "How could you?"

Her expression didn't change when she asked, "What?"

"That Wall of Shame you came up with." Her nostrils flared, and Geneva could have sworn she was looking at Spence, until Alexia spoke. "And for some reason, I can't delete it."

"That's because I knew your first reaction would be to do exactly that."

"I don't see why you'd want to add something like that to *my* site." Alexia turned her head away, huffing as she did. "You agreed not to post anything I don't agree with, or want people to know."

"You're not angry with those people, but you're angry with me?" Leaning back, Geneva folded her arms. "Is that why you're crying?"

Alexia tapped her pen on the desk as if she wanted to ram the metal point through the wood.

Something had happened before she got there, but Geneva had to be patient. Alexia was like her, in that she preferred to deal with issues privately before sharing them with anyone else. While she waited, Geneva worked through an idea that had come to her in relation to *that boy*. She couldn't even bear to have his name taint her brain.

"Chad broke up with me."

Her matter-of-fact tone, that didn't hide the hurt, brought Geneva back into the room. She wanted to comfort Alexia so badly, but sensed now wasn't the right time. If she did, her baby would break down, and it wouldn't solve anything.

She sniffed, then the words escaped in a rush. "He couldn't face me, so he did it online."

"Coward." Geneva stayed silent to hold in the rage that washed over her. She'd known this was coming but couldn't do anything to prevent it. Nor did she wish to do so. "He didn't deserve you, but you know that."

Alexia mustered up a smile. "I knew you'd say that."

"Which is exactly why Chad and Danielle are on that wall with those other people."

"Please take down their pictures." Alexia dried her eyes with the sleeve of her T-shirt and held in a sob. "It's too humiliating. He'll think I did it because he dumped me."

Geneva ran one hand over Alexia's arm. "You have nothing to be ashamed of, Lexi. They are the ones who should be disgusted with themselves for how they've treated you."

"I know, but please do it for me."

Geneva nodded. "Only because you asked."

As she drew a breath, Alexia shuddered. "About the other stuff …"

"That stays."

Her voice cracked as she cried, "But it makes no difference."

"It does, baby." The fury she sometimes couldn't contain flared to life again, and she wanted to hurt someone the way her daughter was hurting. The way an angry dragon would—spewing fire and flicking its tail in a reckless, destructive tantrum. But that was a fantasy, and this was their reality. Geneva slowed her breathing and even managed a smile. "They could have prevented what happened to you, *if* they cared."

"The way things are set up at these parties, people are off doing their own thing. The music was loud. It's not impossible for stuff to happen without everyone knowing."

Geneva didn't want to hear any of that. "Young people share everything. They must have heard the others talking. Someone should have done right by you, instead of leaving you to die."

"*Island Escape* is a big villa, and I didn't die." Alexia rubbed a faint nick on the table. "I've asked myself a thousand times already what I would have done if this had happened to someone else, and—"

"You have a heart of gold, Lexi." With one finger, Geneva rapped the table hard in time with her words. "You'd have done the right thing."

"Why are you so sure?" Alexia asked, staring at Geneva.

"Because I've watched you grow, and frankly, you're a much better person than I am."

Alexia's half smile was crooked as she quipped, "Well, you see how much good that did me."

"Like your father always says, never allow circumstances and people to change your personality."

"But you have."

Alexia's quiet words had the effect of a slap in the face. The seconds ticked by before Geneva could gather a response. If only Alexia knew. The good thing was that she'd never know the depths her mother had plunged to because of one unfortunate incident. When she recovered from her shock, Geneva said, "You're right. But you're my baby, the best part of me, so I'm allowed."

"I've never understood why you always get away with playing outside the family rules."

She chuckled to break the tense atmosphere around them. Alexia had always been perceptive, and she'd forgotten that at her peril. "Because your mama has always been a rebel."

To Geneva's relief, the nurse and physiotherapist appeared over Alexia's shoulder, greeted them, and asked if she was ready for today's session.

"I have to go downtown, so I'll leave you to it." Geneva rose and leaned in to kiss her forehead. "Jaden will be along by the time you're finished."

"Is Daddy coming today?" Alexia's eyes brightened as she gripped the table and stood.

A pang of regret stole Geneva's breath as put out her hands to support Alexia, in case she needed help. "He has back-to-back meetings today. I'm sure he'll be here tomorrow."

"I'll send him a message." Alexia gripped the handles of the walker as the support staff hovered. "See you soon."

"He'll appreciate that. Talk later."

One thing she knew for sure—despite his faults, Spence loved his children. But Alexia had his heart. Always had. Always would. She realized then that she still hadn't found out where he'd disappeared to after watching the video. Much later that evening, he'd returned, sullen and quiet. If she didn't know Spence's habits, she'd think he'd been drinking. But, he hadn't.

She'd left him alone, and when he fell asleep, she watched him, her heart aching. The grief she held at bay was etched into his features. She didn't know what to think as her gaze traveled to his skinned knuckles and returned to the bruise around one of his eyes.

# CHAPTER THIRTY-TWO

## GENEVA

CHAD AND DANNY occupied Geneva's mind on the way to her SUV in the parking lot. She'd made it easier for them to separate themselves from Alexia after their disastrous visit to the rehab center. Of course, she couldn't give her those facts.

"If you can't act like decent human beings, please don't come back."

The pair had exchanged glances riddled with shock and guilt, but Geneva didn't care. They'd shown their hand, and she was only doing what was necessary to protect her child.

If Chad owned a backbone, he'd have defied her, but his response told her exactly who he was—someone Alexia could do without. When it came down to it, Alexia had no friends. Not even Deja.

The detour home and the ride downtown did her good, and by the time she stepped into Officer Harrison's space, she was prepared for any battle she'd be called on to fight. She gave Officer Cruz a charming smile, let her gaze shift to include Harrison, and lied as she sat. "It's good to see you both again."

Cruz tipped his head and returned her gesture, while Harrison acted as if breaking a smile would earn him a demotion.

"May I?" she asked before laying the bags she carried on the chair next to her. Idly, she wondered why both men remained standing. *Probably trying to intimidate.*

Geneva hid her amusement while reminding herself not to underestimate Harrison. It wouldn't serve her well.

"Mrs. Leighton," he said, taking slow steps until he stood behind his chair. He turned the screen of a laptop toward her and continued, "We've analyzed the evidence we have so far and wanted you to see it, only to be sure this is, in fact, your daughter."

Geneva sat still, but could do nothing about the perspiration that rushed from her pores and dotted her forehead. She licked her lip and reached for something, anything to delay what she sensed was coming. "Shouldn't my husband be here to see it as well?"

"This is your third visit. So far, you've done fine on your own."

He clicked the touchpad and the video started. A soft moan rose from her throat. If this ploy was supposed to weaken her, he'd won. But what appeared on the screen wasn't what she expected. The clip was of Phil Reid hunched at an interrogation table, his fingers twitching along with the rest of him.

The policeman's eyes never left her while he asked, "Do you know that young man?"

"Should I?" She frowned and sat back. The clawing sensation in her stomach was like having a gardening fork drawn every which way inside. "What is this? You tell me you're showing me one thing and then produce another."

He sat and clasped his hands, while Cruz shuffled his feet and sat in a chair to Harrison's right. After clearing his throat, Cruz said, "That young man has been accused of several crimes, one of which is assaulting your daughter."

Geneva's attention went back to the computer, where Phil was shaking as if he was in withdrawal, but the fear in his eyes said otherwise. He was terrified. *Good.*

"And you know this how?" she asked, looking suitably concerned.

"From the evidence." Harrison unlocked thick fingers and flattened his thin lips in a scowl. "But he's also in trouble for something we don't believe he did."

One of her eyebrows rose in a question. "What does that have to do with me? Is it not enough that my Alexia will never be the same?"

Harrison's posture—head tipped upward and his dark eyes intense and laser-focused with a knowing glint—reminded Geneva of an iguana. If he had a tail, he'd be whipping it to maintain an air of dominance. "Well, we thought you might be able to help us in that matter."

"And why would I do that, especially since you believe he had a hand in hurting Alexia?" She hiked one shoulder in a half-shrug. "I'm not sure why or how you think I can give you any assistance."

"As a cybersec—"

She raised both hands palm out, now certain the policeman was toying with her. "If I'm to believe you, this young man was part of the evildoers that tried to murder my baby." She laid a hand on her chest. "Some might consider me a good person. But I'm not a saint. Aside from that, I'm certain this police department has a capable cybercrimes unit. You sure as hell don't need my help."

"We solve crimes more efficiently when we're assisted by the victims."

Geneva stiffened her spine. "That's not how I'd describe myself. My child is the victim here." She allowed her attention to shift to the laptop, then back toward Harrison. "I wish you'd remember that."

Cruz crossed and uncrossed his ankles and make a strangled sound, as if he was choking.

In the uncomfortable silence that fell around them, Harrison reached for the laptop, fiddled with the keyboard, and spun it back toward her.

A few hurried footsteps brought Cruz to her side.

Once more, she witnessed the group jumping Alexia. She shuddered as the emotional wound that hadn't healed was ripped open again. Yet, she couldn't look away. Nor did she attempt to hide how she felt. As the tears streamed down her cheeks, she reached into her handbag for a handkerchief. The thin cotton dried her tears, but she carried a gaping hole in her soul. "Please! Turn it off."

The young policeman advanced the video, then paused it. "There's something else we need you to see. Please tell us if you know the persons involved."

With the hanky that smelled of Spence's cologne, which gave some measure of comfort, she dabbed her eyes. "Fine. Just give me a moment."

"Would you like some water?" Cruz asked.

She shook her head. "No, I'm fine. You can go ahead now."

The scene picked up where Alexia lay on the grass with a male and female crouching next to her. The girl said something inaudible, which made the guy stare at her and then Alexia. He reached for the waist of his pants, and Cruz stopped the video.

Geneva pressed the handkerchief to her lips and held in her sobs, knowing this wasn't the place to lose control. Maybe, by a miracle, something would change with this meeting. Perhaps Alexia would receive what was due to her.

She counted to ten, timing her breathing. When she opened her mouth to speak, Harrison asked, "Did you know she was…um—"

"Raped." She stared at the ceiling then settled her eyes on Harrison, whose skin was flushed. "Yes, we knew. The police in Jamaica did a swab because of the condition she was in. I'm sure they sent that to you."

He nodded and pulled the laptop toward him. "Can you identify either of the people on the screen with your daughter?"

In a matter-of-fact tone, she answered, "Christian Skyers and Sancia Jackman."

"I thought you didn't know her." Harrison studied her with new interest.

"Now, I do." She waited a few seconds before adding, "You see, Alexia's grandmother retrieved her phone at the hospital. That's how I know who they are. They're in a messaging group."

She leaned toward the chair a few inches away. "Can I assume you will do something about Mr. Skyers?"

The men looked at each other and nodded. "Of course," Harrison snapped.

"Thank goodness." Geneva placed a small shopping bag on the edge of the desk. "The dress Alexia was wearing the night of the party is in there. It may contain samples you need."

The second Harrison reached for the handles. Geneva swept the bag into her lap. "One more thing. I'm not giving this up unless you sign for what's inside."

The muscles in Harrison's jaw worked while his nostrils flared. "Mrs. Leighton, that's unnecessary, and it's not how this is supposed to work."

His annoyance didn't mean anything to Geneva. All she wanted was for him to agree to her request. She'd had enough of the police's incompetence to last several lifetimes.

"Tell that to someone who hasn't waited months to get to this point." She picked up her handbag and dropped the strap over her shoulder. "The decision is yours."

"We could charge you for obstruction."

"And I could write a post on that blog about how long it has taken the police do to *anything* about my daughter's ordeal." Neither of them attempted to speak, so she continued on her way toward the door, "Like I said, it's your choice."

# CHAPTER THIRTY-THREE

## CHRISTIAN

HE COULDN'T SHAKE the feeling that disaster was coming. A week ago, someone he'd taken to be a madman at first had attacked him outside their front door. The older guy, who packed some mean punches, had worked him over. Even now, his ribs and stomach were sore. Although the doctor said his jaw wasn't broken, Christian wasn't so sure. He'd barely eaten anything for several days, the pain was so bad.

Anoushka had distracted Dad when he asked about his condition. He'd been suspicious but didn't dig beyond Christian's explanation that he'd gotten into a fight over a girl. What puzzled Christian was that the man, who was vaguely familiar, hadn't said a word while he smashed both fists into his upper body. Christian had landed two blows and thought he was going to die when the stranger stared him in the eyes and squeezed his neck.

His stepmother's screams brought the attacker to his senses. Tears welled in the man's eyes and snot dripped from his nostril when he released Christian, who collapsed on the ceramic tiles out front. With a trembling finger, he pointed at Christian. "I hope you rot in prison for what you did."

Christian didn't know what he meant. Since then, no new texts had come in, but as he came and went from the university campus, he kept his guard up. He was tired of being reminded by his friends that his days of playing football were over. Sure, he didn't miss the grueling hours at training, but he needed something else to take the edge off some of his energy.

He paced his room, wanting to punch someone. If he had to make a choice, Anoushka would do. But that wasn't happening any time soon. The woman could not be satisfied, and he wondered what Dad was doing in the bedroom if she had to come knocking on his door this often. He now feared leaving his room when Dad and Anoushka were in the house at the same time. Her sly looks and knowing smile gave him the jitters. She was reckless, and Christian didn't want to pay the price for her stupidity. He'd tried, but couldn't think his way out of this current mess.

His phone pinged, and he picked it up. Another notification from his study group. They did more joking around than anything else. He sucked his teeth and headed to the bathroom. After relieving himself, he sank in the chair, prepared to continue with his finance assignment. The phone pinged several times, and he was tempted to ignore it. These days, he felt it was his master. Whenever it made a sound, he jumped, thinking the worst. He made a slow circle with his head then sighed as he picked up the Samsung.

Agony knifed him in the belly as a video downloaded. The images on the screen made his throat close and his stomach rumble. He looked up at the webcam on the computer, shaking his head. It wasn't possible. But the evidence was in his hand.

Someone had recorded him and Anoushka. He spun toward the bed, thinking how foolish he'd been. Blake, a classmate and ever a conspiracy theorist, warned that "Big Brother" was always watching. His remedy was using masking tape to block his laptop camera.

Nauseous with anxiety, Christian watched the action unfolding on his phone. The worst of what they'd done was spliced together in a raunchy thirty-second display. If he didn't know different, Christian would think he was watching porn. If his father found out, he'd be worse than dead. The only advantage he could think of was that Dad had nothing to do with social media. According to him, that kind of thing was for people who had nothing better to do with their time. He hired people to take care of marketing and promotion and stayed away from everything except handling his email and attending online conferences.

Christian swallowed hard as his stomach dropped. During his summer internship, he'd also learned that those same workers his father hired promoted the company name and scoured the internet for anything related to the Skyers name and business. One hashtag could bring everything tumbling down.

Praying and wearing out the bedside carpet didn't help. In less than a half-hour, his phone blew up. If he believed what his friends were telling him, the reel had gone viral. His stomach gurled and a sharp pain ripped through his belly. He raced into the bathroom and dropped his sweats mere seconds before his bowels exploded.

*Who would let him down this way?*

He was gasping and sweating when the bedroom door slammed back on its hinges. The tap-tap-tap of Anoushka's heels approached before he could move.

She stood in the doorway, her smooth forehead wrinkled and one hand resting on her hip. With the other, she covered her nose. "Disgusting. What's wrong with you?"

"Get out," he gasped. "Just fall back for a minute."

Grimacing, she turned away and pulled the handle until the lock clicked.

He swiped the sweat from his forehead, cleaned himself, and washed his hands. In the mirror, he barely recognized the washed-out skin and large eyes that stared back at him.

Anoushka waited by the desk when he walked back into the bedroom and dropped on the side of the bed. He stared at the floor, wishing she'd disappeared. It was stupid to think he could ride out her foolishness. What he should have done was to tell Dad the first time she attacked him. Now, no matter which way he analyzed it, this whole scenario looked bad.

"What d'you want now?" he mumbled and raised his head. "Dad will be home soon."

"I thought you were smart, but I guess not." She pulled in a breath and folded her arms. "You couldn't help yourself, you had to be a showoff."

Running one hand over his hair, Christian sat up. "Look, I don't know what you're talking about. If you mean that video, I didn't do it. Why would I?"

Her lips twisted as she spat, "So you could embarrass me and your father."

"What would I gain, huh? I have everything to lose."

A smile spread over her face. "I'm glad you recognize that. You're not so stupid after all. You better hope your father doesn't find out about this."

He didn't bother to tell her it was only a matter of time. The poison from the internet had a way of spreading itself everywhere and ruining everything. Just like that recording of him and Sancia that wouldn't stay gone. Now, it even haunted his sleep.

"Christian!"

The thunder echoing through his father's voice made him want to rush to the toilet again, but he couldn't make his muscles work. He was as weak as a sick baby.

"Now, you'll get what you deserve for forcing me to do all of those things," Anoushka yelled.

"What?" Christian glared at her. "Don't think you're going to put this on me."

By the time Dad appeared, Anoushka was deep in drama queen mode. She turned a tearful face toward Radcliff Skyers, who barely glanced her way.

He walked into the room past Anoushka. His face twitched as he raked Christian with a hostile gaze.

When the blow came, it took Christian by surprise. His head twisted to one side, and the next hit spun his neck in the other direction. Then his father's fist landed square on his forehead, throwing him to the floor. Blinded by the pain radiating through his face, Christian curled into a ball.

His father shouted swear words while aiming several kicks to his butt and tailbone. In the background, Anoushka's screams echoed around the room. He blacked out for a moment, and when he came to, Dad's foot connected with his forehead, putting him out again. The silence didn't last long. Anoushka's yodeling woke him that second time. When he attempted to pull himself to a sitting position, Dad stomped on his fingers and ground them into the carpet.

A trickle of urine warmed Christian's boxers as his knuckles cracked and burned.

Dad leaned in, pressing harder with his Oxfords.

Christian inhaled the whiskey on his breath, but didn't cry out. He was beyond the pain. Anoushka had ruined everything, just like he knew she would.

With a rough fist, Dad lifted his chin. "When I come back downstairs, you'd better be gone. You're dead to me."

# CHAPTER THIRTY-FOUR

## GENEVA

"**M**OM, CAN YOU look me in the eyes and tell me none of this has anything to do with you?"

Geneva looked up from her laptop. "What are you calling *this*?"

Jaden slid into the seat in front of her desk. "The people who went to Jamaica."

"What about them?" she asked, peering at the screen again.

He tapped the desk two times, and she raised her head.

"This is important." Jaden stopped and ran a hand over the beard he'd been nursing. "When we were in Jamaica, I warned you about doing anything that might—"

"Jay, stop accusing me of something I haven't done." Her gaze went back to the screen, and he settled more comfortably into the seat.

Geneva slid the laptop a few inches from her and leaned back. "Okay, since you want to talk, let's talk. Is this what you needed to discuss the other day?"

"Actually, no. I wanted to ask what's going on with you and Dad." He frowned, reminding her of Spence. She looked away to get the image of his father out of her head. "I know Alexia's

177

situation must be hard to deal with on top of what you guys have going on."

Her son was no fool, so she wouldn't treat him as such. "Spence and I are working on our issues. That's between us. I don't want you worrying about things that shouldn't concern you."

"I can't help that. We live in the same house."

She gazed at the painting of a seascape across the room as she organized her thoughts. When her attention settled on him, Jaden was watching her. "Your father and I still love each other, you know that—"

"But?"

"We basically have a different approach to the way we do things."

"Meaning, you take action, he's more cautious, and so you disagree on stuff."

She eyed him with new respect. "That's right. This business with Alexia has shown me just how differently we both think, but don't get me wrong, you father keeps me toeing the line—"

"But are you?"

She smiled faintly. "Boy, are you going to allow me to complete my thoughts without interrupting?"

He chuckled and sat forward. "The reason I'm asking is because I see a pattern."

Geneva raised both brows, picked up her stainless-steel flask, and took a sip of cucumber water. "Oh?"

Nodding, Jaden said, "Sancia, Jason, Phil, and now Christian."

With her chin propped on one fist, Geneva said, "You do know that what goes around comes around, right?"

"Yes, but it all seems too convenient."

"Perhaps because you're looking at this from the inside." She shifted and fiddled with the crucifix at her throat. "I'm flattered that you think I'm responsible for all the ill that's befallen these kids, but not even I'm that good or powerful. It's one thing to leak information and quite another to rig a car crash, for example."

Jaden sucked his lower lip into his mouth and angled his head the way Spence did when he suspected her of wrongdoing. "What if I asked you to let me have a look at your computer? Just to ease my mind."

"I'd say have at it…except for the fact this laptop houses sensitive information that concerns my clients."

"I get that." He was silent for several minutes, and she stared at him, wondering if he'd shared his suspicions with his father. If he did, what had Spence said in response? He was loyal, but had concerns that bothered her. Frustration might have made him say something he shouldn't.

Jaden sat up and cleared his throat. "I know you'd do anything to protect Alexia and me, but I feel this last thing with Skyers is up your alley."

"Tell me what happened, please."

He gave a short explanation and meanwhile she did a search, which brought up the images in question. She watched, trying to suppress the annoyance that simmered below the surface. Geneva wasn't used to being questioned by anyone. "I'm not sure how you're connecting *that* with me."

Jaden stared hard at her, then said, "I just needed to have a face-to-face conversation with you."

"And now?" She supported her cheek on one fist.

"You want the truth?" he asked, stroking his beard.

"When did you start lying to me?"

"Moving right along." His lips quirked as he continued, "You haven't said much about how the case is progressing, and I'm afraid you've done your own thing off to the side. I'm grown and everything, but I still need you…*we* need you."

His words touched the deepest part of her, but Geneva had to know if Spence was behind it. She'd give him hell for bringing Jaden into their mess.

"Please tell me your father didn't send you in here to ambush me."

"Dad wouldn't do that."

She rose and took another sip of water before walking to the credenza to pick up a file folder. Jaden had always been his own person, so she didn't know what to believe.

"Are you dismissing me?" Jaden asked, getting to his feet.

Returning to her seat, Geneva chuckled. "Nobody can accuse you of not being smart."

At the door, he said, "I notice you haven't asked me anything more about Lexi's friends, which means you're doing what I asked you not to do."

"Seeking information isn't stalking."

"It is, when you're not on a network and accessing details by other means."

"Come here," she said, walking around the desk. Geneva wrapped her arms around Jaden and kissed his prickly chin. "You worry too much. Everything will be fine."

The door closed behind him, and she settled into the executive chair, wondering if she'd moved too fast on Christian's payback but shook her head. There was no time like the present. Why should she allow him to get comfortable after his sin against Alexia? Let him deal with the fallout in his family. The police should be knocking on his door at any minute with an arrest warrant for sexual assault. It was only what he'd earned.

She went back to work and only an hour had passed before Spence opened the door without knocking. His grimace put her on guard. What accusation was he coming with this time?

Geneva was tired of fighting with him. It was ironic that they weren't bickering over his cheating but about their daughter.

"What is it with you?" he asked as he flung himself in the leather sofa by the window.

"I don't know what you mean."

Spence rose to pace the office. After several trips, he stopped in front of the desk.

"The police came to see me today."

Her eyes widened and she forced herself to sit still. "What did they want?"

"To know about your movements, your skills, what you might have been up to these past few weeks." He leaned toward her with his hands splayed on the desk. "You're a suspect."

"In what crime? Where is this coming from?" Her heart beat a hard tattoo against her ribs as she licked her lips.

"One more thing." Spence's gaze never left her face. "Can you tell me why you've been to see the police without me?"

She opened her mouth to explain, but he held up one finger. "I'm warning you, Geneva, think carefully about what you're going to say."

"What do you want me to tell you?"

Eyes closed, Spence drew back. "I don't know who you are anymore and it worries me."

Geneva folded her arms and fought the stubborn expression that sat on her face. "If I've changed it's because these same police haven't done right by our daughter."

"And of course, you couldn't wait for them to reach out to you."

"I had to be sure they hadn't thrown Lexi's case into some file thirteen."

"You had no intention of waiting for the police to get the evidence from Jamaica before you jumped in." He made a chopping motion with his hand and shook his head. "They told me you've been to see them three times. Three times. You're telling me it didn't occur to you even once to mention your visits?"

"You travel so much, I didn't want to bother you with it."

"Or was it the case that you're the only one who could handle what needed to be done?"

"Don't say that."

"What else can I say, Jen? You operate like you're the Lone Ranger, and it doesn't matter what I say, you do exactly what you please."

Anything she said would make him trip, so she held her silence.

"And don't think I don't know about that letter to the editor you submitted, blasting the police for what Dad said about the business at *Island Escape*. It came out today. The least you could have done was to use an alias."

"For what? So they wouldn't recognize my name? So your father's precious job wouldn't be in jeopardy?" The sour taste in the back of her mouth spread as she added, "Tourism interests and politics shouldn't come before the wellbeing of people like *our* daughter."

"Dad explained the context in which he said it."

"And I'll repeat what I told him when he spewed that bullshit. I. Don't. Care. All that matters is Alexia."

"Don't you think about who you embarrass in your cause? Nothing and no one else counts for anything?"

She shot to her feet. "For heaven's sake, don't make this about you."

In slow motion, Spence slid his hands inside his pockets. "The way you're acting, I'd never make the mistake of thinking anything is about me or us."

Geneva covered her face to help settle her jumping nerves. "Don't do this, please. I have enough on my plate."

"Now, why doesn't that surprise me?" Spence rubbed his forehead and stared over her shoulder. "These days, all you're focused on is yourself and the things you want."

"Don't you dare." Pointing at him, she continued, "Maybe if you paid more attention to me and what happens in this house, I wouldn't feel the need to do everything on my own."

Spence's skin flushed, and a tic danced under his eye. He rolled his shoulders, and she noticed then he was only wearing a shirt and tie. As if he'd rushed out of his office without his jacket, or he'd left it in the vehicle.

The hurt in his eyes haunted her, but she was out of words. She'd already said too much. This was an old argument: her accusing him of being gone too much, and him throwing her self-sufficiency in her face.

No matter what, she'd fight on for Alexia. But in this moment, she was battle-worn. What she wouldn't give to return to the days when her only worry was Jaden and Alexia's safety once they left the house. Too bad she seemed to have fallen into a vortex from which she couldn't escape.

A bitter smile twisted Spence's lips. "Don't worry about it, Jen. It's only what you've been dying to say. All you needed was an opportunity to get it off your chest."

# CHAPTER THIRTY-FIVE

## CHRISTIAN

Everything was happening too fast.

He was on the front porch with his backpack at his feet when Anoushka screamed as if she was being attacked. The door opened and she stumbled outside, propelled by a shove from his father. "I don't care where you go. You're not sleeping under this roof one more night."

"But it isn't my fault. Christian—"

The door slammed in her face.

Christian leaned off the column and picked up his backpack. The movement reminded him of the beating his father had put on him less than fifteen minutes ago. "Guess he didn't buy your story, huh?"

"This is all your fault." She stabbed the air with one finger, then poked him in the chest and grabbed a fistful of his T-shirt. "You've ruined everything."

He raised one hand to ease her off. "Hey, back up."

"Where can I go with only the clothes I'm wearing? Radcliff said—"

"I heard him." Christian rubbed his face, then winced and stared at his kicks. "You're asking the wrong person."

He didn't have a clue what to do next or where to go. If Sancia was around, he could have crashed at her place. Maybe one of the guys would put him up for the night. At least he wouldn't have to make up any excuses, because everybody would know why he looked as if he'd had a run-in with a trash compactor.

Anoushka wasn't much better off. Her hair was a mess, her blouse was torn, and she was sniffling.

At least Dad hadn't taken the key to the Hyundai. Anoushka wasn't so lucky. She didn't have so much as a handbag, and he'd heard Dad yelling about her leaving the way she'd come into his house—with nothing.

His father could be cruel when he wanted to be.

He left Anoushka and went around to the side of the house.

Dad had parked his BMW behind the black Hyundai Elantra SE. No way was Christian going to leave in it. Nor could he ask his father to back up. He flexed his hand, which was swollen. It throbbed, adding to the pounding in his temples. The curse he was about to utter dried in his throat when he turned back toward the driveway.

A police car had pulled up to the sidewalk. Two cops got out, approached him, and confirmed the address. Then, the older of the two said, "We're looking for Christian Skyers. What's your name?"

He swallowed to bring saliva into his mouth, but didn't think to lie. "I'm Christian."

"Christian Skyers, you're under arrest for the sexual assault of Alexia Leighton. Turn around and put your hands behind your back."

His brain had stopped functioning as if was just waking from a traumatic dream. "But…who?"

"Doesn't the name Alexia Leighton mean anything to you?" one of the uniformed men asked.

Christian gulped, but didn't answer.

"I see that it does, now turn around." He continued, "You have the right to remain silent. Anything you say ..."

The roar between Christian's ears was enough to drown the policeman's words. This couldn't be happening. Jamaica and all of that was supposed to be behind him. The videos worried him, but he'd prayed they would stop coming. His approach wasn't practical, yet everything in his world had fallen in place because of his father and the life he'd been born into. So, he expected that somehow the situation would work out. So much for that. First his football career had been shot to hell, then Anoushka screwed him, and now this.

Anoushka stood gaping on the steps and turned back to beat on the front door. "Radcliff! You need to come out here. The police are arresting Christian."

The officer guided him toward the car with an iron grip around his arm. Across the street, someone pulled away a curtain and looked out.

Christian hung his head. The reality of Dad's words hit. He *was* dead. Radcliff Skyers wouldn't come down to the station, so he was on his own. Even the *word* jail freaked him out, and sweat poured off his forehead and stung his eyes. His thoughts raced in circles but didn't make a lot of sense. What was he going to do? He'd be in lockup forever if Dad didn't bail him out. The red and blue lights added to the nightmare-like quality of the moment. He prayed he'd awake to find himself in bed and that all of this was the worst dream he'd ever lived through.

But that wasn't the case when he was escorted into the station, his watch and other personal items removed, and he was seated in a bare room that smelled like the fear of a thousand suspects who'd been there before him.

"This is a mistake," he said to the large man, whose scalp showed through thin, brown hair. His partner leaned against the wall near the door as though he didn't have a care in the world, but he watched Christian as if he'd make a break for it.

The plainclothes police officer, who'd introduced himself as James Harrison, sat on the other side of the table and studied him in silence. Then he reeled off Christian's name and address. A second later, he added, "There is no error."

"What happened to your face?" the Latino policeman asked.

"Had a run-in with a door," Christian mumbled.

Harrison smirked and exchanged a knowing look with the other officer, while Christian threw a panicked glance at the huge pane of reflective glass. Who was on the other side? Couldn't be Alexia. From what he'd heard, she was in rehab. They couldn't pin beating her up on him. He had nothing to do with that bit of madness. Sancia and he had stumbled on her when they came from the beach, where they'd been smoking weed and fooling around.

Now, he knew why people said hindsight was twenty-twenty. He shouldn't have listened to Sancia and messed with that bitch. Staring at his swollen knuckles, which were getting stiffer by the minute, he decided to keep his mouth shut. If he stayed quiet, he had some hope of getting out of this mess. He was supposed to have one phone call, but who could he ask to get him out? That's if the police would let him leave.

The man slid a picture of Alexia across the table, then asked, "Do you know this girl?"

Lying about that wouldn't help him, so Christian nodded.

"Yes or no."

His sharp tone made Christian look up. "Yes."

"And when was the last time you had contact with her?"

He cleared away the rust in his throat. "Months ago."

"Can you say where?"

"School." He winced. Wrong answer. He warned himself to hold his silence.

After sharing a look with the other man, Officer Harrison slammed his fist on the desk. "Stop lying. You. Raped. That. Girl. Things will go easier for you if you admit it now and don't waste our time. We'll need you to do a DNA test."

Christian set his jaw and stared at his hands. "I didn't do anything."

Someone tapped on the glass and Christian peered at it, as though he had any hope of seeing through it.

The younger policeman left the room.

In the tense silence, the click of the lock raised the hairs on the back of Christian's neck. He bit his bottom lip, sensing that his situation was about to get worse.

When the man returned, he leaned next to Officer Harrison and said something in his ear. At the sight of his triumphant smile, Christian lowered his gaze. His stomach twisted into a tight knot that made him want to find a toilet.

The senior policeman brushed the hair at the top of his head and announced. "It seems you'll be our guest for some time."

Christian stared at Harrison and held his breath.

"You've been very busy, Mr. Skyers." He flipped the file shut as a scowl covered his face. "It seems another woman has accused you of rape."

# CHAPTER THIRTY-SIX

## DEJA

**"S**O YOU'RE NOT even going to act like you're sorry?"

"Sorry for what?" Nigel barked.

His screwed-up face, strapping physique, and height made him scary.

Deja jerked and stepped backward, but reminded herself that she wasn't afraid of him, even though she wanted to take off running. She wouldn't get farther than the other end of the yard, and her family would wonder if she'd lost her mind.

She didn't want to be here, but her mother, Hyacinth, used every excuse to bring the family together. Today was her birthday, and she had insisted that everyone show up to celebrate. Deja had been in Florida now for five years but hadn't left the worst of Jamaica behind. Scarcely a year after she landed in the United States, her uncle had made his first visit. Now, he was a resident.

She shifted so her aunt, who sat under a tree, couldn't see her face. Nigel stood facing the other women scattered around the backyard. The children, including his, chased each other across the grass and screamed for no reason.

The man in front of Deja had stolen the ordinary life she should have had when she was living with her grandmother, who was not interested in leaving Jamaica and had been happy to have Deja stay with them after Hyacinth decided to seek what she called "greener pastures" in America.

Her brother, Nathaniel, was two years older, but her mother decided to send for him first to save him from the gangs in Montego Bay. Curtis's father had filed for him, and he also left the island before Deja. *It should have been me. Things would have been different.*

Deja didn't lie to herself. Sometimes, she hated her mother. Hated the fact that she was so busy working toward a better life that she had no idea what was happening to her daughter, whose virginity shouldn't have been given to her uncle. She corrected herself. *Nigel stole it.* Then acted as if she had done something wrong. Telling her that she'd been teasing him by wearing shorts and tights around the house. His threats had kept her silent, and she'd survived being his toy for three long years.

At twelve, she shouldn't have been worried about getting pregnant and being thrown out of his mother's house. At that age, she also shouldn't have been wondering about the next time she'd be forced into an act that was done in love between adults and *not* family members.

*"If you tell, nobody will believe you. Plus, it won't matter. I'll get someone to cut your throat."*

The heat of his breath in her face was as fresh as if he'd threatened her yesterday. She looked up at Nigel. "I don't need to tell you what you should apologize for. You know, *uncle.*"

The word on her tongue made her want to vomit. What he'd done wasn't something any decent human being would do. He'd been twenty-five and knew better. The shadows in his eyes each time he muffled her screams with a large hand told her so.

Night and day she prayed for the abuse to stop, but only had the courage to stand up for herself after Grandma announced that she'd received the embassy documents and that Hyacinth had bought an airline ticket. He'd been bold enough to come to Deja's room on her last night in Jamaica. For a *last lick*, as he called it.

As his palm smothered her face and he pinned her to the mattress, she bit his hand. He'd howled and punched her in the side of the head, stunning her for a moment. She continued fighting until Nigel reared back to slap her. With the steel-tipped pen she'd been using to do her homework, she'd stabbed him in the stomach.

Her uncle wouldn't give up, and in desperation, she twisted out of his grip and stabbed him again. This time, high on the inside of one thigh.

He scrambled away from her with his hand pressed to the wound and blood running through his fingers.

Barely able to catch her breath, she whispered. "That's the only last lick you're getting."

In the morning, she'd apologized to her grandmother for the messy sheets, giving the impression that she was having her period.

She shook her head, loosening her braids. "Pickney gyal, tell Hyacinth to take yuh to di doctor when yuh land. Yuh losing too much blood for a likkle girl."

"Yes, Grandma," she'd said in a meek tone, relieved that she accepted the lie. Perhaps because it was what she wanted to hear.

One of her cousins screamed, bringing Deja back to where they stood.

Nigel scanned the yard, then flexed his jaw. "I don't know what you're talking about. You need to get a life."

Deja closed both hands into fists, wanting to ram one of them into his middle. This man had changed her life forever because of the things he'd done without her permission. The worst mistake she'd made was to watch the video of Christian raping Alexia. It brought back so many issues Deja preferred to bury at the bottom of the pile of unpleasant memories from the past.

Some things she didn't want to remember, others she refused to acknowledge. Like the fact that she still didn't know for sure whether she'd ever healed from the abuse. Why should she alone suffer? The minute she laid eyes on him today, she decided it was time for him to pay. She moved sideways to bring his wife, Marina, into view. One of his daughters stood next to her, sucking on a freezer pop. If she was lucky, he hadn't started putting his hands on her. Predators like him never stopped; they only grew worse with time, and every family seemed to have one cousin or uncle like Nigel that everybody shielded.

One good thing came out of that trip to Jamaica. She'd learned more about how adults handled their business. What happened to Alexia might have caused someone else to fall to pieces, but not Aunt Jenny. Deja wasn't sure what she did with the little bits of information she gave her but was certain they would be put to good use.

Just talking to Aunt Jenny had her thinking of switching her major to computer studies. The data she'd dug into and blasted on social media, plus the stuff she'd learned from Tyler, made Deja feel assured and powerful. The biggest win was knowing the police had Christian in custody. The news had taken the campus by storm, and though Aunt Jenny hadn't said so, Deja knew she'd helped to put the evidence of his crime into the hands of the police.

Tipping her head back, Deja said, "You took the life you're telling me to get, so you still owe me."

The hatred that flashed in his eyes made her shrink.

"I don't owe you shit." He glanced toward Marina then back at Deja. "If you ever mention this again, you'll be sorry."

He turned on his heels and walked away.

Pitching her voice so he'd hear, she taunted him. "I'm sure you'd like that, *uncle*, but since you won't apologize, you'd better prepare to deal with this. Tell the family, or I will."

# CHAPTER THIRTY-SEVEN

## ALEXIA

"**A**RE YOU SURE you can do this?" Geneva asked.

Alexia nodded, but didn't speak.

*I must be cutting off her circulation.* Yet, she couldn't release the grip on her mother's hand. Clinging to the person who had supported her these many months was the only anchor she had in a day that had started like she was sailing under sunny skies and ended up in turbulent weather. Today was the worst twenty-four hours she'd been through in a while.

Aside from the pain that still bothered her, being in the rehab facility was like living inside an ivory tower while she re-learned to do the simple day-to-day activities she'd taken for granted. The world she knew had closed its doors on her, aside from a few friends like Deja who stayed in touch. Mom had taught her to enjoy her own company when she was much younger and had become a nuisance to Jaden. Now, she was thankful she knew how to be independent.

Although she longed for home, she didn't want to complain. Mom tried not to show it, but she'd changed, and it made Alexia sad. The time in her "recovery space" was more interesting since she'd met Cory, a guy who was recovering from a bad motorcycle accident and Angelia, who'd been in a car crash with a drunk driver. They were both older than her, but they were entertaining. She needed them to avoid thinking about what Christian had stolen from her, how Chad had treated her, and how her friends had turned their back when she needed them. Sometimes, she felt she was stuck on a deserted island. Now, she had to face the fear that haunted her since Mom told her they needed to visit the station.

"Do you see the man who raped you?" the officer standing next to her in the stuffy room asked.

She pulled in a breath and released it, wishing she could sit. Coming here in medical transport was not only humiliating, it drained her mentally. What if she saw someone who knew her? What would she do if she couldn't balance her weight with the cane she now used? What if she came face to face with Christian?

Alexia shut off her racing thoughts and focused, calmed by Mom's soothing touch. She scanned the line of men, but her gaze kept going back to Christian. He no longer had the carefree bad-boy air he'd always sported, but stood with his chin tucked toward his chest. His T-shirt was rumpled and he looked tired.

"Alexia?" the officer prompted.

Mom squeezed her hand and she jumped, then pointed. "Yes. Third from the left. Christian. Christian Skyers."

"Are you certain?" the tall man asked, his voice fading.

To think she used to like him. They had even come close to kissing once, and then she'd heard the stories about him and Sancia being freaks. In her short time at the university, she hadn't found out if any of that was true. Sancia had always been standoffish, but Alexia had discovered why that night. She and Christian were an item—although they kept it under wraps—and she was jealous of Alexia, who became living proof of what they liked and shared in their weird relationship. Her fingers went to the scar on her forehead. A gift from Sancia.

She so wanted this to be over. "Yes, I'm sure," she finally answered.

Shifting her weight, Alexia leaned on the cane and held on tight to Mom's hand. "Can we go now?"

"I don't think so, baby." Mom's thumb slid across the back of her hand in a comforting way. "Now they need a statement from you, remember?"

This was turning into an ordeal. Although she hadn't been inside the building for longer than twenty minutes, Alexia was tired, and if she didn't hold it together, she'd burst into tears and shame herself.

"Can't we come back?" she asked, hating the whininess in her voice.

Mom cupped her face in both hands. "Lexi, we've come this far. You can do this."

She sighed and turned her head away, knowing Mom was probably disappointed by her reaction. Sometimes it was tiring being around her mother, even though she adored her. Only God knew how she managed to be strong all the time. Whether she realized it or not, her strength was also a weakness that worked against her. No one had that kind of power without mental and physical wear and tear. Yet, Geneva Leighton kept on going.

*Sometimes, at the expense of all of us.*

"Fine."

Leaning on Mom, Alexia exited the cramped space and when she sat in another room, facing a female officer, she wanted to be back on the top floor of the hospital. She'd hoped this day wouldn't come and had shoved it to the back of her mind, thinking that maybe there wouldn't be a way to take the worst thing that had ever happened to her any further. She was wrong. Being here was ten times worse than she imagined. She was paying in spades.

The dark-haired woman smiled, and her brown eyes crinkled at the corners. "Hi, Alexia, my name is Mandy Black, and I'm here to talk about what happened to you."

She rattled off her rank and number, then continued. "There's no pressure. I'm going to ask you some questions to guide you through the process. Okay?"

Alexia nodded and resigned herself to reliving the horror of that night.

"Mom, do you mind?" She couldn't move any more words past her throat as shock widened Mom's eyes. She gave her a half smile to soften the blow. "It's less embarrassing if you're not here."

Miss Black seemed about to speak, but Mom stood. "I understand. I'll be outside."

It was clear she didn't, but it was easier to talk to a stranger than to be under pressure to watch what she said. Mom might not think she knew it, but Alexia was perfectly aware that her mother was capable of making life difficult for other people if she had a mind to do so. She didn't need any more juice to feed her anger.

Nobody could tell her Mom hadn't cursed out Chad and Danny after they came to visit. The light in her mother's eyes and her following them out of the lounge said everything. They deserved it, but this right here was something Alexia had to do on her own.

Miss Black was good at her job, but it didn't stop Alexia from wanting to run away or shedding a few tears. At the end of their question-and-answer session, she reminded Alexia that she would have to sign a statement to confirm her story. "Do you know why it's taken this long for us to come to this point?" she asked.

Alexia nodded. "The information on…took a while to come from Montego Bay, where it happened."

"And you're aware we have two suspects in custody?"

"I heard about Phil, yes." She touched her forehead as she asked, "What about the rest of them?"

"We're working on it." Miss Black offered a smile. "Don't lose hope. Everything takes time."

She rose and pulled back the chair for Alexia, then opened the door.

Mom was waiting outside and stepped in close to ask, "Are you okay, baby?"

"I'm fine, let's get out of here. Did they send the van back for us?"

"Yes, the team arrived a few minutes ago." She looked over Alexia's shoulder and frowned. "What is the meaning of this?"

With the help of the cane, Alexia lurched sideways to see what caught Mom's attention.

Christian was sandwiched between two police officers, who were crossing the end of the corridor. When he saw them, Christian planted his feet and yelled, "Alexia, tell them what happened. You must have heard her. Please!"

Mom walked away, pointing a finger at the trio as the policemen moved Christian along. "Don't you *dare* speak to my daughter! Officers, how could you let this happen? Best believe you'll hear from me about it."

If fury were a person, Geneva Leighton would be the description. She fumed on her march back to Alexia, who leaned against the wall on one side of the corridor.

Her eyes glittered as she asked. "What did he mean?"

"I don't know."

"You have to know? Who's this 'her' he's talking about? What did you hear?"

Alexia's voice spiked as she answered, "I don't know."

"You *must* know." Mom eyes were wild as she cupped Alexia's shoulders. "Think, baby girl."

"Give me a chance, Mom." She fought the panic spreading through her system and blinked back tears. "I was mainly out of it, when he ..."

"I'm sorry, baby. Forgive me for grabbing you like that." Mom's shoulders went slack and she released Alexia, but her face hardened. "He'd better watch himself or so help me God ..."

Alexia's scalp prickled, and for the first time, she was deathly afraid of her mother. Sharing anything with her at this point was out of the question.

# CHAPTER THIRTY-EIGHT

## GENEVA

**S**OMETIMES, SHE FELT truly alone. Like now.

Solitude wasn't always a bad thing. She enjoyed her own company, except for times like this present moment when she was fighting an uphill battle under her own steam.

Spence was in his feelings again. Jaden was hardly around, and even Alexia wasn't as open these days. All of them were acting as if she was the problem. Maybe she was.

She picked up a miniature Zebra—a character from some animated movie or other—that she'd kept on her desk for years. At the time Spence gave it to her, he said it was to remind her of the family that needed her. The corporate years had taken their toll, and she'd left that world before she burned herself out, but it didn't seem that much had changed. She was still as driven and single-minded as she'd been then.

She'd flubbed badly yesterday by letting her emotions overrule good sense. But those officers were the absolute limit. It shouldn't be impossible for them, in a stationhouse as large as that one, to keep victims and perpetrators apart. Try as she might, she couldn't figure out what the boy meant by that outburst. If Alexia knew, she wasn't saying, and Geneva couldn't force her to talk.

She rose from behind the desk and stretched. Plotting her next move wasn't as easy with the police keeping tabs on her. They hadn't asked to see her again, but she had no illusions that they weren't watching her digital movements. Not that they could stop her from completing her plans. She simply had to be patient. On her mental list, she marked off the Jamaican policeman, who now had a court date to face corruption charges. Most likely, it would be months before he'd be sentenced, but as long as the process was in motion she could focus her attention elsewhere.

Christian's arrest was now public knowledge, but unlike Sancia Jackman's father, Radcliff Skyers had refused to make a statement when contacted by the media. The boy had been formally charged and was being detained.

She'd chuckled with delight this morning when news broke that the Jackmans had been found guilty and would each face a prison term. Their son would be ousted from the university. "Serves them right," she murmured as she shifted a framed photo of Alexia on the credenza.

Her mind flashed back to yesterday afternoon when Deja came to the hospital. The girl had see-sawed between manic excitement and bouts of silence, which made Geneva wonder what was going on with her. She'd offered her a ride after her visit with Alexia because she had an aim in view.

"I'm so glad the police got Christian," she'd squeaked from the passenger seat, irritating Geneva to no end. "It's about time."

"If you ask me, he's not the only one who needs their attention," Geneva commented as she pulled up at a stoplight.

Frowning, Deja said, "I guess you're right."

"I know I'm right," Geneva snapped. "If Alexia hadn't survived, all of them would be facing a murder charge."

That sobered Deja, who fiddled with the strap of her backpack. "That's true."

"I certainly think they could use a reminder." Geneva tipped one brow. "Don't you?"

"Of course." Deja coiled a lick of hair around her finger. "We shouldn't let them forget what they did to Alexia."

"That's my girl." Smiling, Geneva patted her hand. "Did you delete that part of the video?"

Shaking her head, Deja protested, "Oh no. I was sure it would come in handy."

Geneva turned onto the next street, based on Deja's instructions. "Sounds good. Like you said, we can't let them forget. I'm sure it will be useful. Shortly."

"You bet. Thanks, you can leave me here." Deja pointed to a store. "I need to get some things."

"Take care and be smart."

She grinned, as if she'd been given a compliment. "You can count on me."

Now, all Geneva had to do was wait. And if Deja didn't act in a timely fashion, she'd do the deed herself. Nisha. Robyn. Kara. Those girls who called themselves friends wouldn't be able to deny their part when their actions became public. Only God knew if the police had even made an effort to contact them.

The "Ones Who Did Nothing" had been included on that Wall of Shame—Derek, Chloe, Mia, Jonathan, and Mateo. There were a few others, but Geneva had decided early on to spend her energy on those directly connected to Alexia.

With Phil and Christian facing charges, she wanted to keep the momentum going. Memories were short. She couldn't have the police or Alexia's attackers growing more comfortable. Time had passed, and they would already have a sense of security. Now was the time to strike.

She was on her feet and about to move to the desk when her phone rang and Spence's face greeted her on-screen. Geneva had a mind not to answer. What the heck did he want when he'd been treating her like a piece of furniture after their last run-in?

Spence's tone was light when she greeted him. "Deciding whether or not to give me the time of day, right?"

She bit back her smile, as if he could see her. "You know me too well."

"I wanted to invite you to our favorite eating spot."

She pulled her head back and looked at the phone. "Right now?"

"Why not?"

The wall clock with spines like a starfish told her it was late enough for him to be en route to their house. "It's well ..."

"Almost time for me to come home? I know."

Geneva perched on the sofa, staring at her toes—which were due for a manicure—while her mind ran down several tracks. "I don't get why you're doing this."

"So now I need to set an appointment to have dinner with my wife?"

The hint of annoyance in his voice slowed her response. "What I'm saying is that date night is all about dressing up and going out."

"Agreed, but I wanted to do something different."

"Actually, I have a better idea."

"Let me hear it."

"Why not take Jaden and Alexia with us?"

He sighed. "That brilliant, but will take some arranging, so can we do it tomorrow or Saturday? I really wanted time away from our usual space. Minus the bickering. Just us two."

"Awww." This man still knew how to knock her off guard in the simplest of ways. "All you had to do was straight up ask."

"Nothing is *straight up* with you these days, Jen."

"Touché, I think."

"Sooooo, what are we doing, wife of mine?"

"I'll get a cab."

"See you in fifteen, sweets."

<hr>

Dinner was a relaxed affair at the upscale, intimate restaurant that had started out serving Caribbean food when it opened. Over the years, they had branched into mouthwatering Asian cuisine. The staff greeted them by name and gave them a table for two in a corner of the room filled with sturdy furniture, huge paintings, and potted palms.

The Teriyaki special of fish, lobster tail, scallops, and shrimp was delicious and filling. So was the deep-fried, breaded pieces of pork cutlets she stole from Spence's plate. They shared vanilla ice cream tempura and held hands, the way they hadn't in ages, on the way to Spence's vehicle. Before he opened the door to the Hyundai Palisade, Spence hemmed her in and kissed her lips. "I said some stuff the other day that hurt you, but I want you to know I'm trying to see things from your point of view."

Arms around his neck, she murmured, "I could say the same thing."

"And I'll try to be better about not attacking you when I'm hurt."

The truth was, they were both wrong in their approach. One thing she was sure of, she loved Spence—faults and all.

On their trip home, she closed her eyes and listened to the rocksteady music Spence liked. The precursor to reggae, it was popular in the '50s and '60s with a slow and mellow beat. They didn't speak much, and when they arrived, Spence walked into the house with his arm thrown around her neck.

He checked on Jaden, then locked up for the night. After they both showered, he disappeared and returned with wine glasses and the port she enjoyed. He laid the glasses on the bedside table and lowered himself on the side of the mattress.

Kneeling behind him, Geneva hugged Spence and nuzzled his neck.

He turned and when their lips met, she was lost to reality.

"What about the wine?" he mumbled.

Geneva groaned as he cupped her hips and positioned her on his lap. "Later. It can wait."

The sensuous lovers' dance they shared meant they didn't speak for some time, but after she was sated, her thoughts wouldn't stop tumbling. She inhaled the musk from Spence's skin and sighed against his throat. "Can I ask you something?"

He bit her shoulder gently. "Of course."

The lamp cast his face in shadow, but she stared into his eyes. "Where did you go that night after that video I showed you?"

Spence made her wait, rising to pour more wine for them, then staring at the glass before exhaling deeply. "To Radcliff Skyers's house. We play golf together."

She rested the glass on the night table and held her silence, waiting for what he'd say next.

"I recognized the young man. Skyers' son." He swallowed then continued, anger etched across his features. "So, I went over there and beat the shit out of him."

# CHAPTER THIRTY-NINE

## PHIL

**T**HE GIRLS JASON and he had recorded were too embarrassed to come forward, but Phil wasn't safe. He was back at home, but might as well have been in jail. The police had set his bail high, put him under house arrest, and fitted him with an ankle monitoring bracelet. He couldn't even attend school. The university had expelled him over the information he had supposedly accessed. No one, outside of his lawyer, believed he hadn't gotten hold of information from their database. What really looked bad was that Amelia's information was among the girls' files they thought he'd stolen.

"I'm tired of this crap," he yelled in the silent room.

The only good news was that the small stash of steroids he kept on campus hadn't been discovered. His room had become a prison cell. He only had to wander so far outside before the monitor vibrated and started making noise. Phil didn't want to test what would happen after that. He could cut if off, if he was brave enough, but where would he go? The neighbors no longer waved at him, and none of his so-called friends bothered to answer his texts or phone calls. He was like a leper.

Aside from that, the evidence against him kept piling up. His father told him Amelia had changed her mind and was willing to testify about what Jason and he had done to her. The same reel of her outside his house had started making the rounds right before she went to the police with her parents. He was in a black hole he couldn't climb out of or escape from.

He lowered his head to the desk as memories of his return home crowded his mind.

"You're a disgrace to this family," his father had declared, his voice cracking, while his sister stared in disbelief. "After the sacrifices we've made to give you a good life, you turn around and repay us by trampling our name in the mud."

His mother had continued sobbing, while the vein in Dad's forehead throbbed like a snake out to strike. "It's bad enough that you did all of this stuff, but you attacked that girl on vacation and came home pretending it never happened? You're a damn disgrace, you hear me? A monster in our own home."

Phil hadn't answered or hit back after his father whacked him across the face. Since then, he stayed out of his way. Two weeks had dragged by, and being confined wasn't the worst of what was happening to him.

Since the day he returned home, he hadn't slept well. At 11:00 p.m. each night, a pop-up box on the laptop woke him. The first time it happened, he nearly fell out of bed. The automated voice that filled the room still haunted him and seemed to be stuck inside his head. No matter how often he turned it off, the laptop would power up after a few minutes. He was at his wit's end, and couldn't think of anyone who could explain what was happening. The messages, delivered in that doomsday tone, all meant the same thing and were a mantra tattooed on his brain.

- *You won't escape the things you've done. Do the world a favor. Take the easy way out.*
- *You wreck lives, Phil. Rid the world of yourself.*

- *You're a disgrace to your family. Do the honorable thing.*
- *The longer you wait, the worse things will get. Make your exit now.*
- *The world will be a better place without you.*
- *Those girls will get a chance to heal. Do the right thing. Do it now!*

Whoever was toying with him had a mirror image of his thoughts, which frightened him. How did they know what he was thinking?

By the fifth day, he was ready to follow the advice he was being given. He removed his father's Smith & Wesson 642 from the top shelf of the closet in his parents' bedroom and had kept it since then.

He sat up and opened the drawer on his right side to be sure the gun was still there. Its dull chrome finish reminded him of the same nothingness his life had become. If he died, no one would care, except maybe his mother and Kendra, and even they had lost faith in him.

If he believed what Eric Randall had explained about the seriousness of his crimes, based on everything they found on Jason's computer and in his cloud files, he would be charged with multiple counts of sexual assault. His defense that Jason masterminded their activities wouldn't do much good. They had been careless and had also recorded themselves snickering over the fun they'd had with some of the girls.

He stared at the Smith & Wesson, then rubbed his grainy eyes.

Even if his case went to trial, he couldn't see any way out. Maybe even God wanted him dead. That would be best for everyone. If he spoke to Mom, she would tell him different, but he was too out of it to care anymore.

*What's the point of living if I'll be in a concrete cage for the rest of my life?*

He wouldn't give anyone the satisfaction of discovering all the things Jason and he had done. With trembling hands, he pulled the laptop closer, and after two incorrect attempts to use his password, he peered at the screen, perplexed. He couldn't access his cloud files. Using the crook of his elbow, he swiped at the sweat now raining from his forehead. How the hell could this happen? Maybe he'd made a mistake because he was nervous. He tried again with the same result.

He swore, then got up and paced the room. He shoved one hand into his hair and tugged at the roots, wondering if he had changed the password. The last time he'd done that was just after Jason's death. He did it to be sure he wouldn't be caught flat-footed if the police seized his laptop. After several trips around the edges of the bed, he flopped down in the chair. His mind wouldn't settle long enough for him to concentrate.

He slid the drawer closed then stared at the ceiling, trying to slow the frantic pace of his brain. No one else was at home, so if he planned to do anything drastic, now was the time. He opened the drawer again, but didn't take out the Smith & Wesson. Two more tries and he was frustrated by the message that his password was incorrect. Finally, it occurred to him to reset the password. He checked his email, used the new password that came, and opened his cloud account.

*Welcome, Phil, you have no files saved to your cloud account.*

Phil stared bug-eyed at the screen. He blinked a couple of times, then frowned at the empty space that confirmed he had zero files stored. A strong urge to empty his gut came over him, but he clenched his cheeks and tried to make sense of what was in front of him.

Someone had accessed his cloud files and deleted every picture and audio file. It had to be the same person who was tormenting him at night. What was he going to do now? Tears sprang to his eyes. Which bastard would do this to him? Maybe, it was one of those girls, or a relative of theirs.

The fact that he didn't know who had his personal data sent him into a meltdown. They could release it at any time, and the last shred of hope he had would be gone. He lifted the computer and slammed it against the desk, then swept both hands across the desktop, scattering books, paper, pens, and the prized first-place trophy he'd won in his category in a statewide golf tournament.

The proof of his activities was somewhere in the ether and could turn up at any point. What would he do if that happened? Tears streamed down his cheeks, and he could barely see as he scrambled to pick up the gun. One deep breath helped to calm him, and he swiped away the snot draining from his nostrils. Then he attempted to tidy the desk but gave up, reminding himself that it didn't matter anymore.

He glanced at the alarm clock on the bedside table. It was 3:15 p.m. Mom would soon be back from grocery shopping, and Kendra would be home from school. Sniffling, he dragged himself to his feet and wrapped his shaking fist around the gun. In the bathroom, he climbed into the shower, sat in the tub, and drew the curtain.

People said cowards committed suicide, but he didn't think so. The way he figured it, the trouble he had caused would die with him, and Mom and Dad wouldn't have to live through the additional disgrace that a trial would bring.

Before he changed his mind and copped out, Phil closed his eyes, aimed the gun at the roof of his mouth, and pulled the trigger.

# CHAPTER FORTY

## GENEVA

*A*NOTHER ONE DOWN *and just a few more to go.* The thought made her smile.

Across the table, Spence laid the newspaper next to his plate and popped a forkful of liver and onions into his mouth along with a bit of green banana. They had lived away from the island for many years, but he still enjoyed the food from his boyhood. She found being in the kitchen therapeutic, but didn't spend as much time cooking for the family since Alexia's hospitalization.

He picked up the paper and asked, "Did you hear about this young man? The one who committed suicide?"

After a sip of coffee, she said, "Yes. I read about it just before you came down."

"Pity, but that's one less person Alexia has to face in court if the case goes to trial."

"*When*, Spence, not *if*. I won't stop until they all pay."

"Trust me, I believe you."

His close study made her uncomfortable, and she broke eye contact to top up her coffee cup.

"What did the doctor say about Alexia coming home?"

The change of direction startled her, but Geneva couldn't help her spontaneous smile. "He thinks her recovery is something of a miracle. She's improving every day. He says she'll be up to it in another month or so."

"That's wonderful news." Spence nodded slowly, then looked at her over the rim of his cup. He placed it on the saucer and asked, "What about specialized equipment and therapy?"

"He's hoping she'll be strong enough by then so all we'll need is to have a therapist come in and work with her, which reminds me…we'll have to convert a room down here."

"Which one are you thinking?" Spence asked. "We could use my den, and I'll share your office, if necessary."

Her mood dipped because their discussion reminded her of all the reasons for their life changes. She didn't regret any of the money they spent and was grateful for the combined means and resources that took care of Alexia's needs. But all the dislocation and upset could have been avoided if those kids had acted like human beings. She swallowed her sigh and patted his hand. "That's sweet of you, Spence. It's so hard to think that all of this was over a stupid baggie of illegal drugs."

"It's no problem, hon." He wiped his mouth with a paper napkin, then dropped it on the empty plate. "In any case, the only other space we have is next to the laundry room, and it's tiny."

Spence rose and kissed her forehead. "I have a meeting at nine. Talk later." He left the room, and a few moments later, she followed his footfalls as he climbed the wooden stairs.

Geneva reached for the paper and read the story about Phil's suicide a second time. God forgive her, but she couldn't find it in her heart to be sorry for him. From what she gathered, his family sounded like decent people. Kids these days fell under all kinds of influence, but right and wrong were clear choices. Too bad he hadn't made the right one when it came to Alexia. He could have chosen to put a halt to what Jason started, but he decided to be part of the attack. Phil had sealed his fate without knowing it.

With an analytical eye, she studied the article. If there was any thought of foul play, the paper would have said so, but it seemed the police considered his death a clear case of suicide. She sipped the rest of her coffee, then bit into a slice of pineapple, and wiped her fingers. She no longer ate breakfast, or any other meal, the way she used to do. Another thing that had changed since their lives went topsy-turvy. While clearing the dishes, she considered what she'd done lately.

Phil's incident made her feel like a one-trick pony, but she had learned that people were creatures of habit. After she spoofed an email from the school regarding Phil's disciplinary status and he took the bait, she made the next step to invade his privacy. Before doing any of that, she ensured that she operated from an IP address which happened to be a café that Deja had mentioned she liked. Geneva had been there a time or two to scope out the place and make use of their internet service. Her visits served a purpose that would be useful at the tail end of her plans. They served good food, catered to a mostly young crowd, and the atmosphere was pleasant.

Despite the precaution of a different location, she had the nagging worry that using that particular ruse a second time might have made her easier to track. Still, anything more complex than a phishing link would narrow the list of possible suspects for the police if they decided to look at Phil's computer. If she used a more sophisticated method to reel Phil in, they would know they were dealing with a high-level expert. With any luck, his death wouldn't cause a blip on the police department's radar.

While clearing the dishes, she ran through the steps she'd taken. After getting access to the machine, she'd scanned the passwords he saved in the browser. He had a kazillion of them, but she knew what she was chasing. When she found the information she needed, she logged into the site and changed that particular password. Then, she copied all his files and deleted the originals from his cloud storage drive.

She hadn't forgotten to erase the original email with the link that gave her a handle on his laptop. After that, she wiped out every trace of the invasion. Geneva didn't know for certain that the nightly pop-ups had done the job they were intended to do, but she didn't care anymore. The end result was what mattered. Phil was no longer an issue, and she intended to keep Christian on her radar. She didn't trust the police not to mess up his case, but if that happened, she'd be ready to act.

This afternoon, she had several virtual meetings, so she'd visit Alexia early in the day. With Spence and Jaden out of the house, she tidied things up and caught herself singing Marley's "Three Little Birds" on her way to the hospital. That hadn't happened in a while. Alexia's prognosis had to be the catalyst for that. For the first time in ages, she was in a chipper mood. No doubt this morning's news had contributed to the shift.

She greeted the nurse at the reception desk, who told her Alexia had just finished her morning therapy session and was resting. Geneva breezed into the room and took a seat next to Alexia, who was busy with her laptop. "Aren't you supposed to be taking it easy?"

"Hey, Mom."

Something about her greeting made Geneva pay closer attention.

"What's wrong, Lexi?"

Alexia wrapped the strings on her shirt around her fingers and turned stormy eyes on Geneva. "It's Christian."

"What about him?" Geneva asked, shifting to the edge of the chair.

Her baby's fingertips ran over the scar on her forehead, and her voice shook when she said, "He left town. Just disappeared."

Goosepimples broke out on Geneva's skin. "What?"

Her sharp tone startled Alexia, who jumped. She rubbed Alexia's arm and slowed her breathing. "Sorry, baby. Are you sure?"

She angled the laptop toward Geneva. "This was on the news an hour ago. He was released with special bail conditions and was supposed to report to the police, but he didn't."

"Let me see that." Geneva reached for the laptop. "Does it say who bailed him out?"

Alexia nodded and fiddled with the choker at her neck. "It says here that it was his mother."

Geneva was mad enough to spit nails as she speed-read the news report before replacing the computer on the pad in Alexia's lap. She walked to the other side of the room then returned to Alexia's bedside, her brain in turmoil.

"Are you okay, Mom?"

"I'm fine, baby." She mustered a smile while she strangled the strap of her handbag between shaking fingers. "While you rest, I'll run an errand. Before you know it, I'll be back."

Alexia's curious gaze roamed Geneva's face, but she didn't ask any questions.

It was just as well, because Geneva didn't have any words that were fitting for her daughter to hear.

# CHAPTER FORTY-ONE

## GENEVA

**S**HE'D MADE THE same mistake often enough for it to become a habit. Geneva sat inside the SUV, gripping the steering wheel as if her life depended on it. She wanted to storm into the police station so badly, but once more she'd forgotten to clue Spence in on what she was about to do.

A five-minute phone call brought him up to date and he agreed to meet her there. By then, she had calmed down some, but didn't understand Christian's disappearance and how the media had gotten wind of it so fast.

On the sidewalk, Spence held her in place by the shoulders. "I know this is hard to swallow but take it easy on the officers. Please."

She straightened his tie to avoid his eyes. "That will be difficult, so I'm not making any promises. "

"They'll be more cooperative, not to mention sympathetic to our case, if we treat them with respect."

She patted his chest and pitched her voice louder to combat the passing traffic. "I think you should quit while you're ahead. You're not telling me anything I don't know. "

"And yet you've made up your mind to give them hell."

"I've done no such thing." She shook her head and gripped his arm. "But I do want to know how something like this could happen."

"He's young and foolish," Spence said, "That explains a lot. He probably panicked and ran."

"Thank goodness the media picked up on it, otherwise he might have been halfway to Mexico by now."

Spence rested one hand in the middle of her back as they approached reception. The officer on duty asked them to take a seat and nearly twenty minutes went by before they were shown into Officer Harrison's office.

"Good day, Mr. and Mrs. Leighton." He stood to greet them and waved to indicate that they should sit. "It's good to see you both again. I'm fairly certain why you're here."

"Well, in that case, we can go straight to business." Geneva settled into the seat, determined not to give away her anxiety. While placing the handbag on her lap, her gaze never left Officer Harrison. "Please tell me that you have Christian Skyers back in custody."

"Not yet, Mrs. Leighton, but I'm sure that will change by the end of the day."

Smiling sweetly, she said, "The last time we saw each other, I told you this police department could not possibly need my help. Now I'm not so sure."

"Are you offering?" Officer Harrison asked, glancing at Spence.

On another visit, his sly expression might have amused her, but not today. "I don't understand how you can have a rapist running loose on the streets of Coral Gables. And from what I've heard, this might not be his first time."

"You know a lot for someone who's not interested in helping the police," Officer Harrison snapped.

She raised both eyebrows. "When it comes to my daughter, everything related to this case is of interest to me."

His gaze went to Spence again, then slid back to her. "Can I take it that you're serious about assisting us?"

"I didn't exactly say that. What I'm interested in is finding out what you're doing about getting that young man back behind bars."

"There is a process—"

"I don't care about that. What I want to know is when my daughter can feel safe again. She's the one who let me know he was nowhere to be found, and she's understandably upset." She moved to the edge of the seat, frowning. "And by the way, has he done a DNA test yet?"

"I'm not at liberty to say."

"Is there *anything* you can tell me with any level of confidence?" Geneva said, with a nasty edge to her voice.

Officer Harrison's neck flushed, and a pink tide climbed toward his face while Spence squeezed her hand.

"I'm sure you understand my wife's concern, since getting to this point has taken several months," Spence said. "She's been under a lot of stress from taking care of our daughter since the attack."

The policeman dipped his head once. "Please remember we've not had the case that long. We're doing everything we can to move things along quickly, based on the evidence we have."

His words sounded like what they were, useless platitudes. "What the hell else do you need? I'm sorry, but I don't understand what else is necessary after giving you the dress she was wearing when she was assaulted, plus the rape kit you received. In my view, all you need now is to get hold of the criminal you released."

In a chilly tone, the officer said, "Your daughter's case is not the only one we're dealing with, Mrs. Leighton."

"I'm fully aware of that, Officer Harrison."

Spence's soothing voice cut the tension in the air-conditioned room. "Can you tell us anything at all about how the young man disappeared, and when we can expect to receive an update?"

"We're doing all we can to locate young Mr. Skyers. His parents are cooperating, so I have every confidence we will find him soon."

"Can you tell me one thing, please?" She grabbed Spence's thigh to ground herself.

"Sure, if it's in my power."

"You couldn't answer earlier, but I'm asking as a concerned parent. Did that DNA test prove conclusively that Skyers raped my daughter?"

His curt nod surprised her.

She sagged against the back of the chair and looked across at Spence, who seemed stricken. "Thank you. I appreciate that."

Harrison waved away her thanks. "That's okay. In the meantime, I'd urge you not to do anything foolish."

Her response was quick. "The thought never crossed my mind."

"I wish I could believe you." He shifted a file to the side in an impatient sweep of his hand. In a grudging tone, he said, "You may think you're slick, but one day …"

Every shred of good will disappeared, and she snapped, "Why don't you actually do what the government pays you for? To serve and protect, not harass a grieving parent."

His eyes glimmered. "Mrs. Leighton, you're out of line."

Geneva pulled in a breath to speak, but Spence's glare stopped her. A few dozen choice words came to her lips, but she kept her cool and said nothing. He could play Mr. Nice Guy with the know-it-all, slow-acting officer sitting opposite them, but the police weren't leaving her any choice.

Christian Skyers may have run, but he couldn't hide. Not as long as technology was her friend. It didn't matter where he went; she'd find him.

The seriousness of the charges dictated that the law would deal harshly with him, but she didn't have the confidence they would close their investigation swiftly enough to bring his case to trial. Radcliff Skyers was an influential man, which made it possible for justice to fall by the wayside. Either Christian or she would die before that happened.

Her resolve hardened while Officer Harrison pinned her with a steely gaze, as if she were a nuisance he couldn't wait to be rid of. If he knew what was good for him, he'd find that rapist before the sun set this evening. She picked up her handbag and took Spence's hand, urging him out of the chair. "I have to get back to Alexia, plus there's something important I must do before that."

Officer Harrison's eyes sharpened, and she gave him a smug smile. Let him wonder what her next move would be. She had more than enough tricks to keep him occupied.

# CHAPTER FORTY-TWO

## CHRISTIAN

RUNNING HADN'T BEEN part of his plan when he left the station house. Christian wouldn't even classify going below the grid as that. He was simply taking time to think about where to go from here. His father's refusal to post bail made him desperate.

After dragging him before a judge, the police had been only too happy to lock him up again when he couldn't make bail. Anoushka's crazy accusation that he'd raped her was the unbearable topping on an already bizarre situation. The only good thing was that his father didn't believe her.

He hadn't slept that night as his thoughts ping-ponged in his head. In the morning, he'd asked for a phone call and dialed his mother's cell, after racking his brain to shake the number loose. Her voice was as calm and soothing as he remembered, when she asked, "Christian? Why are you calling me from the city jail?"

"Mom?" He winced, because the word sounded weird coming from his mouth. He rushed in with, "I have a situation, and Dad kicked me out of the house. He won't help."

He'd given her a quick explanation but didn't admit any guilt. In the silence, his heel bounced on the concrete floor as he waited for her answer. Over his shoulder, he checked to be sure no one was waiting, so he wouldn't have to cut the call before he was finished.

Bernadette Ebanks had been pitched out on her ear for cheating on Radcliff, who ensured he gained full custody of ten-year-old Christian. Christian's only contact with her was a card at Christmas, and that hadn't changed in years. She'd remarried and had two children. The way Christian figured it, she had her hands full, and he'd managed fine without her.

Five years ago, she sent him her number along with a hundred-dollar bill, and he'd called to thank her. Since then, they spoke once or twice each year. Of course, Christian never mentioned her, or their conversations, to Dad.

"I-I'm desperate. I won't ask for anything else if you get me out of here."

He waited for her response, unsure of what it would be. If she said no, he didn't know what he'd do.

"Give me a couple of hours," was all she said.

Weak with relief, Christian sagged against the wall. "Thank you," he whispered. He couldn't move his mind beyond getting out of jail. When that happened, he'd take the next step.

Bernadette was as good as her word and arrived two-and-a-half hours later. When they stood next to her car, she hugged him. The second she stepped away, Christian knew he was on his own. Then, her gaze went to his hand, which was cradled to his side. "What happened to your face and fingers?"

He explained and watched her cringe. When his story ended, she opened her handbag, pulled out her wallet, and stuffed some bills into his hand. "Do what you need to do."

"Can you at least give me a ride?" he asked, hefting the backpack onto his shoulder.

He thought she'd say no, but she said, "Sure. Where d'you need me to take you?"

That stumped him and he stared at his Nikes, then said the first place that came to mind and was close to her hometown of Westchester. "South Miami."

"Get in the car."

She was a small woman with an air of authority, like a school teacher. He tried to remember what she did for a living but pulled a blank. It didn't matter anyway. From the corners of his eyes, he studied her. He had her complexion and the shape of her face. Other than that, he was his father.

He soon realized his mother was a speed demon, or she couldn't wait to get rid of him. After several questions about his life and what he was accused of doing, she went silent. When they pulled up outside a small hotel property, he sat up. "What is this place?"

She faced him, then quickly angled her body toward the windscreen. "Look, it's clear you don't have anywhere to go, and I can't just leave you on the side of the road. Your father is a harsh man, but he may change his mind about helping you. In the meantime, let's get you checked into this place."

Before he could ask how she knew the bed and breakfast, she said, "Hotel bookings are part of what I do for a living."

Within minutes, she checked him in for three nights. He couldn't help noticing that she pulled out a credit card, then opted to pay cash. After a sweep of her heels, suit, and handbag, he figured she wasn't struggling.

Through the plate glass, he watched her get into the Subaru. Their eyes met, and she forced a smile. The weight of his problem hit him again, and he didn't see a way out. Not without his father's help.

◆──◇──◆

Two days later, Christian was sure he was going mad. That first evening, he'd gone to the emergency room, where they had given him several shots, put a splint on his two middle fingers, and told him to get pain killers. He still couldn't believe Dad had done him like that. But what was there not to believe? Years ago, he'd heard him ranting when he kicked Mom out of their home. Christian also knew she left with only the clothes she wore, no matter how much she begged to be let back inside to pack a few things.

He stared at the ceiling, wanting to get up but not seeing the point.

The room was small but clean, the cable service crappy, and the Wi-Fi iffy. So far, he had only ventured downstairs to walk around the pool area. Not even the water was appealing. While he'd never been someone who needed much company, he was lonely. Also, though he never had any deep conversations with Sancia, he missed her ditziness.

Worry was killing him slowly. After his three nights at the hotel were up, he'd be out on the street. He stood on the balcony and let loose with several curse words. If he had ignored Sancia, none of this would have happened.

Alexia had been the newbie on the scene, and while he was attracted to her, he hadn't done anything about it. Several times, Sancia had teased him about the way he looked at Alexia, but he still hadn't put any thought behind doing anything more. He much preferred that the girls Sancia selected knew, or at least suspected, what games they'd be playing.

One bad decision had ruined his life.

When his mother bailed him out, he hadn't been thinking about leaving town, but she had provided the perfect opportunity. If only he could really disappear...but that would take some doing.

He rushed inside the room and emptied all the pockets of his backpack, plus his wallet. A grand total of one hundred and fifty dollars, plus a credit card, lay scattered on the bed. So far,

Dad hadn't canceled the card, but it wouldn't be long before he remembered and called the bank.

Christian put everything away, and from the bed, he scrolled through the television channels, which was pretty much all he'd done in the last couple of days while avoiding reality. Other than that, he stared at the city through the plate-glass doors. He stayed off the laptop a good deal of the time. That, and the cell phone, were tracking devices. Just in case he decided not to go back to Coral Gables, he wouldn't be trapped by technology.

His face appeared on the television screen, and he jack-knifed into a sitting position. With clumsy fingers, he scrambled to turn up the volume on the evening news and stared in disbelief while the news anchor read a story about him violating the terms of his bail by leaving Coral Gables. But how did the authorities know he'd left? He hadn't told anyone, which was easy. Even the people in his circle who were known freaks had stopped talking to him.

"Oh, shit." He scooted to the end of the bed, placed both feet on the floor, and dropped his head into his hands while the woman reading the news moved to another story. How could he have been so stupid? And his mother was just as bad. She had to know they could lock him up again for leaving the city limits. Maybe he could turn himself in, if he could make it back safely. If he met any police on the way who recognized him, they might shoot him on sight. Sweat broke out everywhere. Too many Black men had been killed just for being born in the skin God had given them. Plus, the thought of being locked up for days on end just about killed him.

He ordered pizza, then threw the phone aside to stare at the television. His eyes closed, and when he opened them again, someone was pounding at the door. Must be the delivery guy—although he'd had to go downstairs for previous orders. They had probably been calling the room while he was asleep. He swung his feet over the edge of the bed and yelled, "Coming. No need to tear the door down."

He turned the handle, and the door hit him in the shoulder, numbing it instantly. "Hey! What the—"

Two men, one Black, one White, stood on the dingy carpet in the corridor. King Kong didn't have anything on them. If they had a mind, they could snap him like a toothpick. Their arm muscles bulged under their shirts, and they weren't even moving.

Christian dried his forehead with his sweater, trying to push the door closed.

"Are you Christian Skyers?" the man pressing against the panel asked.

Stepping back, Christian bluffed. "Who wants to know?"

"Hotel security," the bald one said with a smirk.

"Do I look like I was born yesterday?"

He tried to slam the door, but the taller of the two shoved his foot into the space.

The skinny man who'd been working reception when Christian checked in walked up to them and peered inside the room. He nodded to the other guy, who stood with his thumbs hooked in his belt loops.

His gaze never left Christian when he asked, "Are you sure that's him?"

"Yes, this is the guy that registered under that name."

Before Christian could say a word, the dude wearing what looked like combat gear flung him against the door and twisted both arms behind his back.

"This is bullshit! You're hurting my hand."

The man planted the back of his arm below Christian's neck and pinned him to the wood.

"Who are you guys?" Christian sagged as his feet threatened to give way, but the man's rough hold kept him upright.

"That's not important." His hot, garlic-and-cigarette breath made Christian want to puke.

His continued protests didn't move either of them while they tossed the room, and when they got ready to leave, Christian asked them to bring his backpack.

Ten minutes later, he sat in the back of a metal-gray Honda truck wearing handcuffs and balancing the box of pizza that arrived in the middle of him being scooped up by the pair of Neanderthals.

No matter which way he spun it, he couldn't understand why they came for him. No one was supposed to know where he was, and they refused to answer anything he asked, so he eventually shut up. Then it occurred to him that although they had radio contact with a "base," they were not policemen. For a mission like this, officers would have been in uniforms.

His next thought almost made him wet the seat. Someone had paid them to hunt him down.

# CHAPTER FORTY-THREE

## GENEVA

**I**F SHE KNEW how to make bombs, she'd have blown up something already. As things stood, Geneva couldn't sit still for thinking about how lax the police had been. Roaming around the house brought her to Alexia's room. She stood inside, absorbing her daughter's energy that still lived in this place she hadn't seen in more than eight months. The peach drapes and matching quilt reflected Alexia's sunny personality. Everything was the same as she'd left them. The badminton rackets in the closet, the tube of shuttles, even the books on her night table that she'd been planning to read on her return from Jamaica.

Downstairs, her golf bag remained standing next to Spence's in his den. Spence didn't play often enough to make a membership viable, and Geneva couldn't remember the last time she'd even seen her clubs.

Like Spence, who had run track and field in high school and also played cricket, Alexia was naturally athletic. Sports had always been part of their lives. Geneva had been so busy keeping positive thoughts that any hint of Alexia not being able to compete at her previous level was barred from her mind. Until now.

She sat on the edge of the bed and reminded herself to focus on reorganizing the room downstairs. Her baby was a first-class fighter and doing well in rehab, but it was time to bring her home. The doctor would resist them moving her earlier than planned, but she'd seen the anxiety reflected in Alexia's eyes when she returned from her visit to the police.

After what she had been through, she shouldn't have to worry about anything but improving her physical condition each day. The idea of Christian reaching out to Alexia had crossed Geneva's mind. She was certain the thought had also occurred to Alexia. The facility was a safe one, and Geneva had dictated who could and couldn't visit. She'd done everything to ensure their peace of mind—until the visit to the police.

Geneva still didn't know what Skyers meant when he yelled to Alexia. What was she supposed to have heard, and what did it have to do with anything? He'd committed a crime and needed to pay for it, and that was that.

She neatened the bed and went to stand in the doorway. Coming to Alex's room had been a way to help her arrive at a decision. Christian skipping town brought home the reality that she had no guarantee he would stay behind bars. She needed a foolproof plan to seal his fate, and she needed it fast. Everything she'd come up with felt too contrived, too drastic, and too dangerous. She wasn't focused on hurting the people around those who had wrecked Alexia's life. But the fact was that no matter what she did, she couldn't avoid some collateral damage. If she went through with what she was thinking about, timing would be mega-important.

Deja had been as good as her word and dropped the part of the video with Alexia's attack. She'd also sent it to everyone involved in the incident. When it hit various social media platforms, Jaden was livid.

"People can be so insensitive," he'd snapped and plunked his mug down so hard the cocoa sloshed over the rim.

She'd gauged her words so as not to make things worse.

"You might not want to hear it, but your sister is not as soft as you think." Circling the coffee mug with both hands, she explained, "She knew there was a possibility of it coming to light. Like I always say, you young'uns live your lives out in public."

"Not all of us," he clapped back. "Some of us actually think before we hit that "post" button."

Spence had given her an inscrutable look before Jaden and he rose and left her at the table.

At her desk, she retrieved a copy of the file Jaden had pointed her to—which she couldn't admit to having previous knowledge about—and emailed it to Officer Harrison. In the mail, she asked whether any of the persons captured in the video had been arrested. After that, she called Spence, who had just arrived at work, then included their lawyer on a three-way call.

Milford Bernard had listened to her explanation, then suggested that she wait for a response from the police before taking any further action.

"How long am I supposed to wait before doing anything else? It seems the only way to get any kind of satisfaction is to deal with the issue myself."

"That's not a wise option, as you know, Geneva."

She pictured Milford frowning as he walked around his office with both hands crossed behind him like a school teacher. She'd known him for years and had confidence in his abilities, but her patience had run out.

It was not a good look on the police when she had to hire bounty hunters to bring Christian to heel. He was back in custody where he belonged, and she would keep her attention on him as long as necessary.

His stupidity was mindboggling. How did someone skip town and still use the same devices as when he'd been at home? But then, he wasn't a hardened criminal, just a spoiled boy who had gotten used to taking whatever he wanted.

Her attention returned to the phone conversation when Spence called her name.

"Yes, I'm here."

"Milford was asking you to stand down until he's had a chance to contact the police."

"As long as you keep us in the loop, I'll be fine, but do you have any idea what they will do with the young man since he violated the conditions of his bail?"

"I'll find out. I'll also put someone on your case. Give me until the end of the day."

Gently but firmly, Geneva said, "I don't want anyone else dealing with this but you."

"I have a competent and efficient team of—"

"Milford, please humor me. I've had more than enough."

"Very well, but you know—"

"Yes, yes, you're about to tell me this is going to cost an arm, a leg, and a kidney if you have to deal directly with our case, but it doesn't matter. Do what you have to do."

She replayed the conversation in her mind on the way downstairs. Sad to say, she had no confidence that the police would do their job. She hadn't shared all her thoughts with Milford, but no matter what the police did, she had a plan. They would bring a lawsuit against those youngsters. If she didn't get them one way, she would get them in another.

She stood inside the den, working out in her mind the best possible use for the space. The home hospital bed she rented would make Alexia more comfortable. Before she left rehab, Geneva would meet with Deja one more time. A daring plan had been teasing the edges of her brain. She didn't have all the details worked out, and her biggest challenge was that she was a little afraid of herself for considering it.

# CHAPTER FORTY-FOUR

## DEJA

**N**IGEL WAS PLAYING stubborn. On top of that, he was acting as if she were a nuisance. Three times she'd texted him, and he hadn't responded. He didn't get the message that she was serious about him confessing his nasty deeds. She'd have settled for a personal apology, or something close to it, but he wanted to play hard ball. That's why she'd changed her strategy. Bad enough he'd stolen from her. Now he wanted to act as if he didn't know what she was talking about. The new Deja didn't want to play that game.

On her way to Tyler's place, she drove on automatic pilot as her mind wandered.

Working with Aunt Jenny had liberated her. A week ago, when she visited Alexia, the two of them had talked on their way out of the building. Aunt Jenny had said she could come back and see Alexia before she went home, and that day was today. She'd seemed different in that she hadn't said much but had touched Deja's shoulder and asked if she was all right.

Deja had been filled to the brim with resentment. Outside the building, she'd turned her face to the sun then focused on Aunt Jenny, who was watching her.

"You can tell me what's bothering you," she said. "I won't share what you say with anyone."

Aunt Jenny's brown eyes questioned her, and Deja felt her concern, but it was a moment before she could bring herself to say anything. "It's my uncle. We have some stuff from the past that I need to deal with, but he—"

Adjusting the strap on her bag, Aunt Jenny asked, "What kind of issues?"

Deja traced the line of cement on the pavement with her sneaker, sorry she'd opened her mouth. Now, she was uncomfortable. "Don't worry about it. I shouldn't have said anything."

"No, no." Aunt Jenny touched her shoulder again and studied her for a moment before asking, "Are you saying he abused you?"

Deja's eyes burned while her chest grew tight. She couldn't say a word if it would save her life, so she nodded.

"My goodness," Aunt Jenny gasped, then waited until a man in a suit passed them and entered the building. "Is that why you've been so interested in helping Alexia?"

While wiping her eyes with the sleeve of her sweater, Deja nodded. "It brought back everything that happened to me," she whispered.

Aunt Jenny's hand tightened on her shoulder. "I'm guessing you haven't done any therapy."

She shook her head and stared at her gray sneakers. "This is the first time I've told anyone."

"Oh, dear, I am so sorry. This isn't something that goes away by pushing it to the back of your mind."

And she was right. Since their talk, and Nigel's refusal to acknowledge her demands, all of it had bothered her. Then Christian had gone missing, which made things worse. She was in a better place now, but Aunt Jenny was right. She needed to deal with her issues. For now, she'd put them out of mind and take care of today's business.

She pulled up in front of Tyler's door and climbed out of the car, carrying her backpack in front of her like a security blanket. She'd been giving him space because she was still upset with him. From his one-word responses to her text, she figured he was still salty. They'd spoken a few times since their blowout. She didn't even know why she was here, except for the fact that she missed him. Tyler was her one constant in a world that sometimes didn't make sense. His opinion on what she was doing wouldn't have changed, but she'd been lonely without him. She also didn't realize how much she relied on him to help keep her sane. Outside of a few female friends, including Alexia, Danny, and her roommate, she'd never really fit in.

She hammered on the door and stepped back when Tyler yanked it open. His frown cleared when he recognized her. Leaning in the doorway, he raised one brow. "I don't suppose you're here to tell me you came to your senses."

"You know better than that," she grumbled on her way past him into the house.

She gazed around the living room that hadn't changed since the last time she was there. In a way though, it was as if she hadn't been there in many months.

"So, what have you been doing with yourself?" Tyler asked, sliding both hands into the pockets of his sweatpants.

"School's out, so I've been working." She'd gotten a new gig doing data entry, which suited her fine. It gave her time to be at her computer, monitoring the people she needed to be watching.

"I've been following what's happening with Skyers." Tyler stopped as if he expected her to fill in the blanks for him.

Instead of responding to his comment, she threw her backpack on the sofa and reached for the remote.

He grabbed it, which forced her to look at him. "Since I have to ask, what have you been doing about Alexia's business?"

"Why do you think I've been doing anything?" She shrugged. "Christian dug a hole he won't get out of so easily."

Arms folded across his chest, Tyler studied her.

She used the time to really look at him. He'd tightened his locs and his beard had grown. Deja was startled when he spoke.

"Okay, then, just tell me how you've been keeping busy since the last time you were here."

Deja cut her eyes at him. "You say that like I'm a five-year-old kid who can't stay out of trouble."

"Before you went to Jamaica, I'd say you were fairly predictable. Now? Not so much."

They both sat, and she filled him in on how she'd stayed occupied. When she stopped talking, he stared over her shoulder deep in thought. He finally focused on her. "I hope you won't be offended by what I'm going to say, but ..."

"Come on." She rolled her eyes. "We just started talking again."

"I'm not deliberately trying to upset you. Only stating the facts as I see them."

"Okay, let me hear what's on your mind."

"I don't know why Alexia's situation bothers you so much. It's like you've forgotten you have a life. From what I see, it's been swallowed up in hers."

She could have told him what she'd told Aunt Jenny about her history, but it didn't feel right.

"All I know is, I would want someone to help if that had happened to me."

"Would Alexia do the same for you?"

Without thinking twice about it, she nodded.

"Here's the thing." Tyler fingered one of his locs. "I get where you're coming from. I really do, but it also sounds like you're addicted to approval from Alexia's mom."

She shook her head, irritated with his amateur psychology. "You have it all wrong. She's always been kind to me, so there's a connection there. I keep thinking that I did the wrong thing in leaving without Alexia that night."

"That wasn't your fault," Tyler said. "You couldn't know what would happen."

"Don't you think I know that?" She stared at his T-shirt, then met his eyes. "Trust me, I wouldn't wish that on anyone."

"I understand all of that. Just don't go overboard on any of this stuff, and don't get swallowed up in that family's problems. Let the police do what they do." He linked their fingers and stroked the back of her hand with his thumb. "Promise?"

She gave him a bright smile. "Promise."

He poked her in the side. "Can't believe I actually missed your annoying ass."

"Boy, you know I'm special. Of course, you missed me."

They spent the next half-hour chatting, until Deja stretched and picked up her backpack. "I have to go now. Talk soon."

Tyler followed her to the front door and placed a soft kiss on her forehead. "Take care of yourself, DJ."

She hugged him, taking her time about it. How she'd gone so long without him, she didn't know. When she stepped back, she waved one finger back and forth. "Don't do anything I wouldn't do."

Tyler's lips shifted into a half smile. "I'd tell you the same thing if I thought you'd listen."

"I'll be fine," Deja said over her shoulder, feeling his eyes on her back as she approached the car. The moment she waved and pulled away from the sidewalk, Deja's smile faded. What she'd done wasn't exactly lying. She'd do this one favor for Aunt Jenny, settle up with her uncle, then her life would return to normal.

# CHAPTER FORTY-FIVE

## CHRISTIAN

**H**E WAS BACK home but didn't feel safe inside his father's house. Not after what had happened between them. Plus, his mind had gone bunny-rabbit crazy, hopping from one thought to another. It was impossible to settle on one thing for more than a few seconds at a time.

Why his father came and got him was a mystery. He'd been hauled before a judge again, but this time his father was at the hearing and had hired a lawyer. Despite that, he had sat in jail for nearly a week. He knew better than to try to contact Dad. At the same time, he couldn't think of anyone else. His mother wasn't an option. For all those years when he hadn't made the effort to speak with her more often, he felt he didn't have the right to call her again. Plus, after questioning him, the police had hinted she was in serious trouble for helping him leave the city. This afternoon, he was bailed out and fitted with an ankle bracelet.

He didn't get an explanation from Dad, but if he had to guess, he'd say the embarrassment made him do something to help. His father acted as if he couldn't bear to be anywhere near him. When Christian tried getting into the front of the BMW, he'd barked at him to get in the back seat. That's when the reality of his situation hit. Again. If he had anywhere else to go, he wouldn't have come back home.

The moment they arrived, he directed Christian to sit in the living room and poured himself a drink before he laid down the new house rules. Of course, Anoushka was nowhere in sight. He wondered what had happened to her but brushed that aside, along with the rape accusation that circled and landed in his head. She was like a cat; she'd touch down on all fours.

Dad took a swig of brandy, then slammed the glass on a side table and loosened his tie. "You're only back here because I don't want you roaming the streets and making my life even worse than you already have."

Christian knew better than to speak. He also didn't dare to move, no matter how he itched to explain what had happened with Anoushka, not to mention take a proper shower.

"Rule number one. Stay out of my way. The less I see of you, the better it will be for both of us."

His harsh tone made Christian wince, but he lowered his head and listened.

"Rule number two. My money isn't yours. Give me the credit card."

He stared at his father, who smirked. "You're man enough to stick it in my wife, you're man enough to handle your own finances."

"But—"

"Put the card on the table next to you." He continued after another sip. "Rule number three. Do not address me unless I give you permission."

Christian started tearing up, which took him by surprise. Dad had told him years ago that men didn't cry, so he blinked hard and pulled out his wallet while his father continued reeling off regulations.

"Rule four. If you leave this house and stray outside the confines of where that bracelet says you should be, you will stay in jail, because I won't show up to bail you out a second time." He took a deep swallow of his drink and replaced the glass on the table. "Five, if I find out you've had any interaction with *her*, you are out on your skinny, ungrateful ass."

He didn't chance any questions, but by the time Radcliff Skyers finished all his dos and don'ts, Christian had stopped listening. Only one thing gave him hope, and that was when his father said, "For the record, I know you didn't rape that bitch. That's the only reason I'm helping you. Otherwise, you'd be on your own."

If his father was serious, Christian wouldn't be allowed to do much aside from staying cooped up in his bedroom. Not that he had the energy to do anything else for the next day or so.

"Now get out of my sight."

He dragged himself toward the passage and his bedroom. The smashing of glass made him move faster, but when he opened the door, he couldn't believe what greeted him. The room was a total wreck. His father had gone batshit crazy and destroyed *everything*.

Christian closed the door behind him, made his way to the bed, and crashed on the edge of it.

He stared at his hand in the splint, which he figured was healing, then around the room. How was he supposed to put things back the way they'd been when his father had ripped up the whole place? The closet doors were flung open, and some of his clothes had been destroyed, cut to shreds as if Dad had turned into a human cyclone while trying to do as much damage as he could. The MVP trophies he'd earned lay broken on the floor, his books were scattered on the carpet, the pages ripped out, and his football jerseys stomped on and shredded.

When he finally got his feet to move, he piled his ruined possessions to the middle of the carpet and kept adding as he circled the room. Dog tired, he pulled the laptop out of his backpack and cleared a space on the desktop. He made sure the bit of masking tape still covered the camera before he hit the power button. After logging in, he sat staring at the screen. A pop-up pulled him from the slump he'd fallen into. He sat up and looked closer. A message in bold letters filled the small blue square. *You'll never outrun me. Your life would still be yours if you hadn't touched that girl. Say your prayers, Christian. Your life is over.*

# CHAPTER FORTY-SIX

## GENEVA

**O**FFICER HARRISON WAS the absolute limit. He smirked as if he knew something Geneva didn't, but she was way ahead of him.

"I'm simply frustrated, but don't think I'm blaming you." She crossed her legs and shook her head. "Forgive me if I don't understand why this department would allow Skyers to leave the city, knowing what he's accused of doing."

The policeman struggled not to sigh. "Mrs. Leighton, I assure you we're doing the best we can with the resources we have."

Her lips crimped into a sour expression she was well aware would irritate him. "Well, your best isn't good enough."

"Perhaps you can share with me how you knew where Skyers was hiding." He rested both elbows on the desk. "But then again, maybe you won't, because stalking, even if it's done electronically, is a crime."

"Why don't you ask the guys who brought him in how they found him?"

"When you glibly allowed them to think they located him under their own steam?" He pointed to his head. "I may not have the fastest CPU but my brain still works."

She shrugged and opened both hands. "All I did was point them in the right direction. Stay focused and you might actually close this case."

The pencil in his hand bent but didn't snap. He loosened his grip when her attention went to his fist. "A little respect would serve you better, Mrs. Leighton."

"And it would *serve you better* if you would stop harassing a parent who's grieving over her daughter's condition, not to mention under stress to make arrangements she shouldn't have to even think about." She set both feet flat on the floor. "And *maybe* lock up the people who are the source of my family's problems."

Officer Harrison cleared his throat but didn't speak. He laid the pencil parallel to the sheet of paper on the desk. "I'm going to overlook that because, as you said, you're under stress. Rest assured, you will hear something pertaining to the case by this evening."

"It's about time," she said, getting to her feet.

She was almost of the room when the policeman's voice stopped her. "You're clever, and you've covered your tracks well so far, but don't think I don't know you're behind the inexplicable things that have happened since you first turned up here to see me."

Some would have described Geneva as cocky, overbearing even, but the one thing she didn't intend to prove herself to be was stupid.

"I see you're determined to believe the worst of me." She adjusted the strap of her handbag on her shoulder. "Maybe when you finally clear up this case, you'll find I wasn't behind any of this. I guess we'll see."

On the way out of the building, she hid a smile. For all she knew, the entire place was wired with cameras. The end of her crusade might be in sight, but she had no reason to be sloppy.

She opened the glass door and stepped into the sunshine. The sun on her skin felt almost alien, as if she'd been housebound for many months. She'd been so caught up in making things right for Alexia that life had stopped. Aside from reading, and even that had been shelved, she couldn't remember the last time she'd done anything she enjoyed outside of work. These days, she served her clients as if driven. That was because her time was limited, and Alexia was her first priority.

The four of them celebrated birthdays close to the end of the year, and with the holidays approaching, she hoped they would be able to enjoy their time with each other the way they had in the past. Team Leighton, as Alexa liked to say. With any luck, she'd be home in time for Thanksgiving.

In her head, Geneva compiled a checklist of grocery items that were running low. On the elevator on her way to Alexia's floor, she prayed no negative energy lingered from her encounter with Harrison. A faint smile came to her lips. She didn't know if her prayers made sense anymore, but the habits of a lifetime were hard to change.

Deja and Alexia were laughing when Geneva arrived in the visitor's lounge.

"I was about to go back to the room when Deja came in." Alexia waved one hand over her leggings and T-shirt, which had perspiration marks around the neck. "I'll go do a little switch. You can keep each other company till I come back."

Pulling out a chair, Geneva said, "Take your time. We'll be okay."

She watched Alexia's progress, then turned her gaze on Deja. "How have you been?"

"I'm fine." Her attention strayed in the direction Alexia had gone. "And it's always good to see Alexia. Reminds me to be thankful."

Her words were like a stab in the gut.

Deja's smile faded. She realized she'd said the wrong thing. "I'm sorry, I didn't mean to—"

"I know you didn't mean any harm." Geneva forced a pleasant expression to her face and reminded herself that she didn't have all day with Deja, who leaned in with both elbows on the table. "Did you hear Christian is back home?"

"Yes. Now we wait for his case to come up for mention."

Deja stared across the room with her brows wrinkled.

"What's the problem?" Geneva asked.

"It just seems weird that he would run off, especially after what happened with his stepmother, and now be back at home as if nothing happened. "

"I was thinking the same thing."

Eyes gleaming, Deja asked, "Is there anything you want me to do?"

Geneva wrinkled her forehead, as if she hadn't been dying for Deja to ask that exact question. She stared at her hands, projecting the aura of a woman deep in thought. It wouldn't do to appear too eager. The one thing she could count on was that Deja would be willing to help her. Guilt was such a useful tool.

She laid a hand on Deja's arm. "There's something that would help."

"Anything, Aunt Jenny."

She made Deja wait, and bit her lip as though working out details in her mind. "I want to keep tabs on a certain young man. I want to set up something inside the building where he lives, but I need a diversion. Something that will prove a bit of an inconvenience. But it will also keep tabs on him in case he decides to run again. That's where you come in."

She laid out what she expected of Deja. Then, she asked, "Is that something you think you can do?"

Deja worried the hair at her nape, running her fingers back and forth. "It sounds a bit risky."

Before she could change her mind, Geneva squeezed her arm and whispered, "Yes, it is, but I'll disarm the security cameras when you're going in so no one will see you." She gave her time to think about it before she asked, "Do you trust me?"

"Of course, I do, Aunt Jenny." Her eyes were wide and earnest. "I'd trust you with my life."

Geneva chuckled. "That's a bit dramatic, don't you think? I wouldn't ask you to put your life in jeopardy."

"I know." She combed one hand through her cloud of hair then asked, "So, when do you want me to get it done?"

"You understand the sensitive nature of what we're doing, right?"

Deja nodded quickly. "That's not something I could talk about with anyone. They wouldn't understand."

"Exactly."

They chatted for a few more minutes until Alexia returned, carefully making her way to where they sat. She had changed into a pair of sweatpants and another T-shirt. As she lowered herself in the chair and leaned the cane against the edge of the table, a wave of bitterness swept through Geneva. Her seventeen-year-old daughter shouldn't be moving around with help from a walking stick.

While the two girls talked, Geneva ran through a mental list of everything that was good in her life. She had not forgotten the policeman's promise. With any luck, he'd make contact like he said. It would be easier on the rest of those hoodlums if the law dealt with them, rather than her treating them as they deserved.

"Did Alexa tell you she'll be moving back home soon?" Geneva asked as a way to switch the channel in her brain.

Deja's head swung in Alexia's direction, and she grinned. "That's great news."

"Yes." Alexia pumped her fists in a delicate, clumsy replica of what she'd have done months ago.

No matter. Geneva was about to remind her not to wait until the last minute to pack her things when Spence called.

"Give me a sec." She walked away from the girls and faced the window. "Hey, babe. What's good?"

"I just landed. How's my baby?"

Glancing over her shoulder, she asked, "The cub, or the lioness?"

"Both." He chuckled, then added, "Make sure the lioness comes out to play tonight."

That had become an inside joke for them. It reminded Geneva of years gone by when Alexia used to hog Spence's attention after he returned from one of his trips. She used to remind him that she, and not Geneva, was his baby girl.

"Whatever you say. I'll see you at home."

"Not so fast," he said, "Let me talk to my baby girl."

"Sure, wait a minute."

In the middle of handing the phone to Alexia, the police department's telephone number flashed on the screen.

# CHAPTER FORTY-SEVEN

## GENEVA

**D**EJA UNDERSTOOD THE assignment, and that was important. Three weeks had gone by since they spoke, but Geneva wasn't worried. Deja had already followed through on what she promised to do at the exact time they agreed on weeks ago. In a short while, Christian would be simply a bad memory for their family.

The only other blip on her radar was the news that Radcliff Skyers had filed for divorce. Anoushka's prenup agreement had left her with nothing, and Radcliff was making noises about taking legal action for the false statement to the police about Christian raping her. That was spite, pure and simple. Geneva understood that well.

Geneva swung her legs onto the sofa and laid her feet in Spence's lap.

He massaged her feet, while she relaxed and closed her eyes. "You have such good hands," she murmured.

He growled, then wriggled his eyebrows. "The better to feel you with, my dear."

Alexia looked at Jaden, and they burst out laughing.

"The two of you never cease to amaze me with your gross behavior," she said.

"Then maybe we should excuse ourselves from your company," Geneva quipped while batting her eyelashes at Spence.

"TMI!" Jaden looked at the ceiling, then shook his head as if they were beyond help.

No matter what Geneva did, her smile wouldn't go away. Alexia had been home for a week and was slowly returning to the rhythm of life inside Leightonville, as she called their home.

The therapist had visited three times already. Aside from the nerve damage she'd always have in one arm, Alexia was adapting well.

Spence's cousins and their families had come for dinner and, as much as it irked Geneva, Alexia had insisted that Deja come over in the early afternoon. She hadn't spent more than an hour because she planned to be at her mother's house for their family gathering.

She'd been bubbly to the point of being annoying, and Geneva wondered if she was in her right mind. Being excited was one thing. Her manic energy was another. That wasn't good, considering what Geneva had asked her to get done.

She'd watched the two of them on the back patio, wondering why Deja or another of the other girls on the property that night hadn't been the one the group turned on in a moment of anger. Before her mood was shot to hell, Geneva switched off those reflections.

Alexia had written out everything that happened at the party in her journal, and Geneva had respected her wishes not to share what she had transcribed. She had that right, so Geneva didn't push. She contained her curiosity by reading what Alexia had posted to the blog and what she felt led to share during their conversations.

"Seriously though." Alexia looked at all of them before continuing, "I'm glad I didn't have to spend Thanksgiving in the rehab center. I was so ready to come home."

"Oh, baby." Geneva's heart ached for all the time Alexia had lost. "We all wanted you at home, but if you'd been in there for Thanksgiving, we would have been there with you."

"I know, but it's so much better being here."

Their voices faded while Geneva sank inside her head, itemizing each piece of the new mind map she'd laid out during the last couple of weeks and making sure each fit seamlessly.

While they laughed and talked, she wondered how Christian had taken her warning. She'd have been terrified to receive a message like that, but wouldn't waste sympathy on him. He deserved everything that was coming to him.

He'd blacked out the webcam on his laptop, as if that would make him safe. With his computer connected to their home system, Geneva had more access to their household than she needed. She knew when Radcliff Skyers came and went and what he did when he was home. On top of that, she understood everything about their home security system. She'd been messing with the electrical system over the last couple of weeks—a power surge here, a brownout there—laying the groundwork for anything "accidental" that might happen.

This holiday, Christian was alone at home. Skyers had gone on a weekend jaunt somewhere to play golf. This was part of the reason some kids were so misguided. How did you leave your son alone on a holiday that was meant to be celebrated with family? But Christian had sealed his fate when he'd given in to the lust of the latest Mrs. Skyers.

"What about some ice cream?" Alexia said, looking up from the book she was reading.

"It's like you have a bottomless pit where your stomach used to be," Jaden teased, glancing away from the television.

She poked him in the side. "The food is much better in this joint."

J.L. CAMPBELL

"You want me to get you some?" Geneva asked.

"I'll do it." Spence gently moved Geneva's feet out of the way. "I need some water anyway."

"Thanks, love."

She picked up her phone from her lap and glanced at the wall clock. It was time. She brought the screen to life, opened the program she wanted, then located Christian inside his house. Like most people, his schedule was like clockwork, except that now he didn't eat as regularly as before the bottom dropped out of his world.

In any case, dinner was a certainty to within fifteen minutes either way. She didn't have to do anything more than watch. Her work didn't need any further input or interference. The helper had prepared food for the family the previous day. All Christian had to do was help himself. As his final moments were relayed on the screen, the terror, then despair, reflected in his eyes didn't make her happy. She'd have been worried about her mental state if it did. The cameras went static, and she had no choice but to stop watching.

*Last man down.*

Officer Harrison had confirmed weeks ago in a telephone call, that Nisha, Robyn, and Kara had been arrested for their part in the assault. It would take a bit more time before their cases came to trial. Patience had never been Geneva's strong suit, but she was prepared to let the justice system work on Alexia's behalf this time. They needed to face her in court and see how they changed the course of her life in a drunken and drug-induced haze. If she was disappointed with the outcome, Geneva knew she'd find a way to get even. By now, she'd become something of an expert.

Spence returned from the kitchen carrying a tray, which returned her to the present.

"I didn't ask for ice cream," she said.

"We had a piece of carrot cake left over from dinner, and since you like it with rum and raisin ice cream ..."

He stopped where Jaden and Alexis sat together. "Pistachio for you two."

After handing her the bowl, Spence settled at the other end of the sofa and placed the tray with the loaded saucer on the cushion between them.

Alexia and Jaden wrinkled their noses and made sounds of disgust while Geneva crumbled carrot cake on top of the ice cream.

A half-hour later, when they finished, she washed the dishes and leaned against the arched entryway from the kitchen watching the people at the center of her universe.

Her heart was so full, it made her chest tight and clogged her throat. Having the entire family in the same room on this special holiday meant more than she could put into words.

Spence looked away from the television into her eyes. The admiration and affection in his gaze was undeniable. Sometimes, his reasoning drove her mad but he was a solid man. Their hurdles hadn't all been crossed, but for now she was content to enjoy this day with him.

Jaden and Alexia were teasing each other, as always. In times gone by when they were much younger, he'd have Alexia in a playful headlock. Now, he was forced to be gentle with her at all times.

"What about a game of Monopoly?" Geneva asked, walking into the room.

"Sounds like a plan." Jaden pulled out the drawer on the bottom of the center table and fished out the game. "Let's go."

"Hold on a minute." Spence raised one hand to quiet them, still staring at the television.

"What?" Geneva and Jaden asked at the same time.

"Shhh." Spence frowned, then covered his mouth with one hand. "Good God."

With her heart beating out of time, Geneva perched next to him and rested one hand on his back. She grabbed the remote and turned up the sound to hear the reporter better.

The slender blonde spoke into a microphone that carried a local station's logo. "It appears that the owner of the house, Radcliff Skyers, was out of town when this disaster happened. The police have not yet confirmed the identity of the person who was inside at the time of the explosion."

# CHAPTER FORTY-EIGHT

## DEJA

TYLER'S JUDGMENTAL TONE was getting on her nerves, but Deja didn't react.

"Did you really have to ruin the man's life right now, during the holidays?"

She stared through the window, but didn't see anything other than a blur of trees and buildings as the sun set. "He didn't give a damn when he ruined mine."

"But you didn't have to do it today." Tyler's voice was strained when he said, "The holiday's never going to be the same for anyone who was there this evening."

"*Good*. Because I'm sure as hell not the same." She barely kept her voice steady because an avalanche of tears was ready to fall. "He robbed me of my life."

She felt the sideways glance he threw her way before easing the car to a stop next to the sidewalk. Tyler didn't speak at the same time, and she understood he was figuring out what to say.

"Why didn't you tell me when I asked what was wrong?" he said.

She sniffled, then sat up. "What he did to me is not something I could talk about in casual conversation."

With his head against the seat, he asked, "Deja, do you trust me?"

With a sigh, she said, "You know I do."

He spread both hands, then let them fall on his thighs. "If you did, surely you could have told me what brought on all of this. And only God knows what you've done, because I'm sure you haven't told me everything."

As several cars swept by, she explained, "You wouldn't have understood."

He rolled his head toward her. "Look, I know you're a private person, plus it's not easy to rehash stuff from your past."

Her phone rang, but she didn't move to answer it. Instead, she fingered the choker at her neck and sighed. "What I said back there is only half of what my uncle took from me. He stole my childhood, my sense of safety, my ability to trust. My sense of self."

"Tell me exactly why you had to expose him in the middle of a family gathering."

"I've been trying to talk to him, but he hasn't been listening." Another sigh escaped as she drummed on both legs with her fingers. After analyzing her reasons, she looked Tyler in the face. "It was time."

He tentatively laid one hand on top of hers and squeezed it. Then he pulled in a sharp breath and released it though his mouth. "Is he the reason for these things you've done in the past few months?"

Deja angled her head away from him as a tear rolled down her cheek. "Partly."

"The memories of what he did to you triggered something, and you—"

"Alexia didn't get to say no. Christian and Sancia took that choice from her." She brought her breathing under control, before she whispered, "My uncle didn't give me any options either."

She couldn't even say his name, and calling him uncle somehow always made things worse. That someone who should have protected her chose to abuse her still hurt her soul. He knew better. She saw it in his eyes every time he raped her. But knowing his actions were wrong hadn't stopped him.

"Let's go to my place," Tyler said, gripping the wheel. "Are you okay with that?"

She nodded, unable to speak. Talking about something she'd kept under wraps for years had brought physical pain. She was burning up inside and her chest was raw, the way it would be if someone had used a clawhammer on her.

At first, they hadn't believed her, until she mentioned the scars on his belly and inside his thigh. "Ask him how he came by those," she'd yelled.

His wife, Marina had rushed across the room to claw at Nigel's face and punch him in the chest.

That's when Deja knew the tide had shifted. The paralyzed faces and horrified expressions of her mother, aunts, cousins, and Nigel's wife now haunted her. But she wasn't the one who should feel guilty. He'd been lying and pretending to be something he wasn't all this time. For all she knew, he'd also had his way with her cousins. Maybe even his own daughter.

Marina had covered her mouth with both hands as her gaze shot to her ten-year-old daughter. Deja was certain Marina knew or suspected him of something. The knowledge was in her eyes.

In her peripheral vision, she caught Tyler's slight shake of the head.

"You don't think I have a good enough reason to put him on blast?"

This time, he responded without looking her way. "I didn't say that."

"Your attitude is telling me something different."

He gripped the steering wheel tight with both hands, and she waited for whatever rubbish he might spew. Christian was facing consequences for raping Alexia. Her uncle needed to pay, too.

"Look, you've been fighting enough. I'm not about to do that with you." Tyler glanced at her, then back to the street. "I'm just worried about you. Who d'you have in your corner now that you've alienated everybody?"

Despite how lost she felt, Deja pulled on his sleeve. "I've got you."

The adrenaline she'd been running on had petered out. In no way did she regret the things she'd done to right what she saw as wrongs but had to admit it would take her family time to recover from the tsunami that just hit them.

Tyler's face was in shadow when he chuckled. "You've got your little boy-toy where you want him, right?"

"Considering you're older than I am, that term isn't gonna fly, and that's not how I think about you."

"Seriously though, DJ, all of this has to stop somewhere. One day, your luck is going to run out."

She sniffed and gave him a side-eye. "None of this was for the fun of it."

"Don't you think I know that? What I'm saying is that you've taken this avenger thing to a level that disturbs me, and it leaves you at risk of getting hurt. The next time you run off and decide to do something crazy on your own, it might not turn out the way you wish."

"I just have one more thing to wrap up and then I'll be done."

"That's what you said the last time we talked about this."

That was true, but she still wasn't finished. When she knew for sure Nigel would be punished, she could get on track, back to where she'd been before spring break. For a long time, she hadn't been in a good place. Now that her secrets were exposed, all she'd gained was a small sense of relief and the overwhelming knowledge that she'd complicated a lot of lives.

"You're right, T, but I kept my promise not to involve you in any of the things I've done lately."

"That doesn't mean I haven't been keeping track of what I think you had a hand in doing." He laughed. "Remind me never to piss you off."

Laughing, she tugged one of his locs. "Well, since you already know—"

"Oh, shit!" Tyler's arm slammed across her chest, and the Accord swerved onto the sidewalk.

She raised one hand to block the zig-zagging headlights and police strobe lights rushing toward them. The impact of metal grinding together was the last thing she heard before her forehead hit the windshield.

# CHAPTER FORTY-NINE

## GENEVA

**O**FFICER HARRISON PACED the interrogation room, almost sniffing the air like a bloodhound. "You were in contact with her several times, which is why I'm asking you these questions."

The "she" in question was Deja.

He ran one hand over his scalp and plowed through the brown tuft at the back of his head, before turning steely eyes on her. "And you have no idea if she ever visited the victim before his death?"

"Officer Harrison, with all due respect, where is this leading? Yes, Deja is one of Alexia's friends and we've known her for years. But I'm not responsible for Deja Johnson's movements, or her actions."

Milford dipped his head in agreement. So far, she hadn't given him reason to demand that she close her mouth.

"She was spotted outside the Skyers property. That's why I'm asking."

"By the neighbors?" Geneva asked, arching one brow as if she didn't know exactly what happened.

"That isn't important." He leaned his weight on the table and stared her in the face. "What is important is the fact that the two of them were in Jamaica on that same trip with your daughter."

"And?" Geneva didn't look away. If he thought he could intimidate her with theatrics, he didn't know who he was dealing with.

"Maybe she had something against him because of what happened to her friend." He stood straight and folded both arms. "And *maybe*, she decided to do something about it."

"I still don't see what this has to do with me."

Milford's thick eyebrows pulled together as he centered his leather portfolio in front of him, while listening to her. "Surely, you have something more substantial than that."

A nasty smile crept over the policeman's face. "She's a young woman who would perhaps listen to someone she respects who might convince her to…oh, you know, do something she might get away with."

"I'm all for the police catching criminals, but when you take me away from my business to ask these kinds of questions, which in turn means I have less time to spend with my daughter, I'm afraid I have to draw the line."

She looked at her watch and shifted in the chair. "I have a meeting at one, and you've had me here now for the better part of three hours. If I'm to make that meeting, I need to be out of here now."

She waited a couple of beats, then added, "And by the way, I was helpful enough to let you *borrow* my computer and my phone. I'd like to have them back before I leave."

"While we have you here, we've been following some leads." His thin lips lifted in a half smile. "You'd better make a call now to cancel that meeting you have scheduled."

"What am I supposed to make that call with?"

His focus shifted to Milford and back to her.

At that point, Geneva sighed.

"Are you arresting me?" Not even by the blink of an eye did she reveal her turmoil, despite the way her pulse raced as if her heart would give out at any moment.

"No, ma'am. I'm simply detaining you for now."

Milford protested, but Geneva didn't hear anything he said. She was too busy trying to calm her galloping heart before she had a stroke. Then the analytical side of her brain went to work. *If he had any evidence, I'd be in a cell. He's just working my nerves. Relax, Geneva.*

She had been relatively certain the police would come looking for her after Christian's unfortunate accident, and had prepared herself. In fact, she'd been sure this day was on the horizon because of the interest Officer Harrison had taken in her from the beginning.

His partner, Cruz, watched her as if not wanting to miss even a micro expression that crossed her face. She had one horse in this race and never intended to lose from the moment she decided to gamble.

Deja's confession outside the hospital confirmed what Geneva had suspected for some time—sexual abuse somewhere in her history. Her interest in Alexia's welfare had been brought on by a combination of guilt and that something else, which had suited Geneva's purpose. Deja was the perfect candidate to insert into a war she'd been only too happy to fight.

The police could clone her computer. Copy her passwords. Scan her emails. They'd not find one incriminating shred of information.

Harrison had pulled her in again because he was at a dead end or wanted to toy with her, thinking she'd make a mistake and give away some valuable snippet that would help close Sancia, Phil, and Christian's cases.

Since the car accident a week ago, Deja was still unconscious, but the police wanted to speak with her. Desperately, if Geneva understood the situation correctly.

She hated to think about what Spence would say when he heard she was back on the police's radar. He wasn't stupid, and the first conclusion he'd come to was that she was a person of interest for a good reason. Hopping mad was the only term that fit when Harrison had called Spence in to question him about beating up Christian. They had been inside the station for hours while Harrison tried to spin the few facts he had into an accusation that Spence had some part in Christian's death.

If she was lucky, this latest trip downtown wouldn't end in an argument. She was mentally tired and yet exhilarated at the same time. Although it didn't make the quality of her life any better, she'd accomplished what she set out to do. Alexia wouldn't ever have to cross paths again with those who'd done her the most harm.

Based on what Geneva knew of rape cases, the victims relived their trauma in the courtroom in the worst way. Skyers's lawyer would put Alexia on trial and make her feel guilty for a crime she hadn't committed. Women who were victims of assault shouldn't have to fear being persecuted because of their personality, the things they'd done, or what they chose to wear. She didn't want that for Alexia. This way, none of her attackers would get away with their evil, and Alexia wouldn't end up with bitterness in her soul. Her daughter didn't need that on top of everything else.

"I'm afraid we won't be able to let you have the laptop back today," Harrison said, pinning her with his gaze while circling the room. "And frankly, you won't need it if you end up in jail. We may be able to let you have the phone."

The man could barely keep himself from smirking, which set her teeth on edge, but she let her jaw hang loose. Ten seconds later, she released her breath in a soft exhale. "That laptop is what I use to conduct my business."

"I'm perfectly aware of that, Mrs. Leighton."

"Then you also know I have sensitive information that pertains to businesses nationwide."

"We're doing everything we can not to inconvenience you."

*Right.*

He glanced at his partner, then slipped both hands into his pockets. "We'll ask you to collect it in the morning, *if* you're allowed to go home this evening."

She exchanged a glance with Milford, who tipped his head to indicate that if she was all right with leaving the laptop, he wouldn't raise any objections.

She sat back from the table. "Very well, but if you damage it in any way or destroy any of my information, I will come after you."

"Like you went after those kids?" His cold eyes watched her every reaction.

She sighed, then said, "Milford, perhaps you should remind Officer Harrison that accusing someone without any evidence is slander."

"She's correct." Milford dipped his head and stroked his salt-and-pepper goatee. "If you are going to charge my client with something, please tell us what it is, otherwise ..."

Without a word, both officers left the room.

While they were gone, Geneva called her client from Milford's phone and rescheduled their meeting.

The minutes ticked by in strained silence, and when Milford attempted to speak, she stopped him with a strong grip on his arm. "They're so desperate to pin something on me, I'm not prepared to talk about anything pertaining to this fiasco while we're inside this building."

"Fine. But I'm not sure how much longer I can stay with you."

She gave him a quelling look. "I meant what I told you about my willingness to pay for your services."

Another forty five minutes crawled by before both men returned. Her nerves were on edge and she wanted to prowl the room and think, but she forced herself to sit still when they appeared.

Harrison laid her phone on the table. "You may have this."

"Are we finished?" she asked, picking up the cellular.

"For now." The officer slipped his thumbs into his belt loops and trailed them to the door with sharp eyes.

"Mrs. Leighton, one moment please."

She faced him, and he approached and stopped a foot away.

"You may think you've won the battle, but don't get too comfortable, because I'm sure Miss Johnson will wake up. When she does, you'll be hearing from me again. This time with a warrant."

"For what?" She looked at the toes of her tan pumps before responding further. "You know, this conversation is getting tiresome. I feel we've had it several times already with the same result."

"You won't be so smug if I have to serve you with a warrant."

"Do what you have to. Meantime, I'll be about the business that pays me and taking care of my daughter." Pulling her head back, she snapped, "I just wish you were as preoccupied with keeping criminals where they belong as you are with making my life miserable."

His nostrils flared, but he didn't respond.

"Have a good afternoon," she said in a dismissive tone. "I'll see you tomorrow."

She walked side by side with Milford, and when they arrived at the front office, he touched her arm to prevent her from going through the door. "Maybe it would be best if I collected that laptop for you tomorrow."

"Why would I put you out of your way?" Geneva smiled faintly. "Your service is far from cheap, as you reminded me."

"I'm doing this for you as a friend and not as your lawyer." His stare was intense when he continued, "I'd feel more comfortable if you let me handle things if we have any further meetings with the police, or if this escalates. You don't want to aggravate them."

She nodded and this time her smile was brighter. "Thanks for the offer, but I'll be fine. I promise not to poke the bear."

Milford chuckled, and his eyes twinkled. "One thing about you, Geneva—no one can accuse you of not taking care of your affairs, no matter how difficult."

"I'm a tough cookie. You know that by now."

They said their goodbyes, and when she sat inside the RAV-4, Geneva took a moment to relax. Jaden was at home with Alexia, and Spence was flying back from Trinidad and Tobago this evening.

She was trying to avoid the things he'd accused her of in the past. Now that she was able to, she sent him a message letting him know where she'd been.

His response came a moment later. *Glad you're cooperating, see you when I land.*

<hr />

That same evening, after they ate dinner and lay watching television in their bedroom, Spence threw an arm over her shoulder and asked, "D'you think that girl really did the things they're accusing her of doing? Like Lexi said, I can't believe she'd take what happened to her so personally."

Geneva shrugged and played with his fingers. "Who knows? Trauma has a way of showing up when we least expect it, especially if it hasn't been dealt with properly. She told me she'd been sexually assaulted by her uncle. Never had therapy. Never told anyone. Not even family. I guess Alexia's experience brought it back."

"I'd hate to think—"

Geneva laid one finger over his lips. "I've had enough of everybody else's business for one day. Tell me something good, and make sure it's real good."

Spence grinned, then whispered, "I love you more and more each day."

Cupping his chin, she asked, "And why is that?"

"You've been a trooper through this whole...life-changing journey. You've managed our home and everything else; and I appreciate you so much more than I can ever say. Or repay, for that matter."

"That's wonderful to know."

Looking at her sideways, he said, "There's one thing I do want to know."

"What's that, love?"

"How come you've never used technology to track anything I do?"

The question surprised her, but she only smiled. "How do you know that I don't?"

Spence remained quiet for several minutes, then brushed the side of her arm with his fingers. "We both know you don't."

She thought about that for a while, but didn't comment. No need to say more and raise any doubts. While staring across the room, she had an epiphany. As terrible as the result of it had been, Alexia's disastrous trip had drawn their family closer.

Aside from Camille, Deja's aunt, Geneva hadn't been in touch with any of the few friends she kept. All of them had experienced relationship or marital issues over the years, which kept them focused on their personal business and led to silence at times. They had agreed ages ago that men didn't understand the value of what they had at home until they were in danger of losing it.

She'd found out about Spence's indiscretions by being in the wrong place at the wrong time when his phone rang. Or perhaps she's been in the right place to figure out what was going on. No matter how far Geneva's behavior deteriorated into spitefulness, Spence had never viewed divorce as an option. But more than anything else, Alexia's condition had contributed to bringing them back together.

That was the only positive she could pinpoint from that harrowing experience, and come what may, she couldn't see herself without him. She also didn't want to think about what life would have looked like if Alexia hadn't survived. That eventuality might have shattered what was left of their relationship.

Gently, she pinched his arm. "You know what?"

"No, but I'm sure you're going to tell me."

"I love you, too." With her eyes fixed on the television screen she added, "I want you to promise me one thing."

"Anything for you, Geneva, you know that."

"If anything happens to me, and I'm not around to explain myself, please tell Alexia that whatever I did was to protect her."

The color drained from Spence's face and left his skin pasty. His eyes widened as he searched hers.

She'd said too much in a moment of weakness. With a soft chuckle, she teased, "I was only joking."

The tension left his body after several minutes. His perplexed frown was evidence of his struggle not to continue that line of conversation. The only thing he said was, "You could let Dad know you're sorry for manhandling and exposing him the way you did."

Her eyebrows rose, and she angled her head to see him better. "Really? At least the bad publicity blew over because they did the right thing by sending what they had to the police here. I can't even begin to imagine what he was thinking."

"He told you, Jen."

"Yeah, and I should have followed up to see what the media would have thought of that tourism official who had the bright idea to suppress the story."

Spence tried to sit upright, but she pulled him back down. Snuggling into his side, she poked him with one elbow. "Don't have a heart attack. I wouldn't do anything you wouldn't, if it meant protecting our children."

"Sometimes, I truly wonder about you." Peering at her as if he expected a bizarre confession, Spence stroked his jaw. "Not to mention the things you don't tell me."

# CHAPTER FIFTY

## DEJA

**S**HE GROANED AND opened her eyes, but everything was a blur. A heavy drumbeat in her forehead made it impossible to think. Her hand snagged on the way to her face, and she couldn't free it after trying several times.

Someone called her name, and she managed to pry her eyelids apart. This time, the low ceiling and fluorescent lights came into focus. She scanned the room, trying to find the source of the sound.

"Who is it?" Her voice sounded rusty to her ears. "Where am I?"

Deja searched her brain, wondering what had happened, because she had no memory of this place. She squinted while trying to jog her memory. She remembered being in the car with Tyler. Then the blue lights racing toward her. Bashing her head on the glass. After that, it was lights out until now.

She repeated her question, but this time the squeak of rubber-soled shoes hinted at someone coming closer. A woman she identified as a nurse stood over her, smiling. "I'm Nurse Walcott. You're finally awake."

"How long have I been here?" Her throat was dry, like she'd been hiking through a desert for days without water.

"A week." The nurse hurried back to the door. "I need to get a doctor in here, but can you tell me your name?"

"It's Deja. Deja Johnson."

"Good. Be right back." The petite woman disappeared, then returned after a short while.

Deja searched her memory and moved her hand again, but it wouldn't cooperate. A silver bracelet held her to the railing of the bed.

The moment the nurse reappeared, Deja raised her left hand. "What does this mean?"

"We'll explain later," she said. "Right now, we need to do a full examination. The doctor will be along in a couple of minutes. Here, have a sip of water."

Deja swallowed as instructed, then wet her lips. "Before you came in, someone called my name. Who was it?"

"That would be your friend." Nurse Walcott smiled, showing a row of braces. "He's checked on you every day since you've been here."

The lights hurt Deja's eyes, making her squint. "Which friend?"

"It's me, Deja."

Tyler stood in the doorway as if he didn't know whether to step inside.

She raised her head, but the room spun. Eyes closed, she rested against the pillow and rolled her head toward him. "What's the matter?"

The worry in Tyler's eyes bothered her. He had bad news written all over him. But wait, it was connected to her. He looked back at her hand. She did, too, and opened her mouth to ask him a question, but he shook his head. She took it to mean that she was to wait until they were alone.

The nurse looked at her chart, then left the room. "I'll just be a moment. Tyler, you'll have to leave when I come back."

"What's happening, Tyler?" Deja rattled the handcuff. "And what is this about?"

He glanced behind him and moved in closer. "I'm glad you woke up, but I think you're in serious trouble."

"For what?" She shot another glance at the handcuff, and her heart tripped harder. She hated the pleading note in her voice, but couldn't help it. "Please tell me what's going on."

"The police think—"

A uniformed officer stepped inside, but the doctor who entered behind him shooed the police outside. "As soon as I clear the patient, you may ask your questions."

When she was alone with the doctor and nurse, Deja wanted to slap away their hands but she understood they were only doing their job.

She nibbled her nail while the tall, East-Indian doctor spoke with the friendly nurse. When they stood by the side of the bed, the doctor said she'd be fine, but didn't know when she could leave the hospital. They would confirm that in another day or so.

"Can I see my friend, please?"

"That will be after you talk to the police. They've been waiting to speak with you all week."

The same officer appeared, as if he'd been standing on the other side of the door. With him was a tall man with thin brown hair. The nurse stood against the wall, watching them.

"Deja Johnson?" the policeman asked.

When she nodded, he said, "I'm Officer Harrison with the Coral Gables Police Department, and I'd like to ask you a few questions."

"I just woke up." When the words left her mouth, she realized how stupid they sounded, but it was all she had.

His thin lips curved into a fake smile. "I understand that, but you have critical information that we need."

"I guess it was important since I'm chained to this bed." Her fingers went to the bandage on her forehead. "What's the reason for that?"

"As I said," he smiled again, acting friendly. "We need to find out a few things."

She winced as a stabbing pain attacked her forehead. "I'm not going anywhere."

The smile dropped from his face. "Are you acquainted with Christian Skyers?"

"Yes, we attend to the same university."

"Outside of that, what is your relationship to him?"

Deja paid closer attention. She didn't like how this man was looking at her. Any minute now, he'd accuse her of something. "We're not friends, if that's what you're asking."

"Are you aware of what happened to Mr. Skyers?"

Her scalp tingled, and her gaze darted between the two men. "N-no." She suddenly wanted to throw up. "Is he okay?"

"I'm afraid he isn't." Officer Harrison didn't look away from her as he spoke. "One week ago, on Thanksgiving Day to be exact, Mr. Skyers was killed."

A heavy weight settled across the back of her neck. She massaged it with her free hand and let out a nervous chuckle. "You're kidding, right?"

He scowled as he tapped the screen of a smart phone he pulled from his pocket.

"Miss Johnson, we're the police, so this is not a joking matter."

"But—"

He went ballistic from that point, shooting questions at Deja until her head felt as though it was stuffed with cotton candy.

Finally, the nurse stopped him. "That's enough."

When he insisted he only had a few more questions, she reminded him that it wouldn't do him any good if Deja was not in a condition to give rational answers. Glancing her way, the nurse said, "If you continue, it will be at risk to her health. Come back tomorrow." Deja assumed she smiled to take the edge off her order as she continued, "Since you have an officer outside the door, I'm sure she won't be going anywhere."

Deja's stomach shriveled. This was bad.

The nurse cleared the room, then came back and re-checked the equipment next to her.

"Is my friend still here?" Deja whispered.

"Yes, he's down the hall. I'll get him for you."

"Thank you." She swallowed the knot in her throat and blinked to clear the tears that flooded her eyes.

Tyler walked in and pulled up a chair next to the bed. "This may sound like a stupid question, but how do you feel?"

"Shocked. Confused. Wondering what the hell is going on. What's up, Tyler?"

He gave her a quick rundown of what had happened since the accident, avoiding her gaze.

Grabbing his hand, she said, "Tell me the truth. What do you think about this whole mess?"

He made a weird sound, but still didn't look directly at her. Then, he sat up and stared past her head. Tyler's eyes were full. Wait. Was he about to cry?

"It looks bad." His voice cracked, but he continued, "I hope the things they're accusing you of aren't true."

"Like what?"

"First of all—"

The door opened and the nurse appeared again. "I'm sorry, visiting time is over for today."

"But it can't be," Deja protested.

"I'm sorry, it is. He can return in the morning." Nurse Walcott softened her words with a smile. "He sat at your side when you were under. Now that you're awake, I'm sure he'll be back."

Tyler kissed her cheek, and she wanted to hug him badly but didn't. He'd be back tomorrow. Things had to get better by then.

He walked out, looking the same as he always had—jacket, jeans, and kicks. But his shoulders were slumped, and his defeated air made her want to cry, but it wouldn't help. She had unfinished business she needed to settle.

"Where's my phone?"

The nurse retrieved it from the drawer of the table next to her. Of course, it was deader than dead. "Do you have a charger I could use?"

She shook her head. "I'll see if I can borrow one."

Some minutes later, she came back with one that fit and plugged the phone into it.

While it got some juice, Deja's mind somersaulted from one thing to another. Did her family know she was here?

She put that aside, since it was the least of her issues. Tyler would have told Curtis. But if he had, why hadn't any of them been there when she woke? Maybe they were busy and someone would come in the morning.

And what about that business with Christian? The policeman had hinted at what she was supposed to have done, but the thought of it was impossible. Wasn't it?

Every time she was certain she might be in the middle of a nightmare, the metal bracelet jangled against the side of the bed and brought reality rushing back. Right now, she didn't regret anything she'd done. She hadn't murdered anyone, and Christian's death probably had nothing to do with her.

When the phone had enough charge for her to make a call, she dialed her mother, who picked up after the third ring.

"Deja?" Her voice was cold and questioning at the same time.

"Mom?"

The awkward silence filled her heart with dread. Then her mother said, "I don't know what you were thinking. Do you know how much grief you've caused this family? Not to mention the disgrace?"

"What are you talking about?" She moved her head side to side. She'd been unconscious for a week, and Hyacinth hadn't expressed one shred of concern for her. Had she even been to see her? Deja didn't ask because she couldn't bear to know the answer. "Don't you care that your brother raped me? Doesn't that matter?"

"Yuh never hear about not washing yuh dirty linen in public?" Her mother's use of patois told Deja how upset she was.

"What public?" She said, grinding her teeth. "Everyone there was family."

"The point is, it happened so many years ago. What purpose did it serve to bring it up now?"

For a second or so, Deja had no words. Her mother had slammed her in the chest with a demolition ball. "I can't believe you don't understand why I had to tell."

"As your grandmother used to say, what gone bad a morning can't come good a evening."

She couldn't believe what she was hearing. Hyacinth thought that since the assault was in the past, it couldn't be fixed, so Deja should have let it stay buried.

Her mother's insensitive comment was like a lightning bolt to the heart. Deja wanted to yank out the needle that fed clear liquid into the vein on the back of her hand, but she'd only be hurting herself. Her eyes filled as she said, "I get it. I never mattered with you. Even now, I still don't."

"All I'm saying is that it wasn't necessary. Because of what you did, Nigel took his own life. Does it make you feel good to know his daughter is without a father, and Marina is devastated after losing her husband?"

Deja noticed her mother didn't deny the accusation. Her voice was dull when she said, "I never told him to kill himself."

"You took that decision from him when you posted his business on the internet."

"I gave him the choice of doing it himself. He refused to confess and threatened me." She sucked in a breath that pained her soul. "The world is a better place without him."

"You're a fine one to talk after what the police said you did to that boy," Hyacinth yelled. "I don't know what happened to you, Deja, but you need help."

The tears Deja couldn't hold back rained down her cheeks. She didn't bother to tell her mother goodbye before jabbing the end call button. What was the point? She'd always been on the outskirts of her mother's life, and here it was again, proof that she meant less than nothing. A big, fat zero.

She reattached the phone to the charger then switched on the television. The news was on, and she was about to switch the channel when a familiar house filled the screen. A small figure in a hoodie identical to one she owned appeared around the side of the building and approached the electrical panel box.

As her heart missed several beats, Deja fumbled to turn up the sound. The news anchor's chirpy voice completed the unfolding story.

"...the station received this footage from an anonymous source. Apparently, the explosion that rocked the Skyers home a week ago was not accidental. Christian Skyers, who was accused of rape, died inside the house. At present, Deja Johnson, who was in a vehicular accident on Thanksgiving Day, is being questioned in connection with what the police say is now a case of homicide."

# EPILOGUE

*Six months later ...*

**I**F ANYONE KNEW the lengths to which she'd gone to protect what was left of her daughter's shattered life, they would say her mind had been forged in the depths of hell.

They wouldn't be wrong. She had traveled to Hades and back. For a time, she'd been helpless to do anything about Alexia's condition other than provide emotional and financial support. The ability to compartmentalize her issues and solve problems were life savers.

Those qualities had also worked in Alexia's favor. Mentally, she'd be fine. Time and therapy sessions—physical and mental— would take care of what Geneva couldn't. Her blog had helped Alexia find overwhelming support, and she'd been invited to give cautionary talks to select groups of high school girls. She hadn't made any decision yet, but Geneva would support any choice she made.

Alexia screamed then, which startled Geneva, who lay in the middle of the Olympic-size pool on an inflatable float. She raised her head to investigate.

Jaden had dunked Alexia, who was splashing water in his direction. "You're a stinking, dirty rat," she yelled as he swam in the opposite direction, grinning.

The two made her heart smile. Geneva sipped from her glass of rum punch, then closed her eyes. The two-week stay at the villa in Ocho Rios came to them compliments of Spence's company, which owned the property.

She'd feared the setting would bring back bad memories for Alexia, but so far, she seemed carefree and happy. This holiday was meant to help her remember how life had been before it took a nosedive into pain and chaos. They had landed in Montego Bay, done the family rounds, and headed into Ochi to enjoy their vacation.

Every action that Geneva had taken stateside was relegated to memory. She'd done what was required and prepared herself to live with the consequences. Alexia's happiness was worth the time Geneva would spend in her own mental purgatory. She sometimes saw Christian and his absolute terror at the moment of death in her dreams. Her thoughts drifted to that fateful day.

On the agreed date and time, Deja had done her part. She inserted the miniature control device Geneva provided into the electrical panel box at Radcliff Skyers's house. The computerized widget served a dual purpose: disrupt and destroy.

When Christian stood in the kitchen at dinner time, she'd switched off the electricity inside the house, which lured Christian outside to the panel box to investigate—as if he knew anything about electrics. Having disengaged the locks remotely, Geneva allowed Deja to slide in through the washroom door and access the kitchen.

As far as Deja knew, the holes she punched in the gas line would be a minor inconvenience for the two Skyers men. The tubing ran behind the stove, which was situated close to the fridge with a counter separating them. She'd almost bungled her escape when Christian came back inside the house while she was trying to leave. The girl barely made it through the laundry room, slamming the door behind her, and had to huddle in the bushes outside.

Christian went to investigate, but couldn't find what had made the noise. He'd gone back into the kitchen and raised the curtain. With the wind rag-dolling the hedges, it was hard for him to pinpoint what had happened. A moment passed before he lowered the sheer fabric and flicked a switch by the doorway, testing for electricity.

Two minutes later, Deja was safely off the property. Geneva reengaged all the locks and switched on the power. The moment he opened the refrigerator, she created a localized power surge through her tiny gizmo, sending ten times the regular electricity supply through the house. She'd taken a sure bet that the refrigerator plug would spark and ignite the leaking gas.

The two hundred-pound cylinders housed in a recessed metal cage at the side of the building provided all the firepower she needed. The explosion left a crater where the right side of the house used to be and exposed the foundation.

Christian hadn't stood a chance. His scream as he tried to escape the resulting inferno still dominated her dreams. But that was all right. She'd known what the result of traveling down this particular road would be before she took the first step.

And to think he'd been egged on to rape Alexia by that devil, Sancia. After his death, Alexia had confessed that Christian yelling at her in the station triggered the memory of that exchange. She'd made sure Alexia knew she had the option of surgery to minimize the scar on her forehead—a reminder of that twisted pair.

As she trailed her fingers though the water, Geneva sighed. Poor Deja. Her case came together easily for the police. The incriminating video, plus the social media leaks she'd orchestrated since her return from Jamaica, didn't help her case. Nor did the digital footprints that proved Phil had been set up and hadn't actually stolen information from the university. One layer at a time, Geneva rerouted all her misdeeds through Deja's devices.

Deja's court-appointed lawyer had brought in the sexual assault by her uncle, hoping to arouse sympathy during the trial. The defense that Christian's attack on Alexia had triggered a trauma response fell flat. Deja lost the jury's sympathy when they found out her uncle had committed suicide. The prosecution team painted her as a vengeful, off-balance young woman. Those labels didn't help her case.

A frantic call from Deja came through on the day after she woke from a week-long coma. "Please, Aunt Jenny. If you tell the police I was only there to—"

She'd shut down Deja's cries with one remark. "I'd have told them anything you wanted if you'd done right by Alexia."

The silence that met her soft words told Geneva everything she needed to know.

Deja had received her clear, concise, and unmistakable message.

At the trial, which was carried on the news, she hadn't said much. A resigned air hung around her, and if Geneva could put words to it, she'd say Deja's spirit had been broken. Pity. Her life might have taken a different course if she'd made a better choice when she had the opportunity. She'd have plenty of time to think about her transgressions while serving a life sentence. She had a shot at parole in twenty years. Who knew what might happen by then?

Spence walked through the French door with a tumbler in hand. He stood on the patio watching them. His slow smile told Geneva that her new bathing suit had made an impression. They'd have an interesting time later this evening. He set the glass on the table beneath the beach umbrella and approached the edge of the pool to watch Alexia swimming. He'd taught her when she was little, and joy was evident in his triumphant laughter. He stuck two fingers his mouth and released a piercing whistle, then applauded. "Yeah! That's my baby, Alexia the Great."

Spence watched for a while longer before diving into the water, barely creating a ripple.

Life hadn't given any guarantees of a smooth ride, but they were here, riding hard for each other to the finish line. These people would always be her priority, no matter what it took to preserve their peace and stability. Family and good friends were priceless—too bad for those who didn't know.

Some had to learn the hard way.

# WWW.BLACKODYSSEY.NET

# THE NEED TO RIGHT A WRONG AGAINST AN INNOCENT VICTIM TRIGGERS A HAILSTORM OF REVENGE!

Less than twenty-four hours before Alexia Leighton is scheduled to return to Miami from spring break in Jamaica, a group of friends betray her in a grisly assault that stops a heartbeat away from murder. The seventeen-year-old prays for the mercy of death. She survives. While she's on the road to recovery, Alexia's attackers become victims of mysterious acts of violence, leaving authorities confounded and racing against time to prevent another deadly attack. Concern looms, as the perpetrator has proven to be two steps ahead of them at every turn.

When the attention swings to Alexia's mother, a cybersecurity expert, the family closes ranks. Geneva Leighton must quickly eliminate herself as a suspect, but not without handing down more punishment. The offenders fear for their own safety and the secrets that plague them. Can they trust the police to find the killer before someone else dies, or has their fate been sealed—leaving them with no place to run, and no place to hide...

* * *

"Hell hath no fury like a mother's vengeance! I couldn't put it down!"
—*Shakir Rashaan, author of Neverwraith*

"J.L. Campbell takes thrillers to another level with Flames of Wrath, which starts with a powerful opening and comes to a mind-blowing ending. Campbell has always stretched the boundaries but in this book, she's outdone herself."
—*Naleighna Kai, USA Today bestselling author of King of Durabia*

"Flames of Wrath is a scorching psychological debut with diabolical twists and an ending that will leave you breathless!" —*D. Andrea Whitfield*

PRINTED IN THE U.S.A.

BLACK ODYSSEY
MEDIA
U.S. $16.95
CAN $22.99
WWW.BLACKODYSSEY.NET
@iamblackodyssey

$16.95
ISBN 979-8-9855941-5-7
51695

FICTION

9 798985 594157